P9-AOT-183

ABOUT LAST CALL

A retired cop past her prime...

A kidnapped bank robber fighting for his life...

A former mob enforcer with a blood debt...

A government assassin on the run...

A wisecracking private eye with only one hand...

A homicide sergeant with one week left on the job...

And three of the worst serial killers, ever.

This is where it all ends. An epic showdown in the desert, where good and evil will clash one last time.

His name is Luther Kite, and his specialty is murdering people in ways too horrible to imagine. He's gone south, where he's found a new, spectacular way to kill. And if you have enough money, you can bet on who dies first.

Legendary Chicago cop Jacqueline "Jack" Daniels has retired. She's no longer chasing bad guys, content to stay out of the public eye and raise her new daughter. But when her daughter's father, Phin Troutt, is kidnapped, she's forced to strap on her gun one last time.

Since being separated from his psychotic soulmate, the prolific serial killer known as Donaldson has been desperately searching for her. Now he thinks he's found out where his beloved, insane Lucy has been hiding. He's going to find her, no matter how many people are slaughtered in the process.

All three will converge in the same place. La Juntita, Mexico. Where a bloodthirsty cartel is enslaving people and forcing them to fight to the death in insane, gladiator-style games.

Join Jack and Phin, Donaldson and Lucy, and Luther, for the very last act in their twisted, perverse saga.

Along for the ride are Jack's friends; Harry and Herb, as well as a mob enforcer named Tequila, and a covert operative named Chandler.

There will be blood. And death. So much death...

LAST CALL by J.A. Konrath

The conclusion to the Jack Daniels/Luther Kite epic

LAST CALL
A JACK DANIELS THRILLER

J.A. KONRATH

MYS
Konrath

LAST CALL
Copyright © 2016 by Joe Konrath
Cover and art copyright © 2016 by Carl Graves

This book is a work of fiction. Names, characters, places and incidents
are either products of the author's imagination or used fictitiously. Any
resemblance to actual events, locales, or persons, living or dead, is entirely
coincidental. All rights reserved. No part of this publication can be reproduced
or transmitted in any form or by any means, electronic or mechanical, without
permission in writing from the authors.

June 2016

INTRODUCTION

L AST CALL was written as a standalone thriller and requires no prior knowledge of any previous books.

If you read STIRRED, co-authored by Blake Crouch, you know that novel was supposed to be the conclusion to this particular storyline. But fan insistence, coupled with some unresolved issues at the end of STIRRED, prompted a follow-up. Besides finishing off the Jack Daniels/Luther Kite saga, LAST CALL also concludes the Lucy/Donaldson story from SERIAL KILLERS UNCUT. Characters from previous books also play key roles, including Chandler and Fleming (FLEE, SPREE, THREE, Tequila (SHOT OF TEQUILA, NAUGHTY), and Jack Daniels regulars Phin, Herb, and Harry.

My frequent collaborator, Blake Crouch, was unable to join me on this book, as he's currently committed to two hit television series based on his stories, WAYWARD PINES and GOOD BEHAVIOR. He's given me his blessing to use some of his characters, for which I'm grateful. I hope I've done them justice.

In LAST CALL, the reader will come across occasional hyperlinks when a character first appears, or when a passage nods to another story. These lead to the story being referenced. There is also an index at the end of the novel which lists all of the interlocking books in this universe.

But, as I previously mentioned, this novel can be enjoyed without having read anything else.

A word of warning, though; this book is called LAST CALL. So be prepared for some characters to die. But before you hate me, I humbly ask you to read the preview chapters of WHITE RUSSIAN, the next Jack Daniels thriller, at the end of this book. ☺

As always, thanks for reading!
Joe Konrath

"It is easier to find men who will volunteer to die, than to find those who are willing to endure pain with patience."

JULIUS CAESAR

Somewhere in Mexico

For forever and beyond...

"Ándale, puto!"

The leg shackles were removed, and the captive man was shoved roughly from behind. He still had his handcuffs on—heavy, rusty chains that had rubbed the skin on his wrists raw. As he was marched through the cell hallway, a machinegun at his back, the chains bumped against his broken ribs, causing a spike of pain with every step.

Besides the ribs, he had a laceration on his scalp that had been fixed with superglue, a nasty burn on his chest, a dislocated pinky, and an abdominal wound that had required eight stitches, which had been done without anesthetic. They were given the barest medical treatment; sutures, bandages, splints, aspirin and penicillin sporadically.

No one spoke much.

It made sense, considering their predicament.

Incongruous to their harsh treatment, they were fed well; delicious burritos and tamales, enchiladas, the best huaraches he'd ever eaten. If someone won a match, he got a six pack of Tecate beer. It was so woefully pathetic, it was almost funny. Even funnier, he'd found himself looking forward to that beer. Not because of what it represented, but because downing six was his only reprieve from this living hell.

He wasn't sure how long he'd been here. Judging by his beard growth, at least two days. They were kept underground, no windows, no accurate way of judging time. When they were taken topside, sometimes it was daytime, sometimes night, and it was so disorienting and so brief he couldn't tell east from west to check if the sun was setting or rising.

Another shove from behind, and he was led through a heavy, iron door, and out into the arena. It had probably been an old bullfighting ring. A circle, perhaps twenty meters wide, surrounded by bleachers. He squinted in the lights, portable kliegs running on gas generators, and looked at the surrounding crowd. A hundred, maybe more. Some cheered when they saw him. Others booed.

He'd made a few of them money, and helped others lose theirs.

Above the seats and the lights, covering the arena like a shroud, was a roof of camouflage netting. He guessed it hid the place from satellite photos.

The man looked to the right, to the board, and saw the number that had been spray painted on his shirt when he'd arrived. Number 17. Beneath it were his odds.

1:2.

That wasn't good. Previously, the odds had always been in his favor, or at least 1:1. Now they were against him.

A lump formed in his throat. There were a couple of big guys underground, and one certified monster. But he had an idea who his opponent was going to be.

Number 12. A gringo, like he was. College student, half his age. He gave up two inches and thirty pounds to him, and the kid was built like a linebacker.

As expected, they led Number 12 into the arena, and the crowd reacted with some lackluster applause. The kid smiled, hooting and raising his cuffed hands. He'd won eight matches, but during that time he'd lost his mind.

Which was completely understandable.

The sand underneath their feet was compact, hard, with dozens of rough spots where blood had seeped in and dried to the strength of concrete. The gamey smell of meat left out in the sun mingled with the scent of arid desert. Without wanting to, Number 17's eyes were drawn to the corner of the arena, to the large, wooden cross. The man who'd been hung there days ago had finally died, as evidenced by the birds picking at his carcass. A terrible ending to a terrible murder. He wondered which son of a bitch in the crowd had come closest to predicting the time of death, and how much they'd won.

There was an announcement is Spanish, booming over the sound system. It was repeated in English for the rich white people in the stands.

"*Last call for bets, last call for bets. Number 12, with eight wins, against Number 17, with two. Weight and age advantage to Number 12, and Number 17 pays two to one. The weapons for this match... aluminum baseball bats.*"

A golf cart puttered into the arena, carrying four guards brandishing Tec-9 machineguns. They unlocked the combatants' chains and gave each a bat. More armed guards—never fewer than four— stood at attention in the wings. Mounted on the north and west sides of the ring, shrouded in bulletproof glass, were belt-fed M60s with 7.62mm armor-piercing NATO rounds. Number 17 had been keeping careful watch on the security, noting the egress points, the personnel, the security cameras, and concluded there wasn't even a remote possibility of escape. The only way out of this hellhole was one chunk at a time, in the bellies of crows.

His opponent immediately picked up his bat and raised it above his head, letting out a crazed whoop.

In a moment, this college kid was going to try to kill him.

He didn't want that to happen. He had too much to live for.

The man closed his eyes and stretched his arms out over his head, then touched his toes, flexing to force blood into his tired limbs. He picked up the bat and held it in front of him like a sword, and stared up at the freak show duo presiding over this ongoing crime against humanity.

A man and a woman. They sat in a balcony above the arena. He wore a crown. She a tiara. Both were clad in purple capes, velvet or velour.

But they weren't royalty.

They were monsters.

The puppet king lifted his gold staff, a human skull forming its bulbous top, and banged it against the Chinese gong next to his throne. The clang resonated out over the crowd, who once again applauded and cheered.

Let the games begin.

The man tensed, and the college kid, predictably, charged at him with his bat upraised. He no doubt expected his speed and strength to be enough to win. And in this particular death match, he might be correct.

Previously in the arena, Number 17 had fought with machetes and spears. Weapons that pierced and slashed. It hadn't been toe-to-toe battles with each fighter standing his ground; instead it was about causing one fast and fatal wound, then keeping away as the opponent bled out.

But it would be tough to kill a man via blood loss with a baseball bat. Beating a man to death with a blunt instrument was likely to be a long and tiring task. The only killing method Number 17 could think of was via concussion, and that favored bigger muscles.

When the college kid got within striking distance, he made like A-Rod and swung for the stands, aiming at no particular part of his opponent's body. If it landed, it would break bones.

Number 17 anticipated the move, rolling beneath the swing, and giving a stiff pop to the football player's groin with the butt of his bat. As the larger man doubled over, Number 17 dipped a shoulder, came up behind him, and connected with the spot between the base of the skull and the neck, giving the blow everything he had.

Number 12 went down, face first into the sand, and was still. Maybe knocked out. Maybe paralyzed. But not dead, since his chest continued to move up and down.

The crowd howled a mixture of boos and cheers.

Number 17looked up at the balcony and waited, keeping his scream bottled up inside.

I came looking for this. And I found what I was looking for.

And it's worse than anything I could have ever imagined.

I'm sorry. I'm so, so sorry.

The puppet king held out a gaunt hand, and turned his thumb down.

As Number 17 smashed the bat into the college kid's head, over and over, he focused on the woman he loved, and their child, and tried to picture their faces instead of the atrocity he was committing.

For them.

I have to get out of this for them.

After all, I got into this for them.

When the football player was no doubt dead, the man wearing the number 17, Phineas Troutt, dropped the gory bat and held up his hands to be cuffed and hauled away again, thinking about the six pack of victory beer waiting in his cell, and wondering if his wife, Jacqueline Daniels, had begun to search for him yet.

He hoped, for her sake, and for the sake of their young daughter, that she had not.

Because if she came, Jack, and anyone else she brought with her, would be caught and caged just like Phin had been. Forced to compete in these perverse gladiator games, run by a ruthless Mexican cartel and an insane, sadistic maniac wearing a gold crown and purple robe.

A maniac who now stood up and began to applaud Phin with a feeble golf clap.

A maniac named Luther Kite.

THREE DAYS EARLIER

JACK

Tampa

It was love bug season in Florida, and the sky was filled with so many it looked like it was snowing black. Giant clouds of hundreds of thousands of bugs, joined at the ends as they mated, flying everywhere and getting into everything; hair, drinks, food, mouths, etc. Mom moved to Tampa because she called it paradise, but my version of paradise didn't have copulating insects flying up your nose every time you took a breath.

Samantha was chasing the love bugs around the pool area on wobbly, toddler legs, smiling and giggling. We'd brought her out here to go swimming, but there was an impenetrable love bug layer floating on top, and no matter how quickly the pool boy skimmed them off, they returned.

"How often does this happen?" I asked my mother. I was considering putting on more sunscreen, but I figured the bugs blocked out at least enough sun to be a natural SPF 20.

"Twice a year." Mary Streng took a sip of her virgin Pina colada, through the napkin that had been placed over the glass rim to keep out horny insects. "Isn't it lovely?"

"That's not the term I'd use." I kept my hand over my mouth.

"Lighten up, Jacqueline. When was the last time you had sex in public?"

"Phin and I keep it behind closed doors. And we don't fly into people's drinks."

"I did it two nights ago, with Al Feinstein from 125-B. At midnight, in that very chaise lounge you're sitting in."

"That nice old guy we had dinner with? Who showed us pictures of his grandchildren?"

His bald head had so many liver spots it looked like the constellation Orion.

"Don't let his wheelchair fool you," Mom said. "The man is a sex machine. He can tie a cherry stem into a knot with his tongue."

"Nice."

"I was so pleased I just got that Brazilian wax."

I grinned. "You're such a slut, Mom."

"I like that word. We need to reclaim it."

"I'll drink to that." I clinked my beer against her glass, and then quickly took the cardboard coaster off the top to take a sip.

"So what's wrong, dear?" Mom asked. "Is it a sex thing? I could get Mr. Feinstein to give your man some pointers."

"Nothing's wrong."

"You've been here three days. Why can't you relax?"

Relaxing didn't come naturally to me. My two speeds were heightened awareness, and exhaustion. Lounging around my mom's retirement community pool, watching my toddler run around eating as many love bugs as she could catch, was not conducive to relaxation. Add in the fact that her father had left me a voicemail three hours ago, saying he was going up north to fish with some old friends, and my unease had been steadily growing since.

Phin didn't have old friends, as far as I knew. And he didn't fish, either. We'd recently had a bad experience up north; so bad I couldn't see him going back this soon. My calls to him had gone unreturned—which was something Phin said might happen because he was going somewhere without any cell reception—but I wasn't buying it.

A paranoid woman, especially one who was a decade older than her husband and still hadn't lost the ten pounds she'd gained while pregnant, might think he was having an affair. But my thoughts tended to be darker. While I was a homicide detective in the Chicago PD, I'd made a lot of enemies. Phin also had a violent past, much of it spent on the other side of the law. I would actually prefer him having an affair than getting tangled up in some of the dangerous things we once did.

We'd promised each other we'd given all of that up. I hung up my badge, he stopped doing all the crazy shit he used to do, and we lived off of savings, my pension, and the money I brought in as a part time private investigator. Phin had seemingly taken to being a fulltime father. He did most of the cooking and housework, raised our daughter, and kept the romance alive. Our relationship wasn't perfect, but no one had shot at either one of us in more than three months.

However, his "I'm going fishing with friends" story didn't pass the sniff test. He was up to something, and it probably involved violence. Since he didn't include me, he must have been trying to protect me. And since I hadn't heard from him, I was getting the feeling he'd found the trouble he was looking for.

"It's Phin's fishing trip, isn't it?" Mom said. "You smell bullshit."

"Yeah. Will you be okay watching Sam for a few days?"

"Of course. You're going to go find him?"

I nodded and rocked myself out of the chaise lounge.

"He's a big boy, Jack. And he knows you're a big girl. If he wanted you involved with whatever he's doing, he would have asked."

"I know. That's what's bothering me."

I looked at Sam, swatting at love bugs and giggling. She caught my eye and said, "Mommy!"

I scooped her up and hugged her, then gave her a kiss on the head. "I love you, Sam."

"Love you, Mommy. I ate three bugs."

"Were they yummy?"

"I ate them on accident. Can we go swimming?"

The pool looked like it had a black blanket floating on top of it. A wiggling black blanket.

"How about we get some ice cream instead?"

Sam pursed her lips as she weighed the decision, then said, "Okay."

My mother stood up, taking my daughter's hand. "We'll be back in a few," she said to me. Then Mom's face became hard. "Jacqueline... do you think it's..."

Her voice trailed off, but I knew what went unsaid. Out of all the loose ends in my past, there was one in particular that kept me up at nights.

"Hopefully Phin's just cheating on me," I told her.

Then I took out my cell phone and searched for the next flight to Chicago.

PHIN

Near Chicago

A few hours before he called his wife and told her he was going on a fishing trip, Phineas Troutt was checking the security camera on his computer monitor to see who was at the door. It was a tall, slender woman, mid-forties, black hair done up in a large bun, dressed in khakis, hiking boots, and what looked like a tactical vest over a short sleeved shirt. She was staring into the camera, a neutral expression on her face. The way she stood, legs slightly apart, hands at her sides, reminded Phin of the *at ease* position in the military.

Phin pressed a key on his computer while he checked the other perimeter cameras. No one else was on the property.

"Can I help you?" he spoke into the monitor mic.

"Phineas Troutt?"

Phin didn't reply.

"My name is Katie Glente. I'm here to speak with you and Lieutenant Daniels."

Jack was in Florida with Samantha, visiting Jack's mother. She also hadn't been a Lieutenant for a few years.

"Jack is unavailable," Phin said.

Katie's expression remained unchanged. "I have information you both might want to hear. About Luther Kite."

Phin opened the desk drawer and took out an FNS 9mm, double-checked the seventeen round magazine to make sure it was full, and said, "Hold on, give me a minute or two."

Phin was at the front door within ten seconds. He gave Duffy, their chubby basset hound, the silent hand command for *stay quiet* and watched the video monitor on the wall. Katie was still in the same position. Phin disarmed the burglar alarm and pulled open their steel security door in a quick motion, the 9mm at his side.

Katie didn't flinch at the quick movement.

"It's a pleasure to meet you." She raised her hand slowly to shake.

Phin made no move to take it. "Do you mind if my dog checks you for weapons?"

"Excuse me?"

"Just stand still. Duffy. Weapons."

Duffy padded out onto the front porch and sniffed at Katie. The hound was trained to recognize gunpowder and explosives, and Phin had been working with him to scent various types of metals. When he sniffed Katie's left boot, he growled.

"Folding knife," Katie said.

Phin raised his FNS. "Take it out, slowly."

Katie lifted her leg, bending the knee, and pulled up her pants to expose the ankle sheath. She removed the folder and handed it to Phin. It was an expensive model, a Schempp Tuff. Phin flicked open the thick four inch blade.

"Duffy. Blood."

The dog snorted at the knife, but didn't growl. No human blood or viscera on the weapon.

"You can come in, but I'll hold onto this while you stay," Phin said, folding the knife and placing it in his pocket.

"Understood."

"I'll also need to pat you down."

Katie's mouth curled into a slight smile, and her dark eyes crinkled at the edges. "Duffy the crime dog isn't enough?"

"He's still working on detecting ceramics and polymers."

"So you want to make sure I'm not carrying a ceramic knife, or made my own gun on a 3D printer."

"Something like that."

Katie continued to appear bemused. "Do you go through this routine every time the UPS man delivers a package?"

"We don't allow packages to be delivered here. Are we doing this, or are we saying goodbye?"

Katie raised up her hands. Phin kept his eyes on hers, and the gun on her chest, as he gave her a thorough frisk. He found her Samsung Galaxy cell phone—something Duffy missed—in one of the pockets of her vest. No car keys, but that made sense because he'd watched the cab drop her off a minute earlier. The fact that she hadn't asked the cab to wait spoke of confidence that Jack would want the information she had. It also gave Phin a bit of reassurance that she hadn't come to do harm; everyone knew cabs kept records.

Still, anyone mentioning Luther Kite's name had to be treated with a tad bit more paranoia than was the norm at their happy household. Having a PO box for deliveries, and bulletproof glass windows, and reinforced entry and exits points, and a state of the art surveillance and alarm system, along with a lazy dog who knew a few tricks, wasn't enough to put Phin's mind completely at ease. Even though Jack had retired, there were still bad guys who wanted to do her harm. And the bad guys Jack tended to attract were the worst of the worst.

Phin had been searching for one particular bad guy, Kite, since they'd returned from an ill-fated vacation up north. He'd lost the killer's trail in Texas. If this Katie Glente had some info, it might be worth the risk of letting her inside.

The squirrel who had made its nest in the oak tree in the front yard chirped off-key, sounding like a dying bird. A mating call. Perhaps the most annoying in the animal kingdom. Duffy, for all his training, barked at the squirrel.

Phin looked hard at Katie, and had an uneasy feeling in his gut. That same adrenaline queasiness he used to get when he was on the street, about to get into a dangerous situation. But Katie was unarmed and maintaining a neutral attitude. Phin decided his instincts were overreacting at the mention of Luther Kite. He told Duffy to be quiet, took a step back, and invited the woman into his home.

Katie moved easily, seemingly relaxed but with that state of readiness Phin noticed in a small percentage of the population; cops, military, martial artists, and mercs. It was also shared by ex-cons and predators. He locked the door and showed her to the sofa against the far wall of the living room. Phin sat on the opposing love seat, maintaining a good view of Katie, along with the front door and the video monitor there. He placed the FNS on the cushion next to him, then told Duffy, "Ball."

The hound went off to look for his favorite toy, and Phin waited for Katie to begin talking. She was quiet for several seconds, apparently sizing him up.

"You're not what I expected," she finally said, breaking the silence.

Phin didn't reply.

"I've done a lot of research on Jack. Spoken to a lot of people she's met. Your name has come up. You're unemployed. Had some run-ins with the law. Including with Jack. She arrested you, years ago. You've also been involved in several of her more publicized cases. I find it interesting that a former police lieutenant wound up having a child with a criminal ten years her junior. But maybe, after all those years of catching murderers, Jack wanted to know what it was like to be with one."

Phin had killed before, when it had been necessary. There had been some dark years in his past, but those were gone. His new role was loving husband and father, and it was one he much preferred to wandering dark alleys, targeting urban scum. He didn't consider himself a murderer.

But there probably weren't any murderers that did. People tended to think they were the heroes of their own stories. Even when they were the bad guys.

"I'm giving you thirty seconds to make your point, Ms. Glente. Ten are already up."

She didn't hesitate. "I'm a writer, Mr. Troutt. I write about serial killers, and those who catch them. Your wife has managed to run into more of them than just about any other single person in history."

"Jack doesn't do interviews."

"I know. I talked to her partner at the private investigation firm she works at. Harrison Harold McGlade. He was willing to tell me anything about Jack, over breakfast in bed at the Hotel Monaco in Chicago. I gave him points for effort, but declined."

"Did he give you this address?"

Katie shook her head. "No. He was happy to share old stories about shoot-outs and close calls, but not any personal info. I got this address through the Cook County Assessor's Office. The house is in the name of Jack's mother, Mary Streng. Is that where Jack and Samantha are now? Visiting Grandma?"

Phin didn't like how easy it was for Katie to find them. "Five seconds."

The speed of her speech increased. "Jack has managed to eliminate most of the high-profile enemies she's picked up over the years. All but three. They're the reason for all of this security and caution, no doubt. One is an older man named Donaldson. He likes to kill hitch hikers. Another is a girl named Lucy. She likes to kill people who pick up hitch hikers. But the worst of the three is Luther Kite. He may have killed more people than Lucy and Donaldson combined."

"If you came to talk to Jack about Luther Kite, or Lucy and Donaldson, she's not here. And if she were, she doesn't talk about that part of her past."

"Is it still the past, though, Mr. Troutt? All three are still at large."

Phin had done quite a bit of research on this topic. "I thought Donaldson was dead."

"It's a nice thing to wish for. But his body was never recovered."

Duffy brought over his ball. He dropped it on Phin's lap and waited, tail wagging.

"Your thirty seconds are up," Phin said, taking the 9mm in hand once again. "It's time for you to go."

"I believe I know where Luther Kite is, Mr. Troutt. He and Lucy."

"So call the FBI."

"They aren't in the US. The FBI has no jurisdiction."

Phin put two and two together. This woman claimed to be a writer, but had the bearing of a soldier. She came here knowing Jack wouldn't talk to her, knowing Jack wasn't even home. And she wanted to talk about Luther Kite, who was no longer in the US.

"You're hunting him," Phin said. "And you want Jack's help."

"I'm hunting a story, Mr. Troutt. I've written three books about serial killers. I can show you."

"What branch did you serve in?"

"I don't understand your question."

"Where did you get your military training?"

"I've had no military training, Mr. Troutt."

Phin threw Duffy's tennis ball, hard, at Katie's chest.

Her hand shot up like it was spring-loaded, and she caught the ball with an audible smack as it connected with her palm.

Phin wasn't sure he could have caught it, had their positions been reversed. Her reflexes were exceptional.

They stared at each other for a moment, then Phin raised the 9mm. "The truth," he said.

She shrugged. "No formal training. I've done some mixed martial arts. Firearms courses. But not through the usual channels. You could say my life experiences have been a bit... unorthodox. I've picked up a few things, taken some classes, but I was never in the military." Katie tossed the ball down the hallway, and Duffy went bounding after it. "Yes, I do want to track down Luther Kite. And I'd like Jack's help. She's the best. Once we find him, we can turn him over to the local authorities. This would make a great story, and it would help ease your obvious, ongoing paranoia."

Phin didn't need any time to make his decision. "No one here is going to help you, Ms. Glente. Ever. You can leave. And don't come back."

If Katie felt rejected or disappointed, it didn't show on her face. "Can I use your bathroom?"

"No."

"It was a long trip from the city. You can escort me if you don't trust me."

"A woman with your unorthodox life experiences can no doubt hold it in."

"Okay. I'm taking out my cell to call a cab." Katie reached slowly into her pocket. "I'm also leaving you a business card, in case you or Jack would like to get in touch. On the back of the card I've written down a YouTube URL. I believe it will interest you both."

Katie stood, did a slow stretch, and rubbed her head, undoing the bun so her black hair fell to shoulder-length. She set the card on the table and dialed the cab company. As she spoke, Duffy came up with the ball. Katie gave the dog a pat on the head, a tickle under the chin, and walked to the front door as she finished her call. Phin shielded the security code with his body as he punched it in, then opened the door, handing Katie the Schempp after she'd walked outside.

It took eight minutes for the taxi to arrive.

Phin stood by the door, the FNS in his hand, watching the video monitor until she'd gone.

KATIE

When the taxi had driven half a mile from Jack's house, Katie told him to pull over. She paid him for the time on the meter, both for the trip up and the time he'd waited for her to call back, and tipped him the fifty she'd promised. Then she grabbed the backpack she'd left in the cab and exited the vehicle.

The area was suburban, wooded. The houses were large, with big lawns, and there was plenty of cover between them. It took her ten minutes to hike her way to Jack's house by cutting through back yards. She stopped when she reached the edge of the property. Removing a Bushnell Sentry scope from the bag, she scanned the house for activity while placing the radio bud in her ear. When she flipped her walkie-talkie on, she heard the sounds of slurping.

Duffy, at his bowl. Or maybe helping himself to some toilet water.

She liked the dog. Not only was it cute and affable, but being able to sniff out blood and firearms were handy skills to have.

She also liked Phin. He was attractive in that rough-hewn, bad-boy way, muscular and intense and potentially dangerous. He seemed extraordinarily devoted to Jack, and Katie much preferred the protective type to the predatory type. Like her, Phin had no professional training, picking things up via an unusual lifestyle rather than in the army or the police force. He'd found her knife, and hadn't given up any information, and from the time she'd arrived until the time she'd left he could have taken her out. A careful guy.

But not careful enough; he'd missed the radio bug she'd hidden in her hair and attached to Duffy's collar.

Katie squatted down behind the large oak, invisible to all except the squirrels, and took out a bag of homemade trail mix. As she ate, she watched and listened.

PHIN

Google informed Phin that Katie had written three books. One about the minds of sexual predators. One about FBI agents who'd died chasing serial killers. And the most recent a biography of the horror author, Andrew Thomas.

The books had all been self-published, and Phin downloaded all three to the Kindle app on his iPhone. Katie had gotten several hundred reviews, most of them decent. There was a brief bio, saying she lived in Michigan and was working on her next nonfiction title. He followed her website link, which was basically an advertisement for her three books. There was another bio that said practically nothing, but a photo section showed Katie doing various things. In one she wore a karate gi with a black belt. Another had her proudly holding up a stainless steel revolver and a silhouette target, eight holes in the head and ten in the chest, the groupings tight. There were also pics of her in a volunteer firefighter uniform, and at the Tough Mudder endurance race in Tahoe.

A hard, capable person, who seemed to have been telling the truth.

Phin dialed Jack's office.

"McGlade and Daniels, private investigators," said a falsetto voice. "This is Mr. McGlade's personal secretary. May I help you?"

"Stop acting stupid, McGlade. You don't have a personal secretary."

Harry went back to using his normal voice. "I wish I did. This thing won't suck itself."

"Nice."

"Like it? I'm thinking of having T-shirts made. So what's up? The old lady is out of town, so you want to go tomcatting around town? Hit a few strip joints, get a few lap dances, then drink so much we start talking about our feelings? I'd be up for that."

Phin got an unwelcome image in his head. Chubby, unshaven, unkempt McGlade, his thousand dollar suit wrinkled and drenched in aftershave, being grinded on by some young dancer who no doubt wanted to eat a gun and end it all.

He forced away the picture and asked, "What did you tell Katie Glente?"

"You never want to hang out. Or call to say hello. If I didn't know you had a man-crush on me, I'd be feeling hurt. If I had feelings."

"Katie Glente, McGlade. She just came to see you. What did you tell her?"

"That writer chick? The usual. That I'm two inches longer than I actually am, and that story about how I ran into George Clooney at the Emmy Awards after-party. I left out the part where he told his security guards to beat me up. I was really unhappy-pants after that."

"Did you tell her anything about Jack?"

"Just the stuff that's already public knowledge; she's mean-spirited, she's got crow's feet, she can fit her whole fist in her mouth. Some of the old cop stories."

Phin clenched his jaw. "Did you tell her where we lived?"

"Of course not. Think I'm an idiot?"

"Everyone thinks you're an idiot."

"Yeah? So why am I a member of Mensa?"

"You cheated on the qualification exam."

"I certainly did. Put one over on those stuck-up, snooty, intel-linazis. I fooled smart people, ergo I can't be an idiot. It's simple math. Or something."

"Okay, smart guy, so why am I calling you right now?"

I could practically hear the gears turn in McGlade's pointy head. "The Glente chick showed up at your house."

"Yeah."

"Did you tap that ass? She was a little thin, but had some fire in her eyes. If you did, I won't tell Jack. I made a pass, but she obviously wasn't into guys with high IQs. So she'd probably dig you."

"Did you run a background check?"

"Strange woman, comes snooping around asking questions about Luther Kite? Of course I ran her. No priors. Went through the NCIC, and Interpol, and some big cities. Also ran her prints."

Harry rarely impressed Phin. He rarely impressed anybody. But getting her prints was praise-worthy. "How'd you manage that?"

"I tossed her my snow globe. You know, the one with Santa inside, banging Mrs. Claus from behind? The harder you shake it, the more they go at it. It's the greatest thing ever. I'll buy you one."

"And you lifted her prints from the surface. Not bad."

"Not bad? It's brilliant! Besides getting latents, it's also a good indicator of how freaky the chick is. Erotic snow globes are like a litmus test for nymphos. Katie didn't react at all. Might not be into sex. Or might be queerpants."

"Or maybe she just has some class."

"No difference to me. Queer, classy, I don't score with either type. Point is, she's clean. No record. Credit check was fine, too. Owes about three grand on her Citibank Mastercard, pays monthly. Spends a lot of money at Radio Shack. I didn't even know that place was still around."

"Relatives?"

"Radio Shack is a store, Phin. It doesn't have relatives."

"Katie, McGlade." Phin rubbed his eyes. "Assume my time is more valuable than yours."

"It isn't. And no relatives that I could find. Checked phone records, too. I know a chick, works in telecommunications. She pulls numbers for me, and I occasionally throw her one. She's really old, so her hips creak like a rocking chair. And dry. Like hitting kitty litter. But when she pops out those dentures it's like dying and going to head heaven. Woman has mad skills. Maybe it has something to do with all the hard candy old people seem to like."

"Can we stick with Katie?" Phin almost said *stay on Katie* but caught himself in time. No need to toss McGlade any easy lobs.

"No family. No friends, either. Dunno why she even has a cell. Other than taxis, the last call she made was ordering a pizza. Who still uses the phone to order a pizza? Haven't people heard of the Internet? You can order anything online these days. I found this escort on the net named Sinnamon. Spelled with an *S*. I don't think that's her real name, by the way..."

Phin interrupted. "What kind of surname is Glente? It's not common."

"I looked it up. It's Danish. Means *bird of prey*. Pretty cool-pants. So, anyway, I took Sinnamon to Cracker Barrel—true story—and in the middle of lunch rush she gives me a handy under the table. Totally worth the three hundred bucks an hour. Plus, she barely touched her chicken fried steak, so I took that home with me. It's always a bonus when you don't have to feed the escort. Kinda like getting free undercoat protection at the car wash."

Phin tuned him out and pictured Katie's face. Weren't many Danes with black hair, but that could have been dyed. And those with Nordic ancestry weren't known for their ability to tan, but Katie had an Arizona glow to her skin. Perhaps the name was a fake.

"Did you see that YouTube video?" Phin asked, cutting off a Harry story about how he once had sex in the car wash, but he didn't really count it on his tally sheet because it was with an inflatable doll.

"Yeah. Major yuckypants."

Phin had watched it several times after Katie had left. "Do you think it's Luther?"

"How should I know? Blurry as hell, only lasted a few seconds."

"If you had to guess?"

"Seems like the kind of sick shit Luther Kite would do. Plus he had that ghoul next to him."

"Ghoul?"

"That scarred chick. Skinny little serial psycho. Lucy. After Michigan, I put together quite a little dossier on her and her buddy, Donaldson."

"Can you even spell *dossier*?"

"Yeah. It starts with an F and ends with a U. Why do you have to be an asspants and mock all of my dope detecting skills?"

"What is up with you adding the word *pants* to the end of everything?"

"Oh. I've got an anonymous blog. It's called The Mansplainer. So I did that pants thing once—I called a commenter *dickpants*—and it started trending on Twitter. Hashtag dickpants. Now it's become my signature."

"People actually follow you?"

"Hell yeahpants."

"Okay then, Harrypants—"

"Blog is anonymous. No one knows it's me."

"Okay then, assholepants—"

"That's pretty meanpants, Phin."

"Can you just make your point about Lucy, without saying pants again?"

"I can't make that promisepants. As for Lucy, she's one for the true crime books. Ran away from home when she was a kid, started hitchhiking and killing anyone who picked her up. Same MO as the video; she would drag them behind the car on a chain, pulling them down the street until their clothes scraped off, stopping every few hundred meters to spritz their skinned bodies with lemon juice. So she meets up with Donaldson—he's yet another psycho from Jack's past. He likes to pick up hitchhikers and torture them to death. Donaldson and Lucy hurt each other real bad. We're talking major league freak show disfigurement here. And somehow they bond from the experience," Harry said. "Pants."

Lemon juice. That must have been what was in the spritz bottle on the video. When she squirted that poor bastard, he thrashed around like he was being electrocuted.

"So you think that's Luther in the video?"

"Tough to say. He's got that hood on. He's all scarred up. But I think it is. The clincher is the knife. For someone who has killed as many people as Luther Kite is supposed to have killed, there isn't a lot of information on him. But all sources agree that he favors a Spyderco Harpy."

Phin was familiar with the Spyderco brand. He paused the video, then used his browser to enlarge the picture. The silver knife being used to carve trenches into the screaming man's back had a curved blade, like the beak of a hawk.

"So what's the planpants?" Harry asked.

Phin didn't have to think about it for more than a few seconds before he made his decision. If that really was Luther, and Lucy, Phin wasn't going to wait around for them to eventually come calling. Jack and Sam shouldn't be forced to live in constant paranoia. Better to nip it in the bud.

If that really was Luther and Lucy, Phin would fix it so they'd never bother his family, or anyone else, ever again.

"I'm going to check it out. Don't tell Jack where I went."

"How can I? I don't even know where the hell you're going."

"Just stay quiet, McGlade."

"Want me to go with you? We could make a road trip out of it. Hey! I could invite Sinnamon! You'd have to pitch in for her hourly rate, though. It's okay; getting a handy isn't like cheating. It's more like a rigorous, joyful greeting. Think of it as saying hello, in the nicest way possible. Jack lets you greet people, right? Or if that doesn't work for you, I can bring my inflatable doll. We'd probably need some wet wipes or something if we take turns."

Phin hung up on him before he could say *pants* again.

Then he watched the YouTube video once more and tried to prepare himself for what he needed to do.

KATIE

Screaming filled her radio earpiece.

The video. That would be Phin's sixth viewing.

Katie wanted to ask him about it. Wanted to get his opinion. She had her suspicions about its origin, but her skillset didn't include detective work. When she'd met with that idiot, McGlade, she'd gone there to hire him and Jack to help her track Luther down. But McGlade didn't actually inspire confidence. All he really inspired was a desire to bathe.

Jack Daniels, however, was another story. If anyone could find Luther, it was Jack.

Which was why Katie watched Phin drive away, a duffle bag in hand, and didn't follow him.

Maybe Phin would find Luther. Maybe he wouldn't.

But once Jack knew Phin was gone, she'd go looking for him. And Jack would lead Katie to Luther Kite.

Katie made her way deeper in the woods, past the property lines, into some undeveloped land alongside a creek. Trees, bushes, years of fallen leaves, and an occasional dirt-covered beer bottle with its label obliterated by the seasons. No one came back there.

She stood beneath a large elm, removed a foldable pruning saw from her pack, and spent an hour clearing a line of sight to Jack's front yard. Then she set up her scope on a small tripod, settled in, and waited for the retired cop to come home.

DECADES AGO

Detroit

The voices outside the door had been raised for several minutes now, and the argument was escalating.

Standing by the window, she stared through the iron bars as snow fell onto the street six stories below. For a moment, she touched her fingers to the freezing glass, the closest she could come to experiencing the world outside. Right now, it was cold. In the summer, it would be hot. Because of the orientation of the building she occupied, she hadn't actually seen the sun in over two years.

This room was her world.

She ate here.

Slept here.

Lived in a heroin-laced fog here.

And in between all the forced horror, she escaped into the worlds of her paperbacks and old magazines whenever she had a moment to herself. That was the best thing about her life by leaps and bounds. Once a week, a green-eyed man named Winston would come bearing an armful of tattered, yellow-paged paperbacks from a nearby thrift store.

If business had been good, he'd bring her five, plus a magazine or two.

If it had been a slow week, two or three.

If she'd broken a single rule: none.

But she hadn't broken any rules. Not in a long time. No escape attempts. No suicide attempts. And they didn't even have to beat her anymore. The worst thing they could do was deny her reading material. Deny her that escape. As far as punishments went, she'd have opted for a ruthless beating over no new books or magazines, any day. Pain went away. Pain could be forgotten. But without the escape of her stories, her thoughts inevitably drifted back to all that had been taken from her.

Those thoughts were unbearable.

But the printed word took away the pain, even more than the drug needle.

Ann Rule, Joel McGinniss, Vincent Bugliosi, F. Paul Wilson, John D. MacDonald, Agatha Christie: these writers were her saviors. Without them, she'd have surely wasted away to nothing.

She turned from the window, from the snowy city whose name she did not know, and moved across the one-bedroom apartment. It wasn't much. A gas stove. An ancient refrigerator that hummed constantly like a diesel engine. A couch that had clearly been pulled off the side of some disgusting curb and still smelled like someone else's trash.

Stopping at the door, she put her ear to the wood.

When she'd heard the footsteps coming down the corridor, she'd assumed it was time to go to work.

But something else was happening out there that sounded like trouble.

Two of the voices she immediately recognized.

She couldn't forget them if she'd wanted to. They would haunt her always.

The third...

Sounded familiar.

Low, gravely, with a touch of psychotic mirth.

Yes, she knew that voice. He'd been here many times to see her.

Donaldson.

A heavyset man who wore a paper-thin veneer of good 'ol boy conviviality over something ugly. Even uglier than the men who kept her here.

It was his voice she heard bleeding through the door: "I don't know! File it in your *shit happens* folder. It ain't my problem, gentlemen."

"It is actually," one of her captors said—the short one with massive thighs she knew as Ben. "You were supposed to use a rubber. House rules."

"Really?" Donaldson snorted. "You two want to lecture me about rules?"

"You come here, we have an agreement on how to do things. You can slap the girls around, use them however you want. But you gotta use a rubber."

"Not my problem," Donaldson said. "She's not my property. She's yours. I just rent her. How do I even know I'm to blame?"

"Because everyone else," Winston said, "uses a goddamn rubber."

"I don't even remember the last time I was here. I only blow through town every few months."

"And that's how far along she is. Bottom line; we want three hundred bucks to make this right."

"Bullshit!" Donaldson began to laugh. "You shooting up what you've been pushing, Winston? I'm not paying to fix your whore's condition. It's an occupational hazard."

She took a step back from the door. Through the receding heroin fog, she reached down, put her hands on her belly, realizing for the first time: *it's a bump*. A small one, to be sure, but a bump nonetheless. She'd noticed it last time she was in the shower, but had written it off as bloating.

What if...

"We're all reasonable men," Winston said. "We don't want this to get ugly."

Donaldson's voice got low. "You have no idea how ugly this can get."

"Is that how you want to play it, friend? Two against one? Is that risk worth a few hundred bucks to you?"

"I came here to get laid, and I get a shake down. This how you treat all your longtime customers?"

"We just want to make this right. And we'll even throw in a freebie."

There was a long pause. "Fine. You want me to take care of this?"

"That's all we're asking."

"I've got some equipment down in my trunk that should do it. I'll be right back up. We'll get this done right now."

"Hold up. You're not qualified to do this."

"It ain't rocket science. It's just—"

"We aren't going to trust the well-being of our property to you and your toolbox."

Another pause.

"Fine," Donaldson said. "But if I'm paying, I should get to watch."

"You serious?" Ben asked.

"It's my baby. And I've never seen an abortion before. Could be fun."

"Deal."

She listened as footsteps trailed off down the hall, then went to the window. Outside, a curtain of snow descended on the city in a perpetual loop. The cars below were all frosted now, and the first snowplows had begun to make their rounds.

She was still clutching her belly.

A life was growing inside of her.

A *life* was growing inside of her.

It didn't matter that half the DNA belonged to a monster.

Half the DNA was hers.

She was a mother. The tiny being growing inside her was her child.

Her *family.*

Suddenly, she couldn't see the snow anymore.

The world was a blur through her tears.

JACK

Chicago

The earliest flight to Chicago I could get was a red-eye leaving at
10:15 P.M., and it cost five times as much as I'd paid to come to
Florida. The ridiculous amount I spent didn't stop the plane from
being delayed.

I called my house for the eighth time that day. No answer.
Called Phin. No answer. Called my house. No answer. Called Phin.
No answer. Called my partner, Harry McGlade, to see if he knew
anything and got his voicemail greeting.

"This is Harry McGlade. I'm not picking up the phone because: A – I'm screening my calls and don't want to talk to you, B
– I'm engaged in a business transaction involving the exchange of
sexual favors for money, or C – It's after midnight and I chased a
sleeping pill with four beers."

I left a message for him to call me. Then I tried Phin again.

No answer.

I got to O'Hare at a little after five in the morning, exhausted
because I have a hard time sleeping in a bed let alone in the cattle
call the airlines dub *coach*, then cabbed it to my house in Bensen-
ville. My husband, and my dog, were gone.

My cat was there, but didn't seem happy to see me. I kept my
distance.

I immediately located the whereabouts of my dog, as Phin
had left a note next to the phone with the number for the kennel
he dropped him off at. But there was no evidence that pointed to

where my husband had gone. He'd cleared his computer history. He'd erased the house security footage. I checked call logs to both his cell number, and the house, and the only numbers that came up were mine, and McGlade's.

We only had one car, which Phin had left for me (probably because there was an anti-theft tracker in it and he didn't want me to locate him), so I braved rush hour traffic and got into Chicago a little after nine. Since McGlade never got to the office before noon, I went to his home.

Harry's current place of residence was a condo in Streeterville overlooking the lake. I parked in front, and walked up to the doorman.

"Is jackass here?" I asked.

"Hello, Miss Daniels. I haven't seen Mr. McGlade this morning. Would you like me to ring him?"

"I'll go up," I said. "Can you please watch my car?"

"Of course."

I handed him the keys in case he needed to move it, and then took the elevator to McGlade's penthouse. I let myself in without bothering to knock.

Harry's home was furnished in 1990's rich douchebag; leather sofas, nude Nagel prints on the walls, a Japanese shoji screen, hunter green everywhere. I heard sounds coming from the hallway, and found Harry in his round, king-size bed, watching something on his tablet.

"Hiya, Jackie. I'm watching Waveya."

He turned the screen my way and I saw five cute Korean girls in tiny outfits doing a sexy synchronized dance to the music.

"I've watched this eighteen times," he said, evidently unfazed that I was in his home. "I think I'm in love. Which of the five do you think is cutest? I'm leaning toward Ari. But MiU has that redhead thing going on."

"Don't you ever pick up your damn phone?"

"Nope."

"What if it's an emergency?"

He smiled big and shot me with his index finger and thumb. "That's why I gave you an emergency key."

"And what if I'm having the emergency?"

Harry shrugged. "You refused to give me a key. You were worried I'd show up in your house unannounced, like you're doing right now.

This wasn't getting anywhere. "Where's Phin?"

"Phin told me not to tell you or he'd beat me up."

"And if you don't tell me, I'll beat you up."

McGlade tapped his chin. "Decisions, decisions."

"This isn't a joke, Harry. If you know where Phin is, spill it."

"It's a long storypants."

"Storypants?"

"I'm doing a blog, so now I add the words *pants* to—"

"I don't care," I said, cutting him off. "Where is my husband?"

"You mean physically? Or emotionally? Because, I gotta be honest, sometimes Phin acts pretty darn juvenile."

I murdered him with my eyes. "Where is he, Harry?"

"It's sort of a long story. Where should I start?"

"The beginning."

"Okay. A long time ago, my parents had unprotected sex, and nine months later I was born. I was given up for adoption, probably because they couldn't accept a child with such a freakishly large penis. Want to see baby pictures? You'd be like, *whoa, does that baby have three legs?*"

"Fast forward."

"Okay. Two weeks ago I was in a Cracker Barrel with an escort named Sinnamon. She ordered a chicken fried steak, which she didn't eat. Do you know what a *handy* is?"

"Do you know what a broken nose is?"

I balled up my fist. Harry didn't flinch. He knew I wasn't actually going to beat him up. But if the only way to stop his comedy routine was with threats, I had one that would work. I dug my Colt out of my Michael Kors purse and pointed it at the bronze statue on his nightstand.

"Not my Erté *Prisoner of Love*! Okay, I thought my playful banter might loosen your resolve, but you win. While you were in Florida, a woman came to see you at the office. A writer named Katie Glente. She wanted to hire us to find Luther Kite."

He went through it all, up to Phin making him promise not to tell me anything. Then we watched the YouTube video on his tablet.

I was no stranger to graphic images, but this one made my stomach juices curdle. The screaming of the man being towed along the pavement, plus the obvious delight of his tormentors, wasn't something I'd forget anytime soon.

And the drivers did indeed look like Lucy and Luther. They also fit the profile. Their particular idea of fun.

"That's… awful," I said.

"Yeah. It's kind of a drag."

"Jesus, Harry."

"I also could have made a streaking joke. Because the guy is naked, and leaving a long, red streak."

"You're a horrible human being."

He grinned. "I'm a horrible human being, who also tracked down where it happened."

"And?"

Harry clasped his hands behind his head and leaned back, his victory pose. "Don't you want to know how I did it?"

"You enhanced the video and ran the license plates."

The victory pose vanished. "You're a buzz kill, you know that?"

"Where are they, McGlade?"

"Mexicali. Off of Mexican Federal Highway 5. I'm guessing the owner of the truck is the poor guy being dragged. Roberto Salazar. Single, Mexican citizen, currently between jobs. And by the look of that beaten down truck, not doing very well for himself. You could say he was just scraping by."

Ugh. And I worked with Harry by choice.

"Did you share any of this with Phin?"

"He left before I knew any of it."

"And you haven't been in touch?"

McGlade shook his head. "You've obviously tried to call him."

"His phone is off. I haven't heard from him since yesterday."

"Check the bankpants?"

"Stop saying pants, McGlade, or I'll punch you in yours."

"Geez, no need to be so crabbypa—" He was lucky he stopped himself.

"I checked the bank," I said. "He hasn't been using his debit card."

"Phin's not the sharpest knife in the chandelier, but he's smart enough to figure out the YouTube video came from Mexico."

I didn't bother correcting McGlade's mixed metaphor. Instead I tried to put myself in my husband's head. He was, obviously, going to try and kill Luther and Lucy to protect me and Sam. He would have seen the license plates on the truck, and the highway sign, and headed southwest. I knew Phin was resourceful, and determined, and could find people. But serial killers tended to be harder to track down than the average street thug. Phin could get lucky, but I didn't think his particular skill set would be enough to track down two sociopaths who made a career out of avoiding detection.

That gave me a little bit of reassurance. Because even though I'd bet on Phin in a bar fight over just about any other man I'd ever met, and I knew he had no reluctance when it came to ending a life if the situation called for it, he wasn't equipped to handle the type of evil that serial killers represented. Luther Kite wouldn't want to meet him face-to-face, one-on-one, on equal terms. Luther was more like a scorpion, hiding in a shoe, waiting for someone to slip a bare foot inside. If Phin found Luther and Lucy first, he'd quickly put an end to them both.

But if they found him first…

"The worst thing he could do," I said, "would be to go slumming around Mexico with a picture of Luther Kite, trying to beat information out of lowlifes."

Harry had begun the Waveya video again. "And you think that's probably his plan?"

"He's not exactly subtle."

"So we either need to find him before he finds Luther and Lucy, or find Luther and Lucy before they find Phin."

"We?"

My partner nodded. "I'm in. Harry Junior is spending the week with the Queen Bitch Who Eats Men's Souls—"

"His mother."

"—and we've got nothing pressing on our schedule other than the Morrow affair. I can string him along for a few more days. I'd be doing him a favor anyways. No one likes to see pics of their wife with some stud balls deep in her backdoor."

McGlade, annoying as he was, could prove helpful. At the very least, he'd be able to cover my back.

"Do you still have Katie Glente's card?"

"You want to pump her for more info?"

"Something like that."

McGlade leaned over and grabbed his wallet off the nightstand. "She wrote about us, you know. You, more than me. One of her books was about those Feebie tools in ViCAT. Another was about Andrew Thomas. We were footnotes, but from what I read her research was solid. Ah, here we go." McGlade produced a business card.

"Hand it over."

"This isn't Katie. This is Sinnamon, the escort. I think she's bi, if you're interested. I won't tell Phin." He closed his eyes and sniffed the card. "Mmm. Smells like daddy issues and ruined self-esteem."

I considered threating his art again, but McGlade must have read my intent because he found Katie's card. No address on it, just her name, phone number, and website URL. Michigan area code.

"Can you turn off the Korean dance troupe?"

"I cannot. Waveya and I are in love, and no one can stop us from being together." He noticed my glare and added, "But I can turn down the sound."

Harry continued to bounce his head along to the muted video as I dialed. Someone picked up on the third ring.

"Katie Glente."

"Ms. Glente, this is Jack Daniels. I heard you were looking for me."

"Yes, Lt. Daniels. I'm a big fan of your work. I'd be very interested in meeting with you."

"Ninety minutes," I said. "My house. I assume you know where it is."

"I do. That's great, I'll see you—"

I hung up. There was no need to chat now when I was going to meet her. I much preferred seeing the person when speaking to them, because then I could judge body language.

"What's your take on Katie Glente?"

Harry shrugged. "I'd hit that."

"You'd hit anything with two tits and a pulse."

"Untrue. The pulse is optional. And so are tits." He glanced at the Avon Walk for Breast Cancer poster hanging on the wall. Harry walked last year, and had actually helped raise over thirty thousand dollars for the cause. "Boobs don't make a woman sexy, Jackie. Her heart and courage are what makes her sexy."

"Stop acting noble, McGlade. You played the caring guy card to get laid."

"And I did. Four times, to be exact. But who's counting? Or taking pictures? Did you want to see pictures? I have a lot. About twice as many as I got during the Muscular Dystrophy Walk."

"There are so many words I could use to describe you, none of them flattering."

He shrugged. "I can't help it. I'm a connoisseur of the fairer sex. I also did pretty good at the Alzheimer's Walk, but I doubt any of the women I drilled would remember it."

I only had myself to blame. "Other than wanting to nail her, what was your impression of Glente?"

"Smart. Tough. Has an edge to her."

"Anything... off?"

"I didn't notice anything."

I searched his face, "You sure?"

McGlade probably wasn't the one to ask. He'd married a woman who cut off his hand, so he wasn't exactly the best judge of crazypants.

Shit, now he had me doing it.

"I get what you're saying." Harry raised his rubber-encased prosthesis, and the mechanical gears inside whirred until he was giving me the finger. "No, she didn't seem like she wanted to torture me to death. And I've gotten better at reading people in recent years. Are you just being your usual, paranoid self?"

I frowned. "Phin is gone because she showed up. If something happens to him, Katie Glente is the one I'm going to blame."

"Well, let's get to it, partner," McGlade said. He swung his legs out of bed, giving me an unwelcome view of his Captain America boxer-briefs.

Third leg my ass.

"Before we go anywhere," I said, "You need to get dressed."

"And dress I shall." He looked around the bedroom floor. "But first, help me find my pantspants."

PHIN

Baja

He'd taken five grand in cash with him. Cash Jack didn't know about. There was more where that came from, about $22k more, in a footlocker Phin kept in the garage rafters. Once upon a time, after he'd been diagnosed with cancer, Phin had taken to the streets and made money by robbing gang bangers and crack houses. It had been an empty, pointless, day-to-day-hand-to-mouth existence, and he'd spent much of what he'd stolen on drugs to take away his pain, both physical and emotional.

He might have also robbed a bank or three. But unlike his dealings with scumbags, Phin had always been nonviolent and polite when making those particular withdrawals.

When his cancer had gone into remission, and Jack had become a larger and larger part of his life, much of Phin's humanity returned. He stopped being a criminal, and started being a responsible adult. Rather than feel bad about his past, Phin was reflective. But just because he'd recognized his mistakes didn't mean he was going to give all the money back.

Besides, if anything happened to Phin, Jack would eventually find the cash, and at least part of Sam's college would be taken care of.

After a quick trip to FedEx, he used a near-perfect fake ID (both driver's license and passport he'd obtained through McGlade) and paid cash for his plane ticket at O'Hare. Phin endured an eight hour flight next to a chubby teen who snored, and after clearing Customs at General Rodolfo Sánchez Taboada International Airport he found a rental car place that accepted American cash instead of a credit card, provided he pay extra for the insurance.

His first night in Mexicali, he took a room at the Hotel Calafia, an upscale tourist destination with a well maintained pool and a workout room with flat screen TVs on the walls. He watched movies in his room until the front desk rang him to pick up the FedEx he sent to himself. It contained his FNS 9mm pistol, with four extra magazines, and a DoubleTap tactical pocket pistol. The DoubleTap was flat and no bigger than his wallet; thirteen ounces, 5/8" wide, and snag-proof. It held two rounds in the double barrel, with two extras in the pistol grip on a speed strip.

Phin appreciated the form and function; it was so small he could hold the gun in his palm and it was completely concealed by his hand. But even though it was the size of a .380 it packed the punch of a 9mm. The thin aluminum frame didn't make it the most comfortable weapon to shoot, but as a back-up piece it was unmatched. The coolest thing about it was the barrel detached, and each piece was small enough to fit inside a hollowed-out secret compartment in his Tony Lama cowboy boots. The heels swung open on hinges, like in the classic TV show *Wild Wild West*. They wouldn't get past TSA, but a thorough frisk wouldn't find them, and in a life or death situation it was better to be armed than unarmed.

He'd also sent four boxes of Hornady Critical Defense Ammo, a Bradley butterfly knife with a 4" tanto blade, some brass knuckles, and a shoulder holster for the FNS.

Once his equipment arrived, Phin went hunting.

Usually, if Phin were trying to find someone in a strange city, he would go cab hopping. Taxi drivers were the lifeblood of an urban area. They saw things, heard things, knew things. Phin's Spanish was *así así*, but he knew enough to ask the important questions.

Finding Luther Kite, however, would be challenging. This was a man who spent years, maybe decades, murdering people while staying in the shadows. Flashing around his picture asking, "¿Lo has visto?" wouldn't get him anywhere. So instead, Phin did something he was familiar with.

He went looking for drugs.

Dealers, like pimps, were territorial creatures of habit. If they were paying off the cops, they owned their street corner and advertised their presence, like peacocks displaying plumage. If they weren't protected, they still needed to be visible enough to sell their wares, but casual enough that they wouldn't draw the attention of law enforcement. That would mean spotters, usually shorties with cell phones who could give them advance warning when the police rolled up.

Phin drove around for half a day and found six dealers in the low rent parts of town. He was looking for codeine. Both Luther, and his psycho girlfriend Lucy, had some serious medical conditions, brought on by extreme physical abuse. Phin guessed they wouldn't be seeing a regular doctor for pain meds. He also guessed they were smart enough to avoid the really harsh stuff, like heroin and krokodil.

When Phin had been in his drug phase, cocaine was his palliative narcotic of choice. But to really take away the pain, he needed pills. Strangely, pills weren't easy to come by in Mexico. At least, not of the opiate variety. Phin found ecstasy, meth, GHB, and ketamine, but nothing from the codeine family other than some grubby Tylenol-3 caplets that looked like knock-offs.

He went back to the hotel, ordered some room service enchiladas, and spent ten minutes staring at his cell phone, which was off.

No doubt Jack had called. Several times. He wanted to hear her voice, but if he knew Jack she was probably on her way back to Chicago, if not back already. If he turned his phone on, there was a possibility she could track it.

Best to leave it off. And to not take it with him.

If he did find Luther, and things went sour, he didn't want anything that could be traced back to the woman he loved, and their daughter.

KATIE

Near Chicago

K atie called a taxi, had the driver take her to a nearby McDonalds and wait in the lot while she forced down a burger, fries, and whatever energy drink was at the soda fountain. She kept herself in shape and usually ate well, but sometimes a girl just needed empty calories. A remnant of her past, when she'd gone days without eating. Powerless. A victim. Surviving on the whim of others.

Never again.

Jack had sounded hard on the phone. Cynical. Tough. Which was good. That's what Katie had come for. The ex-police lieutenant was fifty years old, and had been out of the game since having her baby. Katie was concerned she wouldn't be up to the task of hunting Luther. Hopefully Jack would be just as hard in person as she'd been on the phone.

After a second cup of caffeinated sugar water, enough to make Katie's normally steady pulse tick a few more beats per minute, she returned to the cab and went back to Jack's house. Hoisting her backpack, she once again approached the entrance, keeping her face neutral as she stared into the security camera.

The door opened, and Jack, wearing a smart pantsuit with fashionably wide lapels—Donna Karan?—said, "You have five minutes."

Katie forced herself not to smile. She'd written, tangentially, about Jack Daniels in her non-fiction books, had read quite a bit about her, and had seen a lot of news footage, so Katie already knew what she looked like and how she sounded. But meeting her made Katie feel a little like a fan girl. Jack was greyer than her last press conference, and had put on a little weight, but she radiated authority like few people Katie had ever met. This woman had *presence.*

"I only need two," Katie said.

Behind Jack, Duffy stood at attention, his tail ramrod straight. Jack opened the door wider, allowing Katie entry, and she saw Harry McGlade was on the love seat, a leg draped over the armrest.

"Couldn't stay away, huh?" he asked, waggling his eyebrows.

"It's taking all of my self-control not to climb on you right now," Katie deadpanned.

She noted Jack's mouth twitched in a small smile.

"I'll be brief," Katie said. "I want to find Luther Kite, and I want your help."

"I don't care about Kite. I care about my husband."

"I know."

Katie watched the realization seep into Jack's face.

"You sent Phin after Kite because you knew I'd go after him."

"I know more about Luther Kite than anyone. I've spent years tracing unsolved murders and disappearances back to him. I know how he thinks, what he's capable of. That's why I won't go after him alone."

"Do you know where he is?"

"No. But I think he's in Baja."

"Do you know where Phin is?"

"No. He hasn't been in touch since I met him yesterday."

"You've trapped me into going after Luther. You've made it to the top of my shit list."

"Luther should be at the top of your shit list. Him, and Lucy. I see how you live, Jack. You know they're out there. You know they could come for you and your family someday. Phin decided on a pre-emptive strike. But he isn't you. If anyone can find Luther, you can."

"Why should I bring you along?"

"I can fight. I can shoot."

"I can get my own crew to back me up."

"You should. The more people we have on our side, the better chance we'll have at finding Kite... and surviving."

"And this is all for a book?"

Katie didn't reply. She kept her face neutral, revealing nothing, which wasn't easy because Jack seemed to be staring directly into Katie's soul.

"You've experienced violence," Jack said.

It was a statement, not a question, and Katie was a bit taken aback. "Yes."

"This is personal for you."

Katie chose not to lie. "Yes."

"Why?"

Katie didn't answer, but she held Jack's penetrating gaze.

"Give me your pack," Jack said.

Katie didn't hesitate. She handed the pack over. As Jack went through it, Katie noticed that McGlade had a gigantic gun, a .44 Magnum, in his lap. He was still smiling.

"That's a lot of firepower," Katie said. "Overcompensating for something?"

Harry winked. "You're welcome to discover that for yourself."

"And what would you do if I actually took you up on that offer?"

"I'd make love to you in a rapid, clumsy fashion, disregarding your needs entirely, and then I'd send you out for some food."

Katie had to give him points for honesty.

"How long have you been watching my house?" Jack asked.

"Since yesterday."

"From the southwest? I noticed someone had cut down some branches in the woods."

"You don't miss much."

"Where's the bug?" Jack asked.

"On your dog's collar."

"And Phin didn't catch that?"

"Your husband is… cautious. But he was more concerned about me attacking him than planting a microphone."

"Did you plant a microphone at my office?" Harry asked.

"No. I assumed all I would hear is you surfing Internet porn."

"I also spend a lot of time on YouTube, watching fat people trip and fall. Speaking of fatties, heard from Herb lately, Jack? I've got this idea, where I follow his fat ass around with a camera, waiting for him to trip and fall."

Jack seemed to ignore Harry, which Katie could completely understand. She and Jack had a brief stare-down, with neither saying anything.

Jack finally broke the silence. "If I go after Phin without you, you'll just follow me."

"That's the plan. Then I'll catch some fish with my bare hands and hope I impress you enough to join the posse."

Another small smile from Jack. She'd gotten the *Magnificent Seven* reference, where Horst Buchholz was originally rejected by the group, but then tagged along on their journey until they accepted him.

"I could make it difficult for you to follow," Jack said. "By breaking your leg."

Katie was younger than Jack, and stronger than Jack might assume, but there was a good possibility the older woman could make good on her threat.

"Yes. You could."

"Cat fight," Harry said. "Hot."

"I need to make a few calls," Jack said. "Have a seat. And since Harry mentioned cats, I have one. If it comes by, don't try to pet it. Or make eye contact. It doesn't like people."

Katie covered up her excitement at being included by acting nonchalant. "What's its name?"

"Mr. Friskers."

"It's pure evil," Harry said, "Imagine Hitler and Stalin had a baby mixed with feline DNA and Damien: The Omen II. And, speak of the devil."

McGlade's gaze turned toward the kitchen. Katie glanced that way and saw an ordinary-looking cat walking over to her.

"Don't move," Harry said. "Don't. Even. Breathe."

Katie watched, somewhat amused, as Mr. Friskers padded up to her leg and rubbed against it.

"Hitler and Stalin?" Katie said.

"Trust me," Harry said, "that cat is…"

Mr. Friskers screeched, a shrill sound not unlike a steam whistle, and launched himself four feet through the air, landing on Harry's leg and sinking in his claws.

"THE ANTICHRIST! IT'S THE ANTICHRIST! GET IT OFF!"

McGlade tried to push the cat away with his mechanical hand, and it bit onto his rubber index finger. He tried to shake his arm, but Mr. Friskers clung to it like a pit bull. McGlade's movements became broader, until it looked like he was waving a cat-shaped flag over his head.

"This is NOT what I meant by a cat fight being hot!"

Duffy began to howl. Jack's expression remained neutral, though Katie might have caught a small sigh.

"Get it off me, Jack! This prosthetic cost a fortune!"

"And have him attack me?" Daniels shrugged. "No, thanks. It's your fault for making eye contact."

McGlade picked up the Magnum and held it to the cat's head. "I'll shoot it! I swear I'll shoot it!"

"Don't," Jack warned. "We just bought that couch."

Harry made a fast movement, like he was pitching a baseball, and the cat flew off his hand, sailing through the air and letting out a long howl. It flew at least three meters, landed on the far wall, and stuck there like a gecko, all four legs splayed out. A very impressive display of claw strength. Then it dropped to the floor, hissed, and ran off down the hallway.

"I think I peed myself," Harry said.

"Do not piss on my couch."

So this is the dysfunctional little group I've aligned myself with. Katie thought. She wondered if maybe she should have followed Phin after all.

"I'm making my calls," Jack said, walking off.

"So..." Harry said. "Ebooks, huh? Does it pay well?"

"Not bad."

"Wanna make a hundred dollars? You can keep most of your clothes on."

"You and me, Harry, is never going to happen."

"Why not? You play for the other team?"

"No. I have standards."

"Understood. A hundred and five dollars."

"How about I give you a hundred dollars to stop talking to me?"

"For how long?"

"Forever."

McGlade rubbed his chin, apparently thinking it over. Then he said, "Deal."

Katie was surprised he accepted, but true to her word she took a hundred dollar bill from her pants pocket—emergency money— and handed it over to McGlade. In return, Harry handed her a business card. It read:

MY NAME IS HARRY MCGLADE.
I'M RICH, AND I'LL PAY YOU FOR SEX.

Katie turned away so Harry didn't see her grin.

PHIN

Baja

On his second day in Mexicali, Phin tried to buy drugs in some of the trendier areas. His first prospect was a pusher in front of an upscale nightclub. The short, thin man was wearing a light blue Hugo Boss polo, chinos, and Ray Bans. His business was strictly drive-up. Sports cars, luxury cars, limos. No spotters, so the guy paid to be there. After watching him for an hour, Phin pulled up in his rental, and was summarily ignored. He gave a little tap on the horn, and the man still refused to approach. Either overly cautious, or the Ford Fusion Phin had rented failed to impress him.

Phin laid on the horn and held up three hundred dollar bills, waving them until Hugo Boss had no choice but to approach. Phin rolled down the window.

"Can I help you?" The dealer's English was decent, as if he'd spent a lot of time trying to lose his accent.

"Vikes," Phin said.

Phin caught the beginning of a sneer, and saw the man begin to back away. Phin reached out and grabbed the guy's collar, yanking him forward with one hand and pointing the FNS with the other.

"I have some pain issues," he said. "Vicodin, codeine, oxytocin, hydrocodone, Percocet. And nothing with needles. Comprendes?"

"Ease up, brother. You're stretching my shirt."

Phin wondered how stoned the man was that he cared more about his designer top than the gun pointed at him.

"Do you have any pills?"

"Pills are so five years ago. It's all about the drank these days."

"Drank?"

"Slurps, brother. Purple. Lean. Tussin. Sizzurp."

Phin had been out of the drug scene for a while, but he recognized the term Tussin. That was codeine based cough syrup.

"You've got Tussin?"

"Brother, I am the Tussin King of Baja. I can get you more purple than you can carry. Take away your pain issues, no problem."

Phin released him. "What will three hundred get me?"

"Get you higher than a jet plane, brother. See my ride parked up the street?"

He pointed to an older model Benz in a tow zone. Phin nodded.

"I'm going to take a walk over, grab a cold one, be right back. You wait here, okay?"

"If you make a call, I'll take it as a sign of bad faith."

The dealer smiled, revealing his gold tooth. "Make a call? Brother, I got guys on the roofs. You're in the crosshairs. If I wanted you ventilated, I would have given the signal already."

Phin kept his face neutral, but felt like an idiot. He'd been so careful about looking for spotters, but he hadn't thought to check rooftops.

I'm slipping, he thought. *Three years ago I wouldn't have missed that.*

He watched the dealer saunter over to his car, open his trunk without any fear at all his stash would be taken, and remove a plastic soda bottle. He came back to Phin and handed him the bottle. Funny that it was called purple, because the liquid inside was reddish-pink.

"That's three hundred?" Phin said. He knew from experience that codeine cough syrup was about ten bucks a bottle at the pharmacy.

"This syrup is the shizznit, brother. That's four hundred, there. I'm giving you a new customer discount."

He handed over the three hundred, the dealer smiled and waved, and Phin drove off, feeling like he had rifle sights on his head until he'd gotten two blocks away.

He took it slow, careful, watching for tails, and returned to the Hotel Calafia. Once in his room he opened the bottle—the label was some brand of Mexican soda—and took a sniff.

It didn't smell like cough syrup. It smelled like strawberry candy. Phin guessed this wasn't jacked from some pharmacy. This was homemade. Someone was putting their poppy fields to good use. Good, profitable use, because heroin was forty bucks a gram and killed the clientele. If they were selling bottles of this shit to rich users at four bills a pop, they wouldn't even need to bother with cutting or trafficking to make a profit.

Phin raised it to his lips, swallowed a teaspoon, and waited.

Within ten minutes, the familiar warmth set in. Phin's shoulders unbunched. His eyelids drooped. He felt that floating/sinking sensation that was unique to the wonderful family of opiates. Phin stood up, slightly dizzy, infused with a strong sense of well-being and a mellow buzz that made the whole world fuzzy and beautiful.

This was some seriously good stuff. It made Vicodin seem like Pez.

It also made sense why no one else in town dealt with pills. Whomever Hugo Boss worked for owned the market. And they were obviously well-connected enough to keep the market cornered. If he could afford to deal so openly, and had riflemen spotting for him, it meant payoffs and protection and a supply chain that probably went all the way back to the farmers.

Phin knew a little bit about Mexican cartels. They had more in common with the mafia than garden variety street gangs. Organized, powerful, very dangerous, run like a hybrid of militia and white collar business.

If Lucy and Luther were in Mexicali, they'd be on purple. And if they were on purple, they would have dealt with Hugo Boss, or someone in his network.

Phin unscrewed the cap, walked into the bathroom, and poured the rest of the syrup down the toilet. He used the coffee machine in the room to brew three cups, and when he'd finished drinking them all his codeine high had worn off sufficiently. Then it was back in the car, and back to the dealer.

Time to go find Luther Kite.

JACK

Near Chicago

I can do what I can from behind my desk at the precinct. But I can't go with you, Jack."

I was so surprised by Herb's answer that it took me a moment to find my voice. Lieutenant Herb Benedict was the closest thing I had to a best friend. We'd been partners on the force for over a decade. We'd closed dozens of cases. We'd saved each other's lives. Though we didn't stay in touch as often since I retired, we still talked on a pretty regular basis.

I switched the phone to my other hand. "Mind if I ask why?"

I could hear his breathing, but he didn't respond.

"Herb? You know I wouldn't ask this if I didn't need your help."

"Aren't we a little old to still chase after serial killers, Jack?"

"We aren't chasing Luther Kite. We're chasing Phin."

"And Phin is chasing Luther Kite. And then what will happen? People are going to wind up dead. Or worse."

"That won't happen again. I'm not looking for trouble, Herb."

"But trouble finds you anyway."

I wasn't sure how to respond. He was right, of course. Everyone I was close to eventually wound up with some degree of PTSD. Sometimes I felt like I secreted some sort of pheromone that attracted psychos.

But that didn't mask the hurt. I'd been counting on Herb—he was one of the only people I'd ever known that I could always count on—and he rejected me so fast it felt like whiplash.

"No problem," I told him.

"Now I feel shitty."

"Don't. I get it. I'm sorry for asking."

"Now I feel shittier."

"I didn't mean it like that. I know you'd help if you could. It's okay."

Another uncomfortable pause.

"I'm quitting, Jack."

"Quitting what?"

"The Job. I've got eight days until retirement."

I wasn't sure what to say. Eight days meant he'd given notice a while ago.

Given notice and hadn't told me. His best friend.

"Congrats," I finally said.

"Bernice made me promise. No more risks. She's seen too many movies where the cop announces his retirement and then dies twenty minutes later. After Michigan, and Wisconsin... You know I love you like you're family, Jack. If it were my choice, I'd come along."

That made Herb's refusal sting a little less.

"Is there going to be a party?" I asked.

"A party?"

"A retirement party. Knowing Bernice, she probably invited the whole—" I cut myself off as realization hit. "Your wife doesn't want me there."

"It's nothing about you personally, Jack. Bernice loves you."

"But?"

I heard Herb sigh. "She thinks you're bad luck. You know?"

"I don't know, Herb. Tell me."

"People are always getting hurt or dying around you, Jack. Bernice thinks you're jinxed. She doesn't want you around."

First came the sucker punch. Then came the knockout.

"Ever?" I asked, my voice soft and nearly cracking.

"Of course not. Just give her some time."

"Herb, I gotta level with you. This hurts."

"It hurts me, too. I've been dreading telling you all this, believe me. But it'll all blow over. I just need to prove to Bernice that I can go for two months without anyone trying to kill me."

"I hear you."

An awful, painful silence ensued.

"Is jackass going with you?" Herb eventually asked.

For a brief moment in time, Harry McGlade and Herb had gotten along. That didn't last, and they were back to hating each other.

"Yes."

"Anyone else?"

"A writer. Katie Glente."

"Can she handle herself?"

"I don't know yet. It seems like she can."

More silence. I didn't have to read Herb's mind to know he was worried about me.

"Is there anyone else you can call, Jack?"

What he really meant was: is there anyone else who owes me enough to risk their life for me?

I thought it over, and came up with four people. I knew where to find two of them, but one, a cop I'd worked with named Tom Mankowski, was currently in physical therapy and pretty much immobile. The third, McGlade could contact. The fourth I hadn't seen in years, but maybe he was still around. I knew someone at the DMV and could possibly get an address, but Herb was right there on the phone.

"Can you do a quick CPD search for me?" I asked Herb. "Last name Abernathy."

"Abernathy. That sounds familiar. Wait, you mean that short muscle head, used to strong arm for Marty the Maniac? What was his name?"

"Tequila," I said. Back when Herb and I were still transitioning into plainclothes, we'd had a run in with the diminutive mob enforcer, who had once worked for a notorious mob bookie named Marty Martowski.

"That guy's a sociopath."

"He's also one of the toughest people to ever live." Even tougher, perhaps, than my missing husband.

I heard fingers on a keyboard, and Herb gave me an address and phone number. "Kept clean. Only thing on his record the past ten years is a speeding ticket. Maybe he's mellowed out."

I hoped not. I didn't need mellow. "Thanks, Herb."

Herb's voice dropped an octave. "Keep me in the loop, okay? Call, text. If I need to send in the cavalry, I need to know where to send it."

I told him I'd call him tomorrow, and then tried Tequila's number. I got an answering machine with only a beep to signal it was working. I left a brief message saying I needed his help, and then I called Val Ryker, a friend and co-worker from my early CPD days.

Straight to voicemail. Didn't anyone pick up the phone anymore? I asked her to get in touch, then returned to the living room and found Mr. Friskers in Katie's lap, purring as she stroked him.

McGlade had backed away to the other side of the couch. "It's eerie, Jack. She must know some kind of sorcery. She's also able to resist my sexual advances."

"That proves it," I said, "she's a witch."

"Not that I need it," Harry said to Katie, "but do you have any spells that would make a guy a few inches bigger? Like, five or six inches?"

Katie didn't respond. As she pet the cat, her eyes seemed to take on a far-away look.

"Harry, we need to contact some old friends. Do you have any way to get in touch with Chandler and Fleming?"

The women I'd just mentioned didn't officially exist, and those weren't they're real names. They previously worked for a secret government organization, and were experts at staying off the grid.

But they owed me, and they'd be powerful allies… *if* we were able to locate them.

"Sure. I'll just give them a ring," Harry said.

"They gave you their phone numbers?"

"Don't be dense, Jack. They're covert op spies. They don't give out their numbers. What about Herb? Did he confirm?"

"He's… got something going on."

Harry's nose wrinkled. "Fat boy bailed on you? Seriously? I thought you guys were attached at the hip. You have some sort of falling out? Because I was chummypants with El Chubbo for a while, but he's got some serious personality problems."

I didn't want to discuss it. "Chandler and Fleming, McGlade. Any ideas?"

"I can reach Hammett. Though—I'm being candidpants here—my juevos are still bruised from the last time I saw her."

"Don't contact Hammett." That woman was crazier than the people we were looking for.

"Your call." Harry took out his phone and spoke as he pressed his touch screen keyboard.

"Super-secret agent spy post," he said, typing out loud. "Fleming, we haven't bugged you since the White House. Jack Daniels and I need help. Also Chandler. Call ASAP. Harry McGlade."

"How can you text her if you don't have her number?"

"I didn't text. I blogged."

"You just blogged?" I said, incredulous.

"Faster than taking out an ad in the personals. Fleming's a hacker. She monitors the net, no doubt has spiders looking for key terms. When she finds the names *Fleming, Chandler, Jack Daniels, Harry McGlade,* and the words *bugged* and *White House* all in one post, she'll call me."

I cast a gaze at Katie, who was still entranced by the cat. "What if someone else is looking for those same terms, Harry?" I asked.

"You mean the NSA? Hell, who cares? Those paranoid bastards already set up a video camera over my bed." Katie glanced over at him. "It was the NSA," Harry told her, "I swear."

I was more concerned about other, unnamed government organizations. Ones the NSA didn't know about. Organizations that could make me, and everyone I know, disappear without a trace.

I was having this obviously delusional paranoid fantasy when my cell phone rang.

UNKNOWN NUMBER.

I picked up, and with a hint of trepidation said, "This is Jack."

"The place we ate at, with the carrot cake," said a female voice I recognized. "Tomorrow at 2 P.M. Bring the idiot. Make sure you aren't followed."

Then she hung up.

Harry read my face. "Told you so."

"We have to go to Washington," I said, putting away my cell.

"We?"

"She told me to bring the idiot."

"Woo-hoo!" Harry said, doing a fist pump. "I'm in. She's obviously been pining for me. Which one was it? Moodypants? Wheels? Both? They owe me a three-way."

I frowned. Because they were identical twins, the sisters sounded the same. I guessed the caller was Wheels—Fleming—because she was the one there when Harry ordered carrot cake at that diner in DC. But she could have told that to Chandler.

"Book a flight," I told Harry.

"How about the cat whisperer over here?"

Katie and I exchanged a glance.

"I'm just going to follow you," she told me.

I sighed. "Book it for three."

LUCY

The cardboard Amazon box clutched in his scarred hands, K pushed open the door to the playroom at the far end of the hotel.

The smell was... strong.

Death had many scents. Some good. Some not so good.

The aroma of blood excited Lucy, stirring something in her similar to hunger or sexual arousal.

Bile was more of an acquired taste, akin to enjoying a fine whiskey. The first few times, it was pungent. But then it began to develop nuances and different notes, and the complexity became appreciated.

Lucy appreciated urine more as a side-effect than as an odor. Making someone piss themselves in fear and pain was fun, but the smell wasn't something she salivated over.

Rot and shit were just plain awful. That's why there were two main rules when torturing someone to death. First, cauterize wounds to prevent necrosis. Second, don't perforate the bowels.

The playroom smelled mainly of blood. And body odor—a fragrance that had no place in a torture chamber, or anywhere else.

There was also the gag-inducing smell of excrement.

Lucy held what was left of her nose, and she and K approached the man on the rack. She couldn't remember what the young man had done—he was a snitch or a rival cartel member or a witness. Or maybe Emilio—the drug lord who owned the compound—was simply as offended by the man's BO as Lucy was. If being pungent was a crime, this guy deserved at least a dozen death sentences.

And now, to add to his unpleasant stench, he'd crapped himself.

It was a bad one, too. Eyes-watering, taste-it-in-the-back-of-your-mouth bad. Lucy had no idea how women could have babies. Wiping asses every day for two straight years seemed worse than any torture she could dream up.

K seemed equally irritated. He handed Lucy the box, removed his folding knife from his pocket, and held it against the man's throat.

"I was going to give you a chance to go free," he said. "But little boys who mess their pants don't deserve freedom. This is what they deserve."

Apparently little boys who messed their pants deserve a Columbian necktie.

Bo-ring.

Lucy quickly left the playroom, finding a cheap dinette chair in the kitchen area, and sat there with the box in her lap as K went to fetch a clean-up crew and another victim. She yawned. What started off as a potential rekindling of the killing spirit had once again devolved into something rote. Rather than celebrate a fellow human being's suffering, Lucy felt like they were just going through the motions.

It was sad, really.

Some men came and took out the body in a plastic bag. Then a smiling Mestizo woman who had more wrinkles than a Shar-Pei padded into the playroom with a mop and bucket. Lucy wondered what she could be so happy about, cleaning up blood and poo for a living, and then began to envy the cleaning woman for her baseless happiness. The envy became so strong that when the cleaning woman came out of the playroom with the smile still on her face, Lucy unholstered the Springfield XD she carried on her belt and shot her twice in the chest.

"Why did you do that?" K asked, hobbling up behind her.

"She was pissing me off."

"How?"

"She looked happy."

They both stared at the woman, who'd collapsed on the floor but somehow managed to not spill her dirty bucket.

"She was good," K said. "A miracle worker with clothing stains."

Lucy frowned. "Aw, shit. She was the one who did the laundry?"

"Yeah."

"She used just the right amount of starch when she ironed."

"Yeah."

Lucy was angry at herself. Then she noticed the woman's chest was moving. "Hey. She's still alive."

"I'll get the men." K trudged off again.

The men came, put the woman on a blanket, and picked her up. Lucy almost told her sorry, but wasn't sure how to say it in Spanish. Besides, apologizing wasn't one of her strengths. Somehow, she always came off sounding sarcastic. Instead, Lucy sort of gave the cleaning woman the universal *oops* shrug as she went past.

The woman was trembling, and seemed to be trying really hard not to cry.

Awkward.

A few minutes later another group of men came (or maybe it was the same group of men, Lucy wasn't really good with faces), lugging along a man in iron shackles. The prisoner was in his twenties, one eye swollen shut from a recent beating. K and the guards exchanged some rapid-fire español.

"His name is Juan," K told Lucy. "He was caught selling Tussin to school children."

"So kids aren't allowed to get high in Mexico?" Lucy asked.

"They drink too much and OD. Bad for business."

"It was only two kids who died," Juan said, his English pretty good. "Mexico has plenty more."

"You broke the rules," K told him. "Emilio doesn't allow sales to kids."

Juan spat on K's feet. "Hijo de puta. You kill kids in your crazy arena games. I saw you make two ten-year olds fight to the death with machetes."

"True," K said. "But they weren't taking drugs."

Juan's look remained defiant. "I lost three thousand pesos on that match. I was only trying to make my money back."

K unsheathed his Spyderco Harpy knife.

"Another Columbian necktie?" Lucy groaned. "Really?"

K glanced at her. "No. I have something else in mind for this one."

The menacing way K said it gave Lucy goose bumps on her scar-free patches of skin.

"Emilio wants you in the games," K told Juan. "My protégé here wants to cut you into little bits and make you eat yourself."

"Protégé?" Lucy repeated. "K, that's sweet."

"But it is your lucky day, Juan. I'm going to give you a chance to walk out of here. But you have to do something for me. Interested?"

"What do I have to do?" Juan asked.

K motioned for Lucy to hold up the Amazon box. When she did, he sliced open the cardboard with his Harpy. Slowly and seductively, as if undressing a lover. Then he reached inside and gingerly took out—

An electric hot plate.

"What are you going to do to him?" Lucy asked. "Cook him a can of beans?"

"That's racist," Juan said. "I'm Mexican, so it has to be beans?"

"I wasn't talking about refried beans," Lucy said. "I meant like American pork and beans."

"The kind with brown sugar?" Juan nodded. "I like those."

"I'm vegan," Lucy said, "except for occasionally drinking blood. But when I was a kid my mom made pork and beans all the time. There was never more than a few tiny pieces of pork in it."

"I know, right? How can they call it pork and beans when it doesn't have hardly any pork?"

"Stop talking about pork and beans," K ordered. "This idea is from a story in an old issue of Alfred Hitchcock's Mystery Magazine. March 2005. It's called The Agreement."

"What is it about, K?" Lucy asked, though she was still thinking about pork and beans, and wondered if they sold cans of it anywhere in Baja. Lucy was still vegan, but she figured it would be simple enough to avoid the pork when there were only three bites per can.

"The story is about a gambler who loses at cards and is going to be killed because he can't pay. But he's given a choice. If he can keep his hand on a stove burner for ten full seconds, his debts will be absolved."

K took the hot plate out with a dramatic flourish. It was one of those models with a round, spiral burner, and didn't look menacing at all. He unwrapped the cord, had one of the guards plug it into an extension in the hall, and set the burner down on a rickety Formica table. K twisted the only knob on the appliance, and the coil began to glow orange.

"The best and the worst pain is what we do to ourselves." K said, staring hard at Juan. "Do you want to go home?"

Juan nodded.

"Place your palm on the burner and hold it there. If you can last for ten seconds without pulling away, you're free."

Juan eyed the hot plate like it was a small dog known to bite.

"Put my hand on that?"

"Yeah."

"And hold it there for ten seconds?"

"Yeah."

"Here's a better idea. You eat a bag of dicks."

Lucy looked at K, then told the guards, "Hold him."

They wrestled the cuffed man to his knees, and Lucy pressed the red-hot grill into Juan's face, holding it there for longer than ten seconds.

Oddly enough, it smelled sort of like pork and beans.

K then cut off the man's pants and said, "What was your idea? Eat a bag of dicks? How about you tell us what that's like."

Juan never did tell them what it was like, because he choked to death. Which was a shame, because Lucy was curious to see what other body parts they could have forced him to eat.

"So how did that Hitchcock story end?" she asked, as the guards hauled Juan's body away.

"I don't know. Last page was ripped out."

"I bet it didn't end with the guy eating his own junk."

"Probably not."

They went to the sink to wash up, sharing the canister of powdered soap. K squinted at his purple robe and frowned. "Blood stains."

"Sorry about that, K. Maybe she'll survive."

"She really is a miracle worker with stains."

"And ironing." Lucy used a wooden brush to get the bits of tissue out from under her fingernails. "So if he actually lasted the full ten seconds, you really would have let him go?"

K made a croaking sound, like someone with emphysema trying to clear his throat. He made the sound again, and again, and Lucy suddenly realized he was laughing.

She joined in.

PHIN

Baja

Phin wasn't built for surveillance. He was built for action.

Watching a target took a skill set antithetical to the one he had. Phin had been keeping an eye on Hugo Boss, and his spotters, for sixteen hours, and had prepared for the stake-out as best he could. He'd picked three spots where he could have them all in sight while remaining off their radar. Binoculars, with screens on the lenses so they wouldn't reflect and give away his position. A case of water. Beef jerky and candy bars—things packed with calories that wouldn't spoil. A thermos to urinate in. Caffeine pills. A notebook, to jot down the movements and guard changes of the snipers on the rooftops, the car makes and models and tags, the number of deals Hugo made.

For four hours, he'd park in a spot up the street. Then he'd get out of the car and sit in an alley, next to the world's smelliest Dumpster; seriously, it smelled like someone vomited up a skunk with diarrhea and let it bake in the ninety degree heat for a week. But it was close enough to the action that he wouldn't need the binoculars, his cover disguise a stained shirt and half a bottle of warm beer in a paper bag. After four hours in the alley it was back to the car and a new parking spot, in the opposite direction.

It was grueling, boring, mind-numbing work. This spying stuff wasn't Phin's thing, and as the minutes ticked slowly by he felt more and more wound up.

But he learned a lot about their operation. Hugo had a five hour shift, then was replaced by another guy—this one in Armani. Armani was replaced by a third dealer, this one in Bermuda shorts and a Hawaiian shirt, the gaudy ensemble topped off with a straw pork pie hat with a flowery band that matched neither shorts nor shirt. Then back to Hugo.

They dealt some grass, occasional baggies of powder, and a lot of syrup. All three used the same parked car as their storage locker, and Phin had yet to see the supply replenished. He did some quick calculations and figured he'd watched over twenty thousand dollars' worth of transactions in a sixteen hour period.

Now the sun was up, heating up the interior of the car. Neither Luther Kite, nor his scarred ward Lucy, had paid Hugo a visit. Were they getting their painkillers elsewhere, maybe via fake prescriptions? Was the painkiller trail a dead end, and they weren't even using? Were they even still in town?

Phin considered his options. Grabbing one of the dealers and asking him if Luther was a client would be risky, and even if the dealer recognized Luther, that didn't mean he knew where Luther was staying. Trying a different approach meant abandoning this one, and Phin could picture Luther driving up to score painkillers five minutes after Phin left.

He tried to think like Luther, but that wasn't one of Phin's strengths. He knew street thugs, pimps, gang bangers, junkies, hustlers, and whores. Jack was the one who knew psychopaths. Though Phin had encountered a few serial killers—old cases of Jack's—he couldn't put himself in their minds like she seemed to be able to.

Luther came to Mexico with Lucy. Why? To escape capture in the US? Because he had some sort of stake here? A hideaway? A supply of cash? Drugs?

Drugs were available everywhere. And Luther wasn't exactly Public Enemy Number 1. He was no doubt on some law enforcement watch lists, and there were arrest warrants, but he was just one of hundreds, probably thousands, of wanted murderers. And there were plenty of places to hide in the US. Luther and Lucy had been doing so for years.

Why Mexico?

Phin recalled the video that brought him there. A man being dragged behind a car. That wasn't the act of someone on the run, trying to avoid attention.

That was the act of a maniac. A psychopath. Someone insane, who got off on the pain of others.

Maybe Luther and Lucy weren't in Mexico to hide from authorities.

Maybe they'd come to have fun.

Phin played with the idea. Baja had plenty of tourists who didn't know the area. Plenty of poor locals no one cared about. Police that could be paid to look the other way.

It was like a Disneyland for serial killers. They could operate under the radar, having their pick of disposable victims, with impunity.

Maybe, instead of staking out dealers, Phin should go to the police. Find out if there had been any more people dragged to death. If they could be bribed to ignore crime, maybe they could also be bribed to reveal it.

That seemed like a better idea than watching Hugo Boss for another four hours.

Phin tucked away his notebook, and started the car.

He'd driven a block when the steering wheel began to pull right and he heard the distinctive *THWAP-THWAP-THWAP* of a flat tire.

Already twitchy from the caffeine, Phin went into instant paranoia mode, taking his FNS in hand and doing a three-sixty scan of the area as he pulled over to the side of the road. The street looked normal, no obvious threats.

He parked, shut off the car, and waited, continuing to look around. At the next corner were three men sharing a cigarette. Across the street was a parked car, empty. Phin glanced back at Hugo Boss, and he was in front of the club, business as usual.

It could have been regular old bad luck. Maybe he ran over a glass bottle, or a jagged chunk of asphalt—the streets weren't in the best shape.

Phin tucked the gun into the back of his jeans, located the button to pop the trunk, and got out of the car. The cholos on the corner gave him a glance, then resumed their conversation. A car cruised past, slowing down, and Phin tensed until he figured out they were headed for Hugo to buy drugs.

Keeping alert, Phin walked to the front of the car and checked the tire. It was flat, the rubber beginning to tear from riding on the rim. He squinted down the street, but didn't notice anything he might have run over.

He went to the trunk, lifting up the carpet-covered board that hid the spare, and that's when they hit him.

It was a smart attack. Phin had the trunk open so he didn't see them run up, and his hands were occupied with the tire the moment before he was tackled.

They were fast. But so was Phin.

He dropped the spare and pulled his gun just as one of the cholos plowed into him. Phin shot twice as he fell backward into the street, dead weight pinning him down, another Mexican coming at him from the right side. Phin fired four more times, center mass, and then two men sat up in the car parked across the street—they'd been hiding—and hurried over to join the fight.

Phin managed to push the dead guy off of him, emptied his magazine at the duo, sensed movement from behind, and then something hit him in the wrist, the FNS falling from his grasp and clattering to the street. Phin dove away from his attacker, tucked and rolled to his feet, and came up surrounded by four men.

The snipers hadn't tried to take him down yet, but Phin suspected that was what had taken out his tire. None of the cholos he faced carried guns. That could only mean one thing; they meant to take Phin alive.

Well... Phin thought, slipping the brass knuckles on to his left hand and then flicking open the butterfly knife with his right, *let them try.*

Two guys rushed Phin at once. He slashed one across the chest, then did a tight spin-kick and caught the other in the jaw. Both stumbled away, and a pipe clipped Phin in the side of the head and sent him off balance and staggering into the middle of the street. He regained his footing, slipped a punch, then countered with a brass knuckle uppercut that broke bone and teeth.

Phin whirled to face the two Mexicans still on their feet, and saw six more running his way.

This was a coordinated attack. His odds weren't good.

He dared a quick glance at the street, looking for his dropped gun, and then a heavy, muscular dude rushed at Phin's knife, the man's shirt balled up in his hand to deflect the blade. Phin raised the weapon, thrusting at the man's face, missing, and the other guy stepped in and popped Phin in the ear, hard enough to rock him sideways.

Phin spun, letting centripetal force whip out his hand with the brass knuckles, catching his attacker on the temple, a stream of blood spurting out and following him like the string of a kite.

Muscles lunged at Phin again, and Phin ducked under the man's hands, dropped a shoulder, and pushed forward, driving the guy backwards as he stabbed at his side. The cholo fell just as the reinforcements arrived.

Five down, six to go.

The fight-or-flight adrenaline surge still strong, Phin planted a boot in one man's chest, and elbowed another in the chin.

Two guys rushed him, and Phin stepped away but someone he'd dropped earlier reached out and snagged his ankle.

Phin went down.

Three men jumped on top of him.

Phin felt a rib snap, tried to roll away, but two more bodies piled on. Another rib went, and Phin's fight for survival became a fight to breathe as all of the weight on him squashed his diaphragm. Pinned immobile under the stack of bodies, the edges of Phin's vision became fuzzy from the lack of oxygen. Then he felt a jab in the arm, and the blackness overtook him.

LUCY

Somewhere in Mexico

She limped up to the threshold and peered inside.

K called it the *throne room*.

The walls were stone. K had insisted on gray, like a medieval castle, but nothing in this country was gray. He'd settled for light brown adobe, topped by a sloppy coat of charcoal paint the cartel had splashed around with the finesse of men who sold drugs for a living.

There was a single window, squarish and barely big enough to stick your head through, overlooking the fighting arena two floors below. At night, the only light came courtesy of greasy oil lamps hanging from chains, yellow and sickly and not much brighter than candles. Electric light was impossible; when K converted the room he'd bricked over the electrical outlets and fixtures. Every time Lucy entered the room it took a few seconds for her eye to adjust to the darkness.

K preferred darkness. He wrapped himself in it like a vampire in a cape.

Lucy didn't knock before entering the throne room; she couldn't because there was no door, only an arched entryway. She was the only one K allowed inside, and every single time she found him in the same position. Seated at a ratty, stained, purple throne leftover from some second-rate 1970s theater production of King Lear. It was huge, with a high back, and K was always slumped in it, perfectly still, looking small, eyes wide and staring at nothing, his labored, keening wheeze the only proof he was still alive.

The cartel called him El Cometa. Lucy had taken to calling him K, and he hadn't objected.

Others knew him as Luther Kite.

She walked up the scrap of maroon runner to the foot of his throne, proprietarily bowed as deeply as her wrecked back could bend, and then searched his eyes to see if he'd noticed her arrival.

His gaze remained vacant. Lucy couldn't tell if it was the Tussin, or something else. K's pale countenance hadn't darkened a bit in the Mexicali weather; if anything it had become more translucent. The hair he had left was patchy, graying. Looking at him, Lucy sometimes felt like she was staring at an old black and white film.

"I've been thinking," he said, surprising her. "About pain."

It was a subject they both knew intimately well. From the delivery end, and as captive recipients.

"What about it, K?"

She leaned in, smelling lemon candy on his breath; a habit he'd been unable to break even though the part of his tongue that tasted sour had been long ago skinned off.

"The end to our pain is coming, Lucy. Soon."

"How?"

"Why not death rather than living torment?"

Lucy hated when he talked like that. Quoting old, cryptic shit.

"Death? That's the end of our pain?"

"Death is the end of everything. And it closes in on us."

"Are you ill, K?"

K's eyes snapped into focus and pinned her. "No more than usual. He's mad that trusts in the tameness of a wolf."

Lucy sighed, overly dramatic. "More Shakespeare. I hate that guy."

"When I was captive, sometimes he let me read. Shakespeare. Old mystery magazines, with pages ripped out so I never knew how the stories ended. Once, because it amused him, an Italian crime novel. That was my sole entertainment for an entire year. I can't speak Italian, but I read every word. I read the Shakespeare, too. It made about as much sense as the Italian. But sometimes, those wretched lines get stuck." He poked a boney finger at his temple. "The Bard is lucky he died four hundred years ago, because I would love to cut him into tiny bits and make him eat himself, piece by piece."

Lucy allowed the image to worm itself into her brain. Where to cut first. How big the slices should be. "Sounds fun. We should try something like that."

"Maybe. I have another idea. From something I read."

The warmth she was feeling dissipated, and Lucy suppressed a groan. "Let me guess. Shakespeare."

"No. Hitchcock. Let's go to the playroom."

Lucy brightened. "Now you're talkin', K."

K pulled himself up to his feet, using his scepter as a cane. The skull atop the staff wasn't real; a ceramic souvenir for tourists to buy on Día de Muertos. The gold shaft was also fake, the metallic paint flaking off, the colored jewels made of glass. But the hair atop the skull, dark and matted and glued there like a fright wig, was a real human scalp.

Lucy knew it was real, because she and K had taken it from its previous owner as he begged for mercy they didn't have.

The duo walked into the hallway, and the faux castle motif continued, albeit sloppily. The walls weren't adobe, but rather stucco painted to look like stone. There were electric lights, hanging on the low ceiling—original fixtures dating from when the building had been converted into a hotel in the 1950s. K had replaced the bulbs with the kind that flickered like orange candles.

They took the stairs slow, using the railings. Lucy hated stairs. It was painful enough getting around on level surfaces, but something about up-and-down movement ignited her raw nerve endings like cattle-prod shocks to her spine. She clenched the teeth she had left and weathered the pain. When they reached the bottom, some cartel asshole was sitting on the last three steps, smoking a cigarette, his ear buds spitting out tinny *ranchero* music. He didn't notice they were above him until K poked him with his scepter.

The cholo turned, his expression morphing from irritated to spooked in half a heartbeat. It reminded Lucy of a Loony Tunes cartoon character, eyes popping out in surprise.

"Lo siento, El Cometa," he sputtered, quickly getting out of the way and hurrying down the corridor.

On the first floor, the décor was no longer Halloween/medieval, and instead reflected what the building actually was; a renovated mission, built in the 1800s. K stopped at his room, and like the majority of rooms in the crumbling hotel it was cramped, hot, and stank of age. Perched on K's bed was a medium-sized cardboard box. He handed Lucy his scepter and picked it up.

"Dropped off this morning," K said. "A new toy to play with."

Lucy noted that the box was labeled Amazon, and her hopes dimmed. Even though Amazon claimed to be *The Everything Store*, she doubted they sold torture paraphernalia, rare weapons, or interrogation equipment. Whatever K had planned for the playroom was probably going to be lame.

As with any other addiction, it was possible to develop a tolerance to sadism. When Lucy had first met K, she'd been a teenager and had just killed her first man. At the time, K collected antique surgical tools, and each terrible instrument they'd tried upped her level of excitement.

Lithotomes, scarificators, tonsil guillotines.

A vintage speculum made of wrought iron that could be heated on a stovetop until it glowed.

Artificial leeches.

Everything was so exciting back then. To get the same high these days, Lucy needed things to be even uglier. Messier. More extreme.

But what was the worst thing that could be in an Amazon box? Some overpriced hardcover books and a lint roller?

She eyed the package again. No bigger than a breadbox.

Shit, maybe it *was* a breadbox. Lucy wouldn't be surprised. Lately, K had been…

Slipping was the wrong word.

Fading? Losing interest?

Going mad?

When they'd first arrived at the compound, over a year ago, Lucy had felt like a dysfunctional kid in a candy store. She'd always been a nomad, and took her fix on the road when she could find it. That meant passing up a lot of potential opportunities for safety's sake. Killing in public required a certain situational awareness. She could never truly lose herself in a messy death while worrying if the cops were around the next corner. And in a day and age where everyone had a cell phone with a high resolution camera, it had become almost impossible to indulge in her particular tastes while remaining invisible.

South of Mexicali, in this blood-soaked sanctuary known as La Juntita, there were no such worries. Lucy could take her time, really enjoy the moment. Not only were they safe, but they were being protected *and* getting paid for their skills.

Those early times in the compound had been fun. She and K had done everything—imaginable and unimaginable—to cause human beings pain. Highlights included:

Building a working iron maiden.

Frying a mother, father, and their two children in a giant pot of lard.

Ling Chi, also known as the death of a thousand cuts (actually, it took a thousand two hundred and four.)

A pair of iron boots that could be locked onto feet, with holes for molten lead to be poured inside.

Strappado, mazzatello, flaying, even a blood eagle (the back slashed open, ribs broken off the spine, and the lungs pulled out to resemble bird wings.)

And her all-time favorite; the blowtorch toilet, which worked pretty much like it sounded.

Those were in the playroom. In the arena, they'd come up with many other wicked forms of execution that paying spectators could wager on.

Drawn and quartered by ATVs, betting on which limb would detach first.

Crucifixions.

Impalings on long, steel rods.

The living necklace (four men with a thick rope threaded through their bellies, playing a disemboweling game of tug o' war.)

A naked footrace over hot coals.

It had been glorious.

Lately, things hadn't been so glorious. K's last attempt at a spectacular death was a man locked in a cage with a hundred rats. In that case, the crowd had almost died... of boredom. The rats had ignored the man, and he eventually died of exposure or thirst or something equally boring.

And K's current method of punishing the cartel's enemies was a Columbian necktie; slitting the throat and pulling the tongue out of the hole. Not very bloody, not very painful, and over much too quickly.

Luther Kite used to terrify Lucy, with his nature and with his legend.

But the man she called K...

K was a crippled, pale image of his former self.

Where was the bloodlust? Where was the creativity?

Lucy remembered when D...

D.

Donaldson.

There was a serial murderer who died at the top of his game. A killer's killer. D kept his edge to the very end.

Lucy had been born without the ability to care about anything other than herself. But sometimes she found herself missing the old fella. They'd been through a lot together. And they'd shared a bond closer than anything she'd ever shared with Luther.

Lucy could hear someone wailing in pain; they were nearing the playroom. But it didn't excite her like it should have.

She was too busy thinking about D. Maybe, someday, she'd see him again.

But only if hell really existed.

DONALDSON

Phoenix

Hell was real, and it was called Arizona.

The oversized red hoodie was like wearing a sauna in the hundred-plus heat, and it attracted almost as much attention from passerby as Donaldson's exaggerated limp.

But not as much attention as he would have gotten if the hoodie was off.

As usual, he was in constant pain. The parts of him that hadn't been scraped bare, burned, stabbed, or whittled down to bone, had been shot. But he hadn't been identified during his extended hospital stay, even though he'd talked to countless cops about the Michigan ordeal. Donaldson stuck to lies, about both his previous injuries and his current ones, and feigned amnesia for much of his time in intensive care. Incredibly, they'd allowed him to walk out of there (well, *limp* out of there) when they'd deemed him healthy enough.

So the serial killer who'd lost track of how many he'd actually killed was free to do so once again.

Except, seriously, who could bear to kill anyone in this horrible heat? How did anything at all get done in Phoenix? What fool thought it was a smart idea to build a city in the middle of a desert?

Donaldson hobbled up to the massive glass and concrete edifice that was the front of the Burton Barr Central Library, blinded by the sun reflecting off five stories of windows, and entered on the west side.

The air conditioning hit him like a slap, and he passed a handsome male guard in slacks and a polo. The guard glanced at Donaldson, trying and failing to hide his revulsion.

I've raped and tortured and murdered men bigger, stronger, and prettier than you.

It was a pleasant thought, but that seemed like a lifetime ago. Donaldson couldn't remember the last time he'd killed for sport. Or for any reason. His latest crime spree, which was lame by any self-respecting maniac's standards, involved stealing a car from a woman who left it running when she went into a convenience store, and taking the wallet off a drunk passed out in a tavern parking lot. He'd also tried, and failed, to shoplift food on four different occasions. His appearance and gait made it impossible to be inconspicuous, and he'd been caught and told to leave three of those times. On the fourth, the clerk felt sorry for him and told him to keep the snack cakes he'd tried to pilfer. Which was even more humiliating than getting caught.

In some ways, helplessness was even worse than pain.

Donaldson headed for the glass elevator at the south end of the building, standing next to a child who was waiting. A little girl of no more than five or six. She stared directly at Donaldson's scarred face. Donaldson saw revulsion there, something he'd gotten used to. But he also saw something else.

Fear.

And it felt good to be feared again.

"I'm going to come to your house tonight," Donaldson said to her, keeping his voice low. "And I'm going to cut up your mommy and daddy with a knife and eat their guts. Next, I'll slice off your face. Then you'll look… Just. Like. Me."

Donaldson watched her fear become full-fledged terror, watched her shorts soak with urine, and then she ran off, screaming.

Donaldson glanced over his shoulder, saw he'd caught the guard's attention. He shrugged, as if to say, "It's not my fault the kid got frightened by my sad appearance."

The guard turned away. Donaldson climbed into the elevator, alone.

He got out on the second floor, pulling out the stolen wallet and finding the previous owner's library card, and using it to reserve Internet time on one of the many public computers. He sat down, which was painful enough to cause him to gasp, and then got onto Google.

First he checked Google News, looking for the keywords *Lucy + serial killer*. But he only found the old stories. Nothing new.

Then he switched from a news search to a web search, and checked the same terms for the past week. Gradually he expanded the search to include new words. *Hitchhike. Drag behind car. Lemon juice. Female killer. Escaped female serial killer. Luther Kite.*

He winced when he typed in that last term. While Donaldson had nothing in particular against a fellow practitioner of the psychopathic arts, Lucy's fascination with Kite, and the possibility that she might be with him at that very moment, rankled the older man.

Lucy belonged to Donaldson. Not Kite. They were destined to spend the rest of their wretched, pain-filled lives together. The only thing that kept Donaldson from jumping off a bridge and ending his unbearable existence was the thought that Lucy was out there, somewhere.

But after more than a year of searching, Donaldson had gotten nowhere. No leads to her whereabouts. No clues to where she'd gone. His long trek to Arizona had been the result of drifting aimlessly, and he was no closer to finding her than he was when he'd been released from the hospital over eighteen months ago.

He closed his eyes and pictured her face. Before, when she was young and pretty. Then after, when she'd been scarred as badly as he'd been.

Strangely, Donaldson wasn't sure which of her looks he preferred.

He typed in a few more terms—a slow process because of his missing fingers—and came up with nothing. His stomach made an unhappy sound, and Donaldson tried to remember where the nearest food pantry or shelter was so he could get some free food. How ironic was that? Once he'd been an alpha predator, taking whatever he wanted. Now he was forced to rely on the charity of those he once preyed upon. Donaldson had caused much misery, and now endured it every waking moment.

It was almost enough to make a guy believe in karma.

He was about ready to leave, working up the nerve to painfully heave himself out of his seat, when nostalgia got the best of him and kept him rooted. Searching now on Google Images, Donaldson looked for pictures of Lucy's old handiwork. Once again he typed in *dragged behind car* and made sure that safe search wasn't activated so he could revel in the explicit gore.

He saw old photos of many of Lucy's previous victims. The blood, the open wounds, the frozen expressions of pain even after death. They stirred sexual feelings in Donaldson that he was no longer physically equipped to deal with. He tried to lick what remained of his lips, but what remained of his tongue was too dry. He flipped from one carnage-filled pic to the next, his breath coming faster. These atrocities had all been before he'd met Lucy, but Donaldson had viewed them so often over the past months they gave him a feeling of reminiscence.

He clicked through the familiar images, lingering on a particularly oozy one, and then saw a new photo that made his cold heart throb. The photo was smaller than the others, because instead of a regular jpg it was a screen capture off YouTube. On it, a mostly-skinned man was being dragged by chains around his wrists. The caption read, "Dragged to death in Mexico".

Donaldson immediately went to YouTube to search for the video, and when he found it he was treated to the musical shrieks of some unlucky fellow who was being towed behind an old pickup truck down a stretch of highway, leaving a red streak on the pavement behind him. The black bars on either side of the screen, which made the image look like a long rectangle, were familiar to Donaldson. Someone had captured this video with their cell phone.

The footage only lasted about forty seconds, and it was shaky and blurry and not nearly as up close and personal as Donaldson would have liked, but when it ended Donaldson felt a jolt as surely as if he'd been hit with a crowbar.

The last few seconds of video, the driver of the truck got out and began hacking at the man with a curved knife.

And the woman...

She was squirting him with a spray bottle.

The man was gaunt, pale, with stringy black hair.

The woman was younger, scarred, and it appeared that she only had one eye.

Hands shaking, Donaldson watched the video again, pausing it at appropriate spots. Each time he paused, he printed the screen. Once on the blurry license plate. Once on the white road sign in the background. Once on the blurred faces of the man and woman.

Then he hauled himself out of his chair and limped to the reception desk.

"I printed out three pictures," he told the librarian, who was busy on her computer.

"Color or black and white?" she asked without looking up.

"Color."

"Forty cents each. That's $1.20."

Donaldson rummaged his front pockets for change and found a quarter, two dimes, and his last Vicodin.

"I only have forty-five cents."

"Then I'm sorry, but you can only have one print out."

Donaldson popped the vike into his mouth, even though it was covered in fuzz. He leaned forward on the woman's desk.

"I need those pictures."

"You need seventy-five more cents."

Donaldson glanced at the stapler within reach, imagined beating the woman over the head with it and then stapling her lips to her gums followed by chiseling out her teeth and dragging barbed wire across her gums.

"How about a discount, this one time?" he asked, trying to keep the anger out of his voice. "For the disabled?"

Now she finally looked at him, and Donaldson watched her eyes go wide.

"Oh my god," she whispered.

"I was tortured," he told her, truthfully. "It went on for hours. Lips snipped away with scissors. My chin filed down with a rasp. See how many fingers I have left? I have even fewer toes. I have to piss through a tube, and even though it has been years since it happened, I still piss blood." He leaned in closer. "Now how about you show a little compassion, you fucking whore, and give me the print outs before I whip out my tube and piss blood all over your snotty, goddamn face."

The librarian handed over the pictures.

"Thanks." Donaldson winked at the librarian. "Have a nice day."

JACK

Washington DC

After landing at Dulles we cabbed it, and got to the diner an hour before our scheduled meeting, McGlade wearing a wide smile on his unshaven face.

"The girls and I go way back," he said. "Whoever it is, she'll be happy to see me."

I let Harry labor under that delusion. It was easier than arguing with him.

It was pleasantly cool inside when we entered the restaurant, a stereotypical egg and coffee shop in downtown DC, half filled with customers. Chandler—I think it was Chandler—was already sitting at a table, a piece of half-eaten carrot cake on a plate in front of her. Her hair had been dyed dirty blond, cut in a bob. She was younger than me by at least fifteen years, about my height, but slimmer and with much more muscle definition. Her Lycra top was so tight I could see her six-pack. I could also see the bulge in her jean jacket where she carried her gun.

"Chandler, right?" McGlade said. "I know you're not Fleming, unless Jesus came down and performed a miracle so you could walk again."

"Maybe I'm Hammett," she said.

"If you were Hammett, you'd be sucking my face right now. Because, as you recall, I rocked that box. Did she mention me?"

Chandler held her blank expression. "She said you were smaller, and quicker, than average."

"So she mentioned me?" Harry beamed. "Awesome!"

McGlade sat down and began to yell for the server to bring coffee. I held out my hand and shook Chandler's.

"Fleming says hello," Chandler said, tapping her earpiece.

"Hello back," I told her. "How have you both been?"

Chandler didn't answer. She wasn't much for small talk.

"A year and a half ago I ran into a serial killer named Luther Kite," I began. "He got away, and is a threat to society, and to my family. I believe my husband, Phin, went to Mexico to find him. That was two days ago. He hasn't returned my calls."

"Phin knows you know, and turned off his phone so you wouldn't follow him."

"That's my guess."

"And you want to follow him anyway."

"Phin is competent. But Luther is different than what he's used to dealing with."

"He's like your sister, Hammett," Harry said. "Crazypants McButtnutspants."

"Who's the target?" Chandler asked. "Phin, or Luther?"

"Phin."

"And if we come across Luther?"

"We contact the authorities and he gets arrested." I leaned in. "Understood?"

If that didn't sit well with the former government assassin, she didn't show it. "Where in Mexico?"

"A writer named Katie Glente found a video of Luther dragging a man to death behind his car. It's the MO of another killer he's with, a girl named Lucy. The video was taken near Mexicali."

"I know someone from Mexico. He's on a job now, but I can call him for intel." She stood up. "Fleming and I will meet you in Mexicali the day after tomorrow."

"How do I get in touch with you?"

"You don't," Chandler said, heading for the door.

"Couldn't we have done this over the phone?" I asked.

"Fleming said the carrot cake was good," Chandler said over her shoulder. "This was an excuse to try it. See you in a few days."

"Later, babe," McGlade called after her. "Tell Fleming if she gets bored with the wheelchair, she can ride me around."

I tapped my fingers on the table top, a nervous habit. "That was... interesting."

Harry speared at the remainder of Chandler's cake with his fork, cutting himself a big piece and shoving it in his cake hole. "Spies are nuts. Maybe all that espionage and subterfuge has finally destroyed Chandler's brain. A two hour flight for a one minute meeting. At least I was in first class, not in coach with you and the lesbian writer. How can you stand coach?"

"You booked us in coach, McGlade. Then upgraded yourself."

McGlade ate more cake. "I know. Coach is unbearable. No room to spread out or get comfortable. Plus you're sitting next to all of those other, not-rich people. Easy way to catch a disease. Do you know I once caught syphilis from a toilet seat?"

"So stop having sex with toilet seats."

"Funny. I'll think of you on our plane ride home, while you're cramped in coach stuck sitting next to Fat Guy McBodyOdorPants and I'm reclining and getting free martinis."

I kept tapping the table, lost in thought. My worries were piling up. I couldn't stop thinking of Phin. I had an urge to call Mom, check how Samantha was doing. And I hadn't let on how much it hurt me that Herb wasn't along for this one. Add in concerns about Katie, and now Chandler, and I was borderline neurotic, which wasn't the best mental state when hunting serial killers.

"Yeah, spies are crazy," McGlade said. He often continued with conversations after others had moved on. "Or maybe that's just Chandler. You can tell that chick had some serious shit happen to her in the past."

"Hasn't everyone?"

Harry studied his prosthetic hand. "I guess. But some of us deal with it by killing people, and some deal by trying to have as much sex as possible, bonus points if it's free. Speaking of, did you check out Chandler's body? Nice and tight. I bet she could dry hump the skin off an apple."

"Thanks for that mental image."

"She's got those Olympic ice skater legs. I'd strap her on like a feed bag."

"And that one. Remind me again why we're partners."

"You were desperate, and I'm uncommonly generous. It's my giving nature."

"Right now you're giving me a headache."

"Want to go tour the White House? For old time's sake?"

"No."

"Want to hear about the sex I had with Hammett?"

"No."

"Want to—"

"No."

The coffee came. I sipped some. It was sour.

"Should I call Katie, tell her to meet us here?"

I shrugged. "Sure."

Katie was at an art gallery up the street. We'd dropped her off there because I wasn't sure how Chandler would react to meeting someone new. I'd only encountered Chandler a few times, and couldn't claim to know very much about her, either her personal life or her professional one, but she didn't seem to have any qualms when it came to murder. While Chandler had good reasons to be paranoid, I didn't want her snapping Katie's neck if Katie said the wrong thing.

McGlade managed to invite Katie to join us for lunch in the most derogatory, insulting way possible, then said something rude to our waitress that was practically a guarantee she'd spit in our food.

"You know Chandler will kill Luther, and Lucy, on sight, right?" he said, eating more cake.

It was possible, and I wasn't sure what I would do if she tried. Years ago, I'd sworn to protect and serve, and had taken the Law

Enforcement Oath of Honor to uphold the Constitution. That meant due process for criminals, even the worst ones.

But I wasn't a cop anymore. And I was getting a fulltime stiff neck, constantly looking over my shoulder waiting for Luther and friends to sneak up on me.

"Luther is going to jail, Harry."

"Phin didn't go after him to arrest him, Jack."

"I know."

"And you just enlisted the help of someone who used to snuff people for Uncle Sam."

"I know."

"And you aren't exactly a Girl Scout yourself."

"I know all of this, McGlade. But this is a rescue mission. Not an assassination. I'm not a killer."

Harry swallowed more cake. "And what if Luther has done something to Phin?"

I sipped sour coffee and hoped I wouldn't ever have to answer that question.

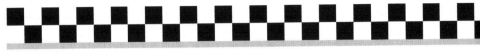

PHIN

Somewhere in Mexico

Someone slapped Phin awake, and for a moment he wasn't sure where he was.

The memories came back, accompanied by pain. His ribs ached. His head hurt. His cheek stung from the waking blow. He remembered the attack on the street, passing out under the pile of bodies, and then...

Nothing.

He blinked, feeling dopey, realizing they must have drugged him. When he tried to move, he discovered he was naked with his hands cuffed behind him, his ankles chained to the legs of a steel chair. Phin looked up at the man who hit him.

For a moment, Phin thought the guy was wearing a Halloween mask. Then he realized it was his actual face. Gaunt and sunken. Horribly scarred. Eyes black and dull as a shark's. Long, mangy black hair.

Luther Kite.

And standing next to him, just as scarred, missing an eye and stooped over, his Bride of Frankenstein, Lucy.

Phin hid his surprise. While he'd been hoping to find them both, he'd also hoped for more favorable circumstances when that happened.

In Luther's hand was Phin's notebook, and Phin reasoned that's what he'd been slapped with, because Luther didn't appear strong enough to hurt with a bare-handed blow.

"Are you with the police?" Luther asked. His voice had a timbre, like a rattle was caught in his throat.

Phin glanced at the stainless steel table next to him. On it were pliers, scalpels, a blow torch. He knew how this would play out. If he stayed silent, he'd be tortured. If he told the truth, he'd be tortured, and also put Jack and Samantha at risk.

He focused on the story he needed to stick to, rather than the pain that was coming. His best bet was a mixture of the truth, with lies. If he could get Luther to believe him, at least Phin's family would be safe.

"No. I'm here for you, Luther. You and Lucy."

Luther's lips twitched slightly. He glanced at Lucy, and she shrugged.

"Who are you?"

"Duffy," he said, using the name on his fake ID. It was an alias he wouldn't forget. The name of a pet, plus the name of the town he was born. "Duffy Hanover. You killed my cousin." Phin let his anger show. "You and your ugly bitch here dragged him behind your car."

"Is that so?" Luther's expression remained impassive, but that might have been because he had limited control of his facial muscles. "So why were you staking out my drug operation?"

Phin didn't understand the question, but quickly put it together. Luther wasn't saying he bought drugs. He was saying he *dealt* drugs. Somehow this human skeleton had wound up working for a Mexican cartel.

"I asked around. You two are pretty distinctive. Found one of your dealers, figured I'd watch until a new supply was dropped off, then follow him to you."

"Asked around? Whom, exactly, did you ask?"

Luther was no longer looking at Phin. He was looking at the tools on the stainless steel table.

"Your pusher. The one who wears Hugo Boss. I flashed him your picture, he said you ran the syrup market."

"And where did you get my picture?"

"YouTube," Phin said.

Luther looked at Lucy. She said, "It's a website, you can upload videos."

"I know what it is," Luther said. He turned back to Phin. "What video?"

"You and your girlfriend dragging some other poor bastard behind his car."

Luther drew a finger over his misshapen nose. "And how did you link that video to us?"

"It's called the Internet, asshole. Ask Google. That's Lucy's thing, isn't it? Dragging people? And it's not like either of you would be hard to pick out of a line-up."

Luther's eyes seemed to drill right into Phin's skull and expose his thoughts. Phin focused on how much he hated this guy.

"What was your cousin's name?" Luther finally asked after their stare down.

Phin went with something easy to remember. His middle name, and a street he lived on.

"Joseph Cermak."

Again Luther glanced at Lucy. She shrugged. "Who can remember them all?"

"Where are you staying in town?" Luther asked him.

"Nowhere yet. Been living out of the car." The mess in the rental would confirm it—empty food wrappers and water bottles, a thermos full of urine. Phin had also been smart enough to hide his room key and cell phone in the car's trunk. So far, his story was sound. Phin figured it was simple enough for him to stick to.

Jack and Samantha would be safe.

"Well, you've found us, Mr. Hanover. Now what are you going to do to us?"

Phin set his jaw. He remained defiant as Lucy, stuck her crab-like hand, which was missing a few fingers, into her shorts and pulled out Phin's butterfly knife.

"Be careful with that," Phin said. "You might lose a digit."

Luther made a barking sound, which Phin realized was a laugh. "You wounded six of my men, and killed three. Do you like to fight, Mr. Hanover?"

"Untie me and I'll show you."

"What do you think, princess?" Luther asked Lucy. "We can burn all his skin off, or we can put him in the games."

Lucy's lip twitched. "Let's burn his skin off."

"Not many good fighters in the games. He could be worth a lot of money."

"Burn him," she said again.

Phin couldn't think of anything worse than having all of his skin burned off, but the way Luther insisted on the games made him wonder if that was indeed the crueler option.

"Do I get a vote?" Phin asked.

"No, Mr. Hanover. But we can take your opinion under advisement."

Phin forced bravado. "Kill me now, because if I get free, you're both dead."

Luther's eyes widened. "He's feisty. I think we'll keep him around."

"Then why did you even ask me for my opinion?" Lucy said. Her face made an ugly, pouting gesture, and she looked down at her shoes. Pink Crocs.

"I'll tell you what, princess. We'll put him in the games, but I'll let you burn off one of his nipples. Would that make you feel better?"

Lucy nodded. Luther picked up the blowtorch and handed it to her. "I don't like to disappoint her, Mr. Hanover. You know how it is with women."

Lucy pushed a button on the torch, igniting the blue flame. As she brought it to his chest, Phin closed his eyes, determined not to give them the satisfaction of hearing him scream.

He lasted almost nine seconds.

DONALDSON

Phoenix

When you have very little power, your only recourse is to prey on the less powerful.

In Donaldson's case, that meant the impaired, little children, or the elderly.

Children didn't own cars. Donaldson could have waited for the bars to close and picked off someone drunk, but besides obtaining a vehicle he also needed a passport to get into Mexico.

That meant finding some old fart.

A nursing home wouldn't work, because those living fossils were already too far gone to have vehicles. Casing a retirement home made sense, but Donaldson had tried that in other towns, and they were unusually well protected—probably because the elderly were so easy to victimize.

So Donaldson thought outside the box and hung out in the parking lot of a discount medical supply store. The heat was stifling, made more unbearable because Donaldson was mostly scar tissue, and scar tissue didn't have sweat glands. He waited, slowly simmering, for two hours before the perfect opportunity presented itself.

Old man, at least eighty, driving a Cadillac from some long ago year when they still made them big. He parked crookedly, and when he got out he had one of those aluminum canes with four legs at the base. Donaldson watched him walk, slow and stooped, into the store, and he made his way to the Caddy.

Dumb old fool didn't lock his doors. Donaldson slipped into the back seat, which was so roomy he was able to hide on the floor.

It being Arizona, the heat in the vehicle quickly rose to that of an oven baking cookies. It made the heat outside seem like the Arctic. The elderly bastard took his time, too. Donaldson sat there for at least twenty minutes, sure he could feel his eyeballs shriveling up as the goo inside them evaporated, before the driver finally returned.

Naturally, he got into the car without checking the back seat, and even threw his bagged purchase directly on top of Donaldson without noticing him. Donaldson checked the contents.

Enemas, and petroleum jelly.

Old people were just plain nasty.

Thankfully, the geezer cranked the AC, and for the first time since the library Donaldson felt relief from the punishing heat. Seriously, anyone would have to be certifiably insane to live in Arizona.

Donaldson couldn't see the dashboard, but he knew they were going at least ten miles an hour under the speed limit. Each intersection required a full, six-second stop. And the driver managed to hit a curb every hundred meters, causing electric ripples of pain to shock through Donaldson's body. By the time they arrived at the geezer's house and parked in his attached garage, Donaldson was ready to kill the guy even if he didn't get a car or passport out of the deal.

The old man reached behind him, his hand blindly seeking the bag, and Donaldson actually handed it to him. A moment later the garage door was closing and Methuselah was getting out of the Caddy.

Donaldson chose that moment to make his move. He let himself out of the rear door, and the dinosaur squinted at him as if he was watching television.

"What in the hell are you doing in the back of my car?"

"Do you live alone?"

"What was that?"

Donaldson raised his voice. "Do you live alone?"

"What?"

Jesus Christ. "Do! You! Live! Alone!"

"What in the hell were you doing in the back of my car?"

And the state still allowed this guy to drive?

Donaldson looked around the garage for some kind of weapon, and found a crow bar hanging on the near wall. He picked it up, the weight in his hands oddly comforting.

"What in the hell are you doing with my crowbar?"

Donaldson limped within pummeling range, and the old man grimaced. "Damn, son. What happened to your face? Someone hit you with an ugly stick so hard the stick broke."

Donaldson countered the barb by hitting him with a stick of his own, bouncing it off the geezer's dome. The old man staggered a few steps, then collapsed.

"Why in the hell are you hitting me with my crowbar, you ugly bastard?"

Donaldson bent down to get closer, even though the act was painful.

"Do you live alone!"

"No, I live with a whole church choir, you idiot."

Donaldson smashed the crowbar against the man's knee.

"My wife is inside!" he moaned.

"Where is your passport?"

"Airport?"

"Pass-port!" Donaldson rapped him hard with each syllable.

"It's in my desk! Please stop hurting me!"

Donaldson was so tired, and so irritated, that he didn't even enjoy beating the old man to death. It felt like work, not pleasure. A shame, since the fellow was tougher than he looked, and it took over two dozen whacks before his brainpan cracked open and spilled the goodies.

Skull piñatas usually cheered Donaldson up. The first time he ever split someone's head, he walked barefoot on the warm, gray matter, letting it squish between his toes, and sang, "I'm always on your mind" to the corpse.

But now all he felt was tired.

After catching his breath he limped over to the house door and warily opened it up.

"Irving?" a woman called from another room.

No. It's not Irving.

It's the boogeyman.

Home invasions weren't normally Donaldson's thing. But he perked up at the idea. The air conditioning was deliciously frigid. Once he got rid of Irving's wife, perhaps he could stay a while. Shower and rinse out the catheter. Fill his belly. Maybe even sleep in an actual bed.

He locked the door behind him, then lurched into the kitchen. A moment later, an old woman with a bowed back and a wooden cane came limping in. She didn't even notice Donaldson until she practically bumped into him.

"You're not Irving," she said, squinting through thick glasses.

"Good grasp of the obvious."

The woman touched her neck.

"There's an intruder in my house," she said. "Real ugly fucker."

Donaldson was momentarily confused, and then noticed she was holding a medical alert necklace.

She'd just alerted the authorities.

And then she whacked him in the mouth with her cane.

Donaldson didn't have many teeth. Most of them had been chiseled out. So the four he had left in his lower jaw were important to him.

The old bitch knocked them out. All four.

Donaldson swung the crowbar so hard he broke her neck on the first blow. He had a strong urge to continue bashing until she was pulp, but he didn't have time. After stuffing his mouth with paper towels, he quickly found the den and the office desk. The passports were in a cubby hole. He began tugging open drawers and also found a silver dollar collection in a binder, a large, glass jar of change, and a Rolex Datejust. The back of the watch was engraved, "To Irving, for 50 Years". Reading it made Donaldson wistful, almost sad inside. Why the hell did those fools ruin a beautiful watch by adding an inscription? That took at least 40% off the resale.

Time running out before the pigs showed up, Donaldson hurried to the bathroom. When he opened the vanity, he gasped so deeply he almost choked on the paper towels.

Merry Christmas.

There for the taking was a pharmacy's worth of prescription drugs. Muscle relaxants, sleep aids, anti-anxiety pills, and best of all; a full bottle of Tylenol-3 and a box of fentanyl patches.

Donaldson gathered everything in a pillowcase and hurried back to the garage. He relieved Irving of his wallet, which held eight dollars in cash and assorted ID and credit cards. Donaldson looked nothing like the man, and his age was way off, but he knew if he flashed it no one would question him. No one had the balls to ask a guy who had a face like chicken cartilage why he didn't match his driver's license pic.

He also noticed something in the pile of brains. False teeth. On impulse Donaldson reached for them, tucking the dentures into his pocket, then getting into the Cadillac just as distant sirens approached.

He breezed past the cops as they came screeching down the street.

Donaldson drove to a supermarket, parked in the busy lot, then checked his mouth in the mirror. Only five teeth left, all on top. He wondered how he was supposed to chew anything now. Maybe put food on the edge of a table, and then ram his upper teeth into it?

That didn't sound very appealing. But what was the alternative? Eating baby food for the rest of his life?

He dug through the pillowcase, dry-swallowed four Tylenol-3s, and considered his options. Maybe he could get a battery-powered blender, and liquefy his meals. A cheeseburger smoothie would taste the same as a whole one, wouldn't it?

Then he remembered Irving's false teeth in his pocket. Donaldson had wondered what impulse made him grab the dentures, but apparently his brilliant subconscious mind had solved his problem. Donaldson wiped off some bits of cerebrum and wedged the falsies onto his lower gums.

They were too big, and didn't fit right, sticking out at a weird angle, giving him a huge under bite.

Uppers. They were uppers.

Donaldson glanced in the mirror.

I look like the world's ugliest bulldog.

He took the dentures out, then pondered his next move.

The car had three-quarters of a tank of gas, but Cadillacs weren't known for their terrific mileage. The Mexican border was about four hundred miles away, and he had no idea how long it would take to find Lucy. He needed cash.

He fiddled with the GPS and drove to a pawn shop a few blocks away. When Donaldson walked inside, he was surprised how much they'd changed. Back in the day, hock shops were seedy places where junkies could fence stolen radios. Apparently, they'd been modernized into retail chains. None of the customers looked strung out. None of the smiling clerks looked shady.

Donaldson limped up to the cashier window and presented the silver dollars, watch, and Irving's ID.

As expected, they didn't question him. And watching the smiling clerk try to maintain a smile while staring at him was oddly amusing.

It amounted to over four thousand dollars. A fortune.

Donaldson was so flushed by the excitement of his windfall that he didn't notice the two teenagers, who'd been waiting for him outside the pawn shop. One shoved him to the ground and held him, and the other did a quick frisk and found the roll of bills.

After a high-five and some celebratory hoots, they jogged off.

The smiling pawn shop cashier came out and helped Donaldson up, asking if he wanted him to call the police. Donaldson made an excuse about driving himself to the hospital, and then got the hell out of Phoenix, close to tears because life was so blatantly unfair.

JACK

Chicago

When we arrived at O'Hare, Harry took a cab back to his condo to pack for the trip, and I drove Katie back to my place. She'd been surprisingly quiet on the plane, and stayed that way in the car.

Odd behavior for someone writing a book. I'd encountered a few journalists in the past, and they usually had to be cut off because they seemed eager to pump me forever. So after ten minutes of silence after picking up the car in short-term parking, I finally asked, "Why Luther Kite?"

Katie seemed to gather her thoughts before responding. "All the books I've written have been about things that have already happened. Kite is still happening. Him, and Lucy, aren't headline news. But they're out there, killing people, getting away with it. So instead of covering the story, I want to be part of the story."

"You don't strike me as someone out for fame."

"I'm not. It's... well, you can go through life as an observer. An observer is a victim, in a sense. They react, but they don't act. There are too many people watching, not enough of them actually doing anything."

"You're a writer." I'd checked my Kindle earlier, saw all of Katie's books already pre-loaded. Phin must have bought them after meeting her, and we shared an Amazon account so they downloaded to mine. "That's doing something."

"I'm doing something after the fact. I've read all there is to read about you, Jacqueline Daniels. All the books. All the articles. I've watched the video clips of your press conferences. I've even got the Blu Ray set of *Fatal Autonomy*."

"I'm sorry about that." Fatal Autonomy was a TV drama supposedly based on the exploits of Harry McGlade. In exchange for a favor I signed away rights for the producers to base a character on me. Harry got rich. I got sent adult-sized diapers every Xmas by Fatal Autonomy fans, because my character wet her pants whenever she got scared.

"You've made a difference, Jack. You've saved lives. You're not a victim, you're a hero."

I shook my head. "A victim is anyone harmed by actions beyond their control. Could be a drunk driver, a tornado, a perverted uncle, a fire, a rapist, a con artist, a psychopath. I've been a victim many times. That doesn't mean I let it define me. No one gets to define me but me."

"Spoken like a hero."

I frowned. "*Hero* is another loaded word. Most people get scared. Being able to act while afraid, being able to face fears and keep going; that's learned. I'm no different than anyone else. I'm just…"

I searched for the word. *Unlucky?* I chose to be a homicide cop, so a lot of the shit I'd gone through I brought on myself. *Stupid?* It was true I had to be either dense or a masochist to do what I did for as long as I did. My job hurt me, and those I cared about, and I was still unable to live a normal life without taking care of loose ends like Luther Kite.

"Driven," Katie said.

I tried on the word, and it fit. Not perfectly, but enough for me to be comfortable with it. "Yeah. Driven. There are predators out there, hurting people. I'm compelled to do what I can to stop them."

"Why?"

Why, indeed?

"My mother was a cop. Maybe it's genetic."

"Nothing happened to you? When you were younger? Made you want to chase killers?"

I recalled my childhood. There had been rough spots, to say the least, but I didn't feel comfortable sharing these with Katie.

"Being a kid isn't easy," was all I revealed.

"I've read you're an insomniac."

I glanced at Katie. She was staring at me like I was some sort of strange animal she'd never seen before.

"I used to be. Sleep better now. The baby changed a lot. Or maybe it was me quitting the force. Or both."

"You're not driven anymore. Maybe that's why you were so good at your job, and why you couldn't sleep."

"Maybe."

"When you did catch someone bad, could you sleep?"

"Yeah," I admitted.

Katie turned away and nodded. Then she stared out the window.

"So you think that catching Luther Kite will make things better for you?" I asked.

"Let's just say I've had more than my share of sleepless nights."

I considered pressing her, but her body language had changed. She'd gone from animated to withdrawn within a few seconds. I concentrated on the road, tried to clear my head of worries, when my phone rang. I hit the button on my steering wheel that enabled hands-free Bluetooth.

"This is Jack."

"Jack? Val Ryker. Been a while."

I'd worked with Val on the CPD years ago. She went on to pursue law enforcement in Wisconsin, and we didn't see each other often. Val was one of the few people I could call a friend, and someone I could normally count on.

"Yeah."

"How's the baby?"

"Cute. And exhausting. How's everything with you?" That was always a loaded question.

"Good as can be expected. I take it this isn't a social call."

"My husband went to Mexico to look for Luther Kite," I said.

"You're going after him, and need help."

"Yeah."

"I'm not... at 100%."

My stomach clenched, and I wondered if she'd bail out on me like Herb had. I couldn't blame her if she did. Val had been having a tough time these last few years. She tended to collect bad luck like it was a favorite hobby.

"I don't know what we'll run into, so I'm assembling a team of people I trust."

"So, the idiot," she meant Harry, "And Herb."

The words hurt coming out. "Herb can't help this time."

"Really? Is he okay?"

"I'm not sure what's going on with him. I think he's burned out on serial killers."

"I can understand that."

"Well," I said, ready to end the conversation. "Thanks for calling me back, and—"

"I didn't say no, Jack. Only that I'm not 100%."

"You're sick?"

Val didn't answer.

"How bad?" I asked.

"I... don't know how much use I'd be, if things go sour."

"Can you still hit a bull's-eye from two hundred meters with a three-aught-eight?"

"You need a sniper?"

"I don't know what I need. But it wouldn't hurt to have someone watching our backs."

"Well, then, have Winchester, will travel. Where are we going?"

"Mexicali."

"When?"

"Two days."

"I can call you when I'm in town. How many rounds should I pack?"

I'd been wondering the same thing. Best case scenario, we got Phin out of there, Luther and Lucy go to jail, and not a single round is fired.

Worst case, the O.K. Corral.

No. Scratch that. Worst case, Little Big Horn.

"I'll bring guns and ammo," I said. "Mexico doesn't allow firearms to be brought in, but Harry has a trap in his RV."

"A trap?"

"A smuggler box. He's got some complicated switch system to open it."

"I take it the baby won't be coming."

"No."

"Bring the latest pictures then."

"I will. Thanks, Val. See you soon."

She hung up, and I let out a stiff breath, surprised by how relieved I was.

"Val Ryker?" Katie asked. "She's coming?"

"Yeah."

"She's the cop who had that altercation with Dixon Hess."

"Yeah."

And it was a lot more than an altercation. Hess was another serial killer, operating out of Wisconsin. He'd taken a serious toll on Val and those she cared about.

I glanced at Katie again, saw she was staring back at me. "Do you have family, Katie?"

She didn't answer.

"Because if you do," I continued, "you should reconsider going with us. You know the Nietzsche quote?"

"I used it for my Andrew Thomas book. *He who fights with monsters should look to it that he himself does not become a monster. And when you gaze long into an abyss the abyss also gazes into you.*"

I nodded. "But Nietzsche only got part of it. The abyss doesn't just gaze into you. It also focuses on those you love. The more you have, the more you have to lose. And monsters, like Hess, and Kite, and so many others, know this. If you're born without empathy, if you get your kicks causing pain... well, there are more ways to cause it than physical torture. Such as targeting your family."

"I haven't had a family in a long time," Katie said, turning and staring out the window.

I'd never been alone, and couldn't imagine what it was like. My mother had always been there for me, and now I had a child of my own.

A child, and a husband, who put himself in danger to protect us.

Maybe Phin was okay. Maybe he would be there, waiting, when I got home.

Or maybe the abyss had him.

PHIN

Somewhere in Mexico

After Lucy had her fun with the blowtorch, causing enough pain for Phin to pass out, he awoke in a cell. Iron bars on four sides, dirt floor, the size of a large closet. It was one of many cells, lining a hallway. It smelled of piss and shit and sweat.

And blood.

The overhead lighting came from bare 60 watt bulbs, hanging at intervals from extension cords, tacked to a ceiling supported by wooden pillars, like a mine shaft. He was underground. And he wasn't alone. In adjacent cells, for as far as the dim light allowed, Phin saw other prisoners, at least thirty or forty. Men, mostly Mexican, a few Caucasians mixed in. Some were sleeping. Others sobbing.

Phin wore a peasant outfit; a dirty, itchy cotton top with a split in the collar, and matching pants secured with a length of twine. The top had #17 spray painted on the front. His wrists and ankles were bound with rusty shackles. He checked his chest, which hurt as bad as anything he'd felt before, and found it to be bandaged.

Phin sat up. His cell consisted of a bucket, a plastic cup, a plastic plate, and nothing else. As he was orienting himself, a Mexican walked down the aisle with a large, tin watering can. He stopped at each cell, sticking the spout inside and pouring water as prisoners held out their cups. Phin held out his, and his twenty ounce convenience store cup was filled to the brim. He gulped down half, then set the rest aside.

Two cells away another prisoner took off his pants and squatted over a bucket, leaving no doubt what it was for. White guy, twenties, fit, a #12 on his shirt.

"What are you staring at, asshole?" he said. "You want a closer look, I'll throw the bucket at you when I'm done."

So much for making friends with another gringo. Phin turned away.

"That's right. Keep your eyes to yourself, dickpants."

Dickpants? Seriously?

Phin avoided making eye contact with anyone else and spent the next twenty minutes carefully checking his bonds. They were old, but solid. No worn links. The locks were heavy. Maybe, with a paperclip or something similar, he could pick them.

Another ten minutes were spent checking the bars on his cell. They looked makeshift, but the iron and the welds were solid. As he was conducting his examination, a hulk of a man, swathed in prison tattoos, entered the corridor with a mustachioed guard behind him.

The guard wore Phin's Tony Lama cowboy boots.

He locked the scary-looking musclehead in the cell across from Phin's, then handed him a six pack of Tecate beer. Phin noted that his ink was mostly white supremacist nonsense. He didn't know his name, but written across the man's abs were the words JEW KILER. Missing an L.

Kiler. It rhymed with Tyler.

Then the guard faced Phin. "You. Come with." Phin noted the cattle prod hanging from his belt. He also saw another guard at the end of the aisle, who was armed with a Tec-9.

"If you win, new blood," Kiler said, "you give me the beer. You hear me? Give me the beer and I'll kill you quick."

Phin stayed docile as the guard opened his cell with a key from his ring, and allowed himself to be ushered past the rows of cells. Walking in chains wasn't easy, and he had to take small, awkward steps. After twenty meters he came to a metal door. The Tec-9 guy kicked it twice, and an eye-level slot in it slammed opened. After a visual check, a third guard unlocked the door, and Phin was led up an incline paved with cement. A waft of fresh air, hot and dry, caught him as he walked to the surface and into—

What the hell?

Phin found himself standing inside some kind of open arena, completely surrounded by a circular wooden wall. Beyond the wall, bleachers stretched out in a bowl-shape, stadium style, twenty rows high. An audience of maybe a hundred people looked on, some cheering, some booing, Phin was forced into the center of the ring.

Already standing, wearing chains identical to Phin's, was a man who looked to be in his late fifties. Mexican, short and stout, his expression somewhere between terror and disbelief.

Phin saw a scoreboard. Someone had scrawled in large numbers:

8 v 17 / 2:1

Opposite the scoreboard, in a balcony, were Luther and Lucy, dressed in purple and gold Halloween costumes, capes and crowns and robes. They looked like Mardi Gras versions of royalty.

It was night, but Phin couldn't see the stars because of the bright lights illuminating the area. He spotted several more guards, including two with mounted 7.62mm machine guns. And at the far end of the arena...

A man bound to a large, wooden cross. His head was down, and Phin couldn't tell if he was dead or not. If not, it wouldn't be long.

The loudspeaker crackled.

"Last call for bets, last call for bets. Number 17, new blood, against Number 8, with one win. Weight and age advantage to Number 17. Bets on Number 8 pays two to one. The weapons for this match... machetes."

A guard approached and dropped two machetes into the dirt at their feet, then unlocked their chains. Phin rubbed his wrists and watched as his older opponent quickly reached for his weapon, wielding it with two hands.

"A la muerte?" Phin asked.

The man nodded, already sweating and obviously terrified.

A sick feeling began in Phin's stomach, quickly growing to the point where he had the need to vomit.

"Vamos!" a guard ordered.

Phin watched as both machine gunners swung their long barrels in his direction. He bent down and picked up the machete. The handle was sticky with blood, the blade nicked with dozens of indents. But the tip was sharp, the weapon lethal.

However, the last thing Phin wanted to do was kill the poor, old bastard standing in front of him.

There was a crashing clang, and Phin saw Luther had hit a large Chinese gong with his scepter.

Letting out a strangled war cry, the old man raised the machete and ran at Phin. Phin used his own weapon to parry the blow, then dropped a shoulder and knocked his opponent to the ground.

A lackadaisical cheer rippled through the crowd.

Phin had a chance to land a killing blow, but he lowered the machete. He had no inclination to kill the poor son of a bitch. Especially for the amusement of Luther and his twisted brood.

"Debes luchar, o va ser crucificado!" the guard yelled.

Fight, or be crucified.

The man got up off the ground and began to attack Phin, slashing back and forth as if he was cutting through a cornfield, leaving himself open again and again. Phin backed up, countering the swings, not wanting to hurt him.

Boos from the onlookers. Phin wondered how much each of them paid to gain admission, how many pesos to witness this sick spectacle. He noticed the crowd was mostly men, mostly well dressed, roughly half Caucasian and half Hispanic. Rich perverts, each of them no doubt involved with some illegal enterprise. Phin couldn't see any of them up close, but he was able to spot a few bodyguards among the crime lords. So along with the guards, there were armed protectors as well.

Escape was looking less and less likely.

Countering his adversary's swinging machete was growing tiring. Phin ducked a strike, and then punched his opponent in the nose, staggering him backward. He caught his breath, and found he'd gotten close to the crucified man. Phin glanced up at him, saw the unlucky son of a bitch's chest was still rising and falling, though in an intermittent, labored way. On the crosspiece several crows had assembled, waiting for their chance to feast.

There were a lot of ways to die in this hellhole, none of them good.

Phin again had to back up as his attacker advanced. One swipe was so close it caught Phin's shirt, cutting a swath across the front, bisecting the painted number on his chest.

"I don't want to fight you," Phin said. "No lucha."

"Tengo familia," he sputtered, eyes wide.

"Yo también. A child."

"Lo siento." As the man apologized, he lunged again, but had switched to an overhead attack. Phin blocked, but the back of his own machete hit him in the scalp, hard.

There was a bright flash, followed by dizziness, followed by blood streaming down into Phin's eyes, blocking his vision.

The crowd applauded.

The old man advanced.

On blind impulse, Phin lashed out, catching his fellow contestant across the throat.

The man immediately dropped the machete, both hands clasping his neck, trying to staunch the flow. But the cut was deep, a vein or artery. Within ten seconds he dropped to his knees, the sand around him turning to crimson mud as the blood spurted in time with his heartbeat.

Phin's first impulse was to help the man. But how? This guy needed an ER and a surgeon with a full medical team. Unable to save him, Phin squatted, put a hand on the man's shoulder, and forced himself to hold his gaze. The doomed man's eyes went from panic, to something softer.

Acceptance?

Forgiveness?

One last human connection before the mortal coil shuffled off?

After a minute, his eyelids fluttered, and he slumped onto his side.

The gong rang.

Phin stood. Armed guards ordered him to drop the machete. He did, and was put back in chains and led back to his cell. A Mexican in a dirty white lab coat was waiting for him. He motioned for Phin to bend down, and repaired the gash in his scalp with superglue. Then he gave Phin some blisterpacks of pills.

"Antibiotics. Tylenol."

"Hippocratic oath," Phin said.

The man smiled, revealing a gold tooth. "I'm not a doctor, gringo."

"Got anything stronger than Tylenol?"

"That's coming up right now."

The guard wearing his Tony Lama boots locked Phin in his cell and gave him a lukewarm six pack of beer.

"Nice work, new blood," Kiler said. "Now hand over the brew."

Phin was sick to his stomach, and his head thrummed steadily in the key of C. He closed his eyes, and saw the face of the man he'd just killed.

"You hear me, asshole? Give me the beer. Do that, and I'll kill you quick when we face each other. If not, I'll make it real bad for you."

Phin turned his back to Kiler, and popped the tab on a tepid Tecate.

"I'm talking to you, you little punk!"

The first beer went down in three sips.

The second one just as fast.

By the third, Kiler had stopped yelling, and Phin was able to keep himself from crying by thinking about Jack and Sam. Hopefully they were still in Florida with Grandma.

Hopefully.

LUCY

There was something off about that new guy, Hanover.

While it wasn't beyond reason that Hanover could be related to someone they'd killed, he'd remained too cool when they'd had him in the playroom. Revenge was a hot-blooded thing. And being tortured tended to break people's minds. But Hanover didn't seem to have that vengeance streak, and he weathered the blowtorch like a man who'd been at the mercy of sadists before.

Then, in the arena, Hanover had carried himself like a seasoned fighter. Someone with experience.

Someone with secrets.

K should have spotted that something was wrong.

But, then again, K had something off about him, too.

The Luther Kite that Lucy had met so many years ago was as savvy as he was deadly. The word that came to mind was *meticulous*. He had a cunning, deliberate way about him, like a dancer whose every step was calculated. Not a single, wasted move.

This Luther was sloppy. Slow. A shadow of his former self.

Lucy watched them bring the new guy back to his cell. She decided to have some one-on-one time with Mr. Hanover. To find out what his secrets were.

She looked at K, almost told him—

And didn't.

Hanover was an easy problem to solve.

K, not so much.

Lucy, like almost all of her type, was genetically free from empathy, and knew love only in the capacity it benefitted her. K used to be fun. Lately, not so much.

"Want to go into town later?" she asked. "Pick up some lemon juice, drag someone around?"

"Just watch the games."

"I want something hands-on, K. Want to go down to the play-room? We can try your hotplate thing."

"I want to watch the games."

"The games are boring."

"Maybe they wouldn't be boring to you," K said, turning to her, "if you were participating."

Lucy caught no hint that it was a joke. K's eyes were as dark and expressionless as always.

He's serious.

Her anger flared. For a millisecond Lucy pictured pulling the straight razor she always carried, giving K one of those stupid Columbian neckties. But she reigned in the rage and managed to stay calm.

"Actually, I think I'm fine right here," she said, smiling. "Best seat in the house."

K turned his attention back to the arena, where two women fought with pitchforks. Lucy tried to process what had just happened.

K just threatened me.

He's never done that before.

What's happening here?

Is he losing it?

What if that's what he really wants? To put me in the games?

K was feared. Respected. Obeyed. Emilio—who was the fifth or sixth most powerful cartel leader in Mexico—let K run the compound with impunity, and supplied him with anything he needed. He was lord and master of this domain, and his orders were always carried out.

Lucy had no power here. The men were afraid of her, but beneath their fear was disgust and disdain. She had no allies other than K. And if he turned against her…

Lucy had thought of this place as a sanctuary.

But what if it was actually a prison?

JACK

Near Chicago

When the doorbell rang, I figured it was McGlade, ready to drive us to Mexico. But a look at the video monitor showed it to be someone else. Someone I hadn't seen in years.

I went to the door, Katie behind me. Phin had previously dropped Duffy off at the kennel, but I did a quick look around for Mr. Friskers, who sometimes liked to pounce on new arrivals. The cat wasn't around, so I let the man in.

"Thanks for coming." I wasn't sure a handshake or hug was in order, and he didn't make a move to do either. But he did nod, and gave me the barest hint of a smile. His crew cut was gray, as was the stubble on his square chin.

"Good to see you again, Jack." He unslung the duffle bag from his shoulder and set on the floor. From its weight, I guessed it contained guns. Lots of them.

"Katie, this is Tequila. Tequila, Katie."

They shook hands, and I watched as they sized each other up. Neither appeared impressed. People tended to underestimate Tequila. He was a former gymnast, and stood only 5'5". But he might as well have been built out of iron, and his biceps were every bit as massive as when I'd met him all those years ago. With the possible exceptions of Chandler, and maybe Phin, Tequila was the toughest person I'd ever met. And if I had to put money on it, Tequila could probably take them both on at the same time. Besides his strength and athleticism, he had an unorthodox fighting style that was pretty much unbeatable.

"You're coming with us?" Katie asked.

Tequila nodded. "You?"

"Yeah."

Tequila glanced at me. "Can she handle herself?"

I answered honestly. "We'll see."

Katie's eyes narrowed. "I can handle myself fine. Can you? It's obvious you keep in shape, but you look like you're past your prime, Gramps. Also, you're short."

"I am? I never noticed that before."

Katie stared pointedly at me. "Does he have a Napoleon complex we're going to have to compensate for?"

I knew she was doing the same thing Tequila had; asking me a question as if he wasn't there. But he'd done it out of sincere interest, and she was doing it to bust his balls.

She was going to have to try harder.

"It's not a complex if you're actually Napoleon," I said.

"What do you practice?" Tequila asked her. "Judo?"

"Karate. I'm a 2nd dan Shotokan black belt."

"Do you think you could hit me?"

I took a step back. If they needed to test each other, my foyer was as good a place as any. Room to spar, not much that could break. It was always impressive to watch Tequila fight, and I was curious what Katie was able to do.

"Are you serious?" Katie looked at me. "Is he serious?"

I nodded.

"I'll pull my punches so I don't hurt you," Tequila said.

Katie's eyes narrowed. She widened her stance and raised her hands. Then she threw a palm-heel strike, which was impressively fast, but before it reached Tequila she was flat on her ass. His block and throw had been so quick I wasn't even sure what he'd done.

Rather than be surprised, Katie looked pissed. She rocked to her feet and attempted a crescent kick, and Tequila caught her thigh and then tossed her onto my couch like she was a discarded

Raggedy Ann doll. The fact that my couch was three meters away made the move all the more impressive.

"She's strong and fast," Tequila said. "And she knows how to fall."

Katie didn't take well to being thrown, and when she walked over it was obvious she was trying to keep her rage under control. Again she assumed a karate stance. "How about you try to hit me, tough guy?"

"Quick to anger," Tequila said. "That's not good."

"Hit me."

Tequila dropped and spun, his body a blur, and did a foot sweep, knocking Katie down again.

Katie kipped up to her feet, lunging with an elbow strike. Tequila blocked it and gave her a tap in the stomach, pulling his punch short. Katie followed with an uppercut, which Tequila slipped, and he gave her a two handed shove, knocking her onto her butt again.

Apparently undeterred, Katie twisted around on the floor and snapped her leg out in a reverse kick. Tequila caught the leg and threw her on the couch once more. This time when she stood up, she was flushed and grinning.

"Do you give lessons?" she asked.

"I just gave you several."

"Jack has a black belt in taekwondo. Could you take us at the same time?"

Again the barest hint of a smile. "Yes."

Katie caught my gaze. "Jack?"

"I'm wearing Donna Karan."

"C'mon. I just want to see what he does."

Watching them made me wonder when the last time I sparred was. I managed to get in workout a few times a week, but hadn't been to a dojo or a firing range since Sam was born. And if this did turn into a rescue mission, a little practice couldn't hurt.

I pointed my chin to the living room and kicked off my heels, folding my blazer over a chair. Tequila followed, and stood between us, looking relaxed.

"Whenever you're ready," he said.

I snapped my hips and did a reverse kick, aiming low, knowing he'd block it. When he did, I immediately countered with a hammer fist aiming for his chest. I landed it, because he was volleying a barrage of strikes from Katie, but it was like hitting a mattress. I followed by driving my shoulder into his belly and grabbing his back pockets. His abs and his glutes were just as hard as his pecs, but I had a purpose beyond copping a cheap feel off a ripped guy.

Tequila stepped away and did a back flip, making it look easy, and then scissor kicked Katie in the chest while punching at me. I took the hit on my bunched up arm—it hurt but he hadn't given it everything—and then dropped down to sweep him. He jumped over my leg, tossed Katie onto the couch for a third time, and then pinned me to the floor between his knees, his fist raised.

"That was over faster that I would have guessed," he said.

"Yes, it was," I told him, then tapped him on the side. He looked, and saw I was holding the folding knife I'd taken from his back pocket. I was touching him with the handle, but we both knew it could have been a blade sticking in his ribs.

"Nice," he said. "I thought grabbing my ass was a bit... unorthodox."

"Age hasn't slowed you down."

He stood and gave me his hand to help me up. It was like grabbing the end of a two by four.

"Yes, it has," he said. "Twenty years ago, you wouldn't have gotten that knife."

Katie had snuck up behind Tequila, and raised her leg for a lunge kick.

A millisecond later she was on the couch again.

"I feel both humiliated and exhilarated at the same time," Katie said, staring at the ceiling.

I handed Tequila his knife, and he put it back into his pocket.

"Who else is coming?" Tequila asked. "That skinny partner of yours?"

"Herb isn't skinny anymore, and no. Besides Katie, there's a cop named Val Ryker I used to work with. And private eye named Harry McGlade."

"I know McGlade."

He said it in a way that bespoke a lack of affection. Which was normal for people who knew Harry.

"Also, two sisters who you might also know. They used to work for Uncle Sam. I referred you to one of them."

Tequila nodded. "Chandler and Fleming. Glad to know they're still in circulation. They're... exceptional." He said it with a hint of admiration in his voice. Then his face became stony. "Someone just drove up."

I checked the wall monitor and saw a recreational vehicle filling my driveway. A large, red recreational vehicle.

"What is that?" Katie asked. She'd sat up and was squinting through the blinds.

I sighed through my nostrils. "That's our ride."

Years ago, Harry had bought a Winnebago and converted it to be his company vehicle. He dubbed it the Crimebago, pronounced *crim-ee-bay-go*. It met with an unfortunate end, but he'd recently gotten a replacement, the Crimebago Deux. With the high cost of gas and parking in Chicago, it cost slightly more to keep running than our posh office downtown. Harry said he'd painted it red, "to hide in plain sight, like a blimp." But I didn't buy that, because stenciled in huge letters on either side was "Harry McGlade Private Investigator" with a large cartoon magnifying glass and caricature of his face. Tough to be discreet tailing cheating husbands in a vehicle that announces you're a PI. Especially a vehicle that can be spotted from five miles away.

In McGlade parlance, it was *failpants*. But, in all fairness, it would be more comfortable taking Harry's souped-up land barge to Mexico than a car. Especially with all the gear we were bringing.

McGlade honked the horn, which played the first eight notes of the Peter Gunn theme. I experienced the same feeling I did many times a day when dealing with Harry; a profound disappointment

in my decision-making abilities. The money I made as his partner was a nice supplement to my pension, and as much as I loved
being a mom, it tended to make me a little stir crazy unless I got
out of the house every few days. Still, pretty regularly I questioned
my decision to work with a guy who once got us kicked out of a
McDonalds for loudly demanding McSushi. When they tried to
sell him a Fillet-O-Fish, he stood on the counter and threatened to
call his congressman. He thought he was funny. All I wanted was a
damn cup of coffee.

No, Harry was no Herb Benedict.

And yet, Harry was here, and Herb wasn't.

I went to my gear—an oversized Samsonite bag on wheels, a
plastic footlocker, a padded metal case—and began pulling the lug-
gage out to the driveway. McGlade was standing next to the side
door of the Crimebago Deux, beaming like a child on Christmas
morning.

"Got a surprise for you, Jackie."

"I bet." Harry's surprises were never good.

"You know your obese buddy Herb said he wasn't coming
along? Well, guess what?"

He pointed to the doorway, like Vanna White presenting the
letter A, and against my better judgment I climbed into the vehicle
expecting to see my best friend.

I saw something else instead. Something four legged. Fat.
Wrinkly. And covered with dark brown hair.

A pot-bellied pig.

"Jack Daniels, meet Herb Bacondict."

Herb Bacondict was knee-high and had to weigh at least a
hundred pounds. His flappy jowls and creased brow ridge gave
him a pensive look. The pig's round snout was black, speckled with
pink, and sniffed at me.

"He's like a dead ringer for the real Herb, isn't he?'

"You're an idiot," I told him. "And this is the ugliest animal
I've ever seen."

Herb farted, so loud it actually startled me.

Harry walked up beside the pig and patted him on the head. "She's wrong, Herb. You're a handsome hog. Yes you are. Want a treat?"

Herb oinked, his curly little tail wiggling. Harry pulled a dog bone out of his pocket and dropped it in front of Herb, who snorted at it then gobbled it up.

"He can do tricks," Harry said. "Herb. Sit."

Herb stared at him.

"Herb, sit."

Herb snuffled Harry's pocket, then began to gnaw on the fabric.

"We're working on it," Harry said, giving him another treat. "Pigs are just as smart as dogs. Which puts him about ten IQ points above his namesake. And this Herb is so much slimmer and better looking."

Tequila boarded the Crimebago and stared at the pig, his expression blank. "Is this so we don't have to stop for food during the drive?"

"Don't listen to the Oompa Loompa, Herb," Harry said, covering the pig's pointy ears with his hands. "He's angry with the world because he has to shop for clothes at Kids-R-Us."

Tequila dropped his duffle bag and found a seat in back, ignoring Harry. He put up his legs and stretched out.

"Nice to know you guys get along" I said.

"Me and Tequila go way back," Harry said. "We see eye-to-eye on a lot of things. But only when he's standing on an apple crate."

Tequila folded his arms and closed his eyes. Herb walked over to Tequila and began to rub up against his leg, then made a sound that was kind of purring, kind of gargling.

"That's a pig," Katie said, climbing aboard.

"Your grasp of the blatantly obvious is startling," McGlade said.

Katie looked at me. "This is a joke, right? We're not driving sixteen hundred miles with a pig."

"With two pigs." I pointed my chin at McGlade.

Harry made a face. "I thought women went crazy over cute pets. Are you sure you both aren't actually dudes?"

"That's not a pet," Katie said. "That's lunch."

Harry's history with pets had been spotty at best. Years ago, he had an aquarium full of dead fish, which amused him because they sprouted colorful colonies of bacteria as they rotted. Later there was a parrot with a meth addiction that kept plucking off all of its feathers. The only word it said was *homeboy*, so that's what Harry named it. McGlade also had a former research monkey he called Slappy, so-named because he kept slapping himself in the head. Last I heard, Slappy was loose in the suburbs.

"I'm not sharing a trailer with a pig," Katie said. "They're disgusting."

"That's a myth," Harry said. "Pigs are actually very clean animals."

Herb lifted his curly little tail and dumped at least three pounds of pig shit on the floor. Then he turned around, sniffed it, and began to munch on his own waste.

"See?" Harry said. "He's cleaning up after himself."

"The pig isn't coming with us," I told McGlade.

"Call him by his name. Herb."

"Herb isn't coming with us."

"He has to. This is called the *socializing* stage. It's a very important part of pig ownership. He needs to learn who the members of his herd are, so he doesn't become mean and nasty. Like your Herb. I once tried to take the last donut, and he bit me. Your Herb, not the pig. But the pig bites, too. When you pet him, curl your fingers under your hand."

"Katie and I will grab a flight and meet you there," I said, turning to leave.

Herb walked over, bumped up against me, and pressed his fat face against my hip.

"He wants you to pet him," Harry said.

I gave Herb a little pat on the head with my closed fist, and he oinked.

"He likes you."

"I don't care."

"If you abandon him at this stage," Harry said, "he may become suicidal."

Tequila snorted, which might have been a laugh. I looked at him, but his eyes were closed and his face devoid of humor.

"Animals aren't suicidal, McGlade," I said.

"Tell that to my parrot, poor little Homeboy. It still haunts my dreams."

Herb made that pig purring noise again. I gave him a scratch behind the ears.

"Aren't pigs contagious?" Katie asked. "Swine flu?"

"That doesn't infect humans," Harry said. "Much."

I wrinkled my nose. "He stinks."

"That's his breath. Probably because he just ate his own feces." McGlade reached into his pocket and removed a tin of Altoids. Herb gobbled up a handful. "We drive during the day. At night, you guys can get a hotel room, and I'll stay in the Crimebago with Herb."

I frowned. "I can imagine the flies you both will attract."

"I bought him for you, Jack."

"You shouldn't have. I mean that. Did you save the receipt?"

"I got him on Craigslist."

"Not at a livestock auction?" Katie asked.

"Don't say that. He's no doubt lost many relatives to mankind's carnivorous habits. How would you like it if the main ingredient in hot dogs was your Cousin Lem?"

Herb began to snuffle at the floor of the vehicle, discovered a cardboard coffee cup, and ate it.

"Look at that. He's also eco-friendly," Harry said. "Maybe I can get rid of the recycle bin. Think he eats glass?"

I continued toward the exit. "Katie? Tequila? Should I book three seats on the next flight?"

"I'm okay with the boar," Tequila said. "I'm also okay with the pig."

"Ha," Harry said, without humor. "I get it. I'm a bore. But at least I can ride all the attractions at Disneyworld. Maybe they'd let you on Space Mountain if you brought your child seat along."

"You sure talk a lot," Tequila said, closing his eyes again.

McGlade folded his arms. "Yeah? Well, you're below average height."

Tequila didn't respond.

"Katie?" I asked.

"He's actually kinda cute." She gave Herb a pat on the rump.

"Seriously? Am I the only one with any sense?"

"There's enough room," Katie said. "Maybe it will make the trip more interesting."

"Come on, Jackie. Don't be a hog hater. Don't be pig prejudiced. Don't be a swine scorner."

"Don't be an alliterative ass," I told him. "See what I did there?"

McGlade blinked. "Good golly."

I rubbed my eyes. I'd been hoping to learn more about Katie during the long ride. Her refusal to talk about her past was odd. Not necessarily odd enough to send up red flags; Tequila didn't talk about his past either. But I had Tequila pegged. He was a sociopath, and used to work as an enforcer for the mob, but he had a predictable code that he followed.

Katie was a mystery. She had apparent combat training but was never in the military. Wrote non-fiction but didn't ask a lot of questions. Seemed obsessed with serial killers without saying why, and knew more than she was letting on. Twenty hours in an RV would give me the chance to pick away at some of her layers, and perhaps understand whom I'd actually aligned myself with.

Of course, I'd also have to spend the same twenty hours avoiding the persistent affections of the other white meat.

Decisions, decisions. Put up with a smelly, needy pig to learn more about a woman I was working with? Or take a quick flight to Mexico and start looking for Phin immediately?

"Okay," I said. "Let's get this travelling circus on the road."

Herb celebrated the decision by crapping on the floor again, then eating it.

This was going to be a swell two days.

Swell.

DECADES AGO

Detroit

She rode in the backseat between Ben and Winston, through the frozen city streets. Kept trying to read the time on the dashboard clock of the filthy Cutlass Ciera, but the digits were moving and fading in and out.

It didn't matter.

It was late.

Too late.

And she couldn't find any reason to care.

They must have doubled up on her dose, because she hadn't been this high in months. They passed people on the street. People who could help her. But the heroin might as well have been duct tape, binding her arms, gagging her mouth.

She glanced over at Donaldson. Watching him drive reminded her of something. Something familiar, but at the same time out of reach. She focused on it, and an image popped into her head like she was staring at a snapshot.

Car trips.

I used to go on car trips with my family.

She tried to study the picture, memorize, see their faces, but it faded as the next wave of the drug overtook her.

My family.

"Fam... ily," she mumbled.

"Goddamn blizzard out here," Donaldson said, turning up the speed on the windshield wipers. "How much further?"

"You turn on Woodward, next right."

Her mind began to wobble, but she knew something about her thoughts were important. "Family…" she said, trying to figure out the meaning.

Donaldson glanced across the back seat at Winston.

"How much you give her?"

"Enough."

"If she dies before we get to the doctor, I ain't paying for nothing."

"She won't die. My shit is good shit. You want to try some for yourself?"

"No thanks," Donaldson said. "Never cared much for needles."

"Family," she said again.

"Don't you worry, sugar," Donaldson said, reaching back and patting her belly. "We're going to take care of that family problem for you."

She stared out the windshield at all the lights from oncoming vehicles reflecting off the cascading snow, and began to cry without knowing the reason, her hands cradling her stomach as she fell asleep.

When she woke up again, she was staring at the ground, piled high with snow. For a moment, she thought she might be flying, but as she moved out of the cold, into a dim corridor, she realized Winston had thrown her over his shoulder. He was carrying her.

The alarm bells in the back of her mind were more prominent now. The horse had lost its grip, and in its place, a wave of total confusion washed over her.

Where am I?

Not in the apartment that, for what seemed eons, had been her World. Her brain felt like sludge, and her thoughts so scattered, like a puzzle dumped right out of the box, the pieces everywhere, no image evident.

"Where are we?" she asked.

No one answered. Ben was there, and someone else was whistling.

Donaldson. She hated Donaldson, but couldn't remember why. Or even how she knew him.

They passed through several doorways, she briefly lost consciousness, and then suddenly she was sitting in a straight-back chair, leaning against Donaldson's shoulder.

It took her a moment, but soon she put the room into focus.

A bare light bulb swung overhead.

A fly buzzed nearby.

Donaldson said, "Where the hell is he?"

They were in a waiting room of some sort. Dirty concrete walls. Mismatched chairs. A strong odor of disinfectant.

Through a pair of double doors, a man in a white coat appeared.

She sat up a little straighter.

His white coat made him look like a doctor, only there were blood stains all over it.

"Who's paying?" he asked.

Winston and Ben pointed at Donaldson. "This guy," they both said.

The doctor held out a hand. "Two hundred fifty."

"Two fifty?" Donaldson exploded.

"Non-negotiable."

"How about one twenty-five to take out half of it?" Donaldson said. "The other half will eventually fall out on its own."

The doctor glanced at Winston. "Your friend is wasting my time."

"You wanted to watch," Ben told Donaldson. "Pay the man."

"Watch?" Donaldson grumbled. "For what I'm paying, I'm taking it home. You got a plastic bag, doc?"

"Don't be an idiot," Ben said. "You get caught walking around with something like that, we're all fucked."

"I'm not going to get caught. Just be nice to have a souvenir."

"Just pay him," Winston said.

Donaldson dug a handful of sweaty, dirty bills out of his pocket.

"What's she on?" the doctor asked after sticking the money into his coat.

"What's the difference?" Winston asked.

"If it reacts with the drugs I give her, she could die."

Winston shrugged. "So don't give her anything."

"If she doesn't get drugs, shouldn't I get some money back?" Donaldson asked.

She still wasn't sure what was happening. But some of the puzzle pieces had started assembling.

Ben and Winston.

They own me.

They took me from my family when I was young.

I can't remember my family.

I can't remember their faces.

I can't remember their names.

I can't remember my own last name.

But I know they exist.

I was with them when I was a kid.

So long ago.

So many years, it was another life.

Before I became Ben and Winston's slave.

They own me.

They pimp me out to other men for money, and keep me drugged up and locked in a room.

Donaldson is one of their clients.

He did something to me.

She wrinkled her face, trying hard to remember it.

What was it Donaldson did?

"Get her up on the table," the doctor said.

She looked at the table.

Saw the stirrups.

Her hands cleaved to her belly as all the pieces suddenly snapped together.

I'm pregnant. There's a baby inside me.

And they want to take it away from me.

"I'm sick," she said, the vomit spewing from her cheeks. All the men stood back, Winston said, "Where's the goddamn bathroom?" And then she was being yanked across the floor, thrown into a stall, and told to clean herself up.

She looked around. Saw a toilet. A sink.

A window.

Unlike the window in her room, this had no bars. She grasped the edges of the sink, pulling herself off the floor, getting a knee up next to the faucet.

I can get away.

I can get away!

I can be free!

I'll be safe!

MY BABY WILL BE SAFE!

It was more clarity than she'd had in years, and then she was up on the sink, pushing the window open, wiggling through face first and dropping into an alley.

A snow drift caught her, saving her from a broken neck. She scrambled to get up, shoveling snow out of the way in big handfuls, making it to all fours, and then onto her feet, sinking up to her knees.

The mouth of the alley was only a few meters away. Beyond it, the street...

Freedom. Cars driving past, with headlights shining like giant diamonds.

"The little bitch got through the window!"

Ben, from above her. She looked, saw him forcing himself through the opening.

She managed to take another step. And another. Then—

I can't move.

The snow sucked at her feet like hungry mouths. She shifted from foot to foot, trying to get free, but the suction was too strong.

Ben had his head and shoulder out the window, and was trying to push his other arm through.

She reached down, the snow so cold on her bare fingers that it burned, and managed to unzip her boot. Winston had bought the boots for her—boots with pointy toes and spikey heels that were too small and hurt her feet—demanding that she take care of them or he'd beat her with the car antenna again.

Her foot slipped out and she left the boot stuck in the snow. Chancing a look behind her, she saw Ben had his whole upper body hanging out the window.

They locked eyes, and he pointed with all the ferocity of him hitting her. "You stay right there!"

"I want to keep my baby!"

"If you move, I'm going to rip that baby right out of your body and make you eat it."

She turned, gazing at the street once again—

—and kept moving forward.

Her other boot became stuck, and she unzipped it just as Ben fell into the alley just a few feet behind her. Diving forward, she clawed through the snow, arms and legs pumping, swimming more than crawling as the cold enveloped her.

The street got closer...

And closer...

And—

Ben grabbed her ankle, squeezing so tightly she cried out in pain, yanking her toward him.

She flipped onto her back, bringing up her free leg, snapping it straight and driving her bare heel into his snarling face once, twice, three times before he let go.

Then she continued to claw her way through the blizzard, her face and hands pink with snow burn, her breath coming in rapid puffs that intermingled with the falling flakes.

Almost there...

Almost—

"Where are you going, sugar?"

Donaldson stood between her and the street, reaching down. Large hands encircling her wrists and lifting her out of the snow.

She kicked wildly, catching him between his legs, and then she was free—FREE—sprinting as fast as she could, into traffic, determined to run until she—

The car struck her hip, sending her twirling through the snow-fall and landing on her side.

She heard honking.

Yelling.

Then someone was kneeling next to her.

She lashed out, her arms not working correctly, the scream in her throat no more than a whimper.

"Don't... hurt... my baby..."

As she fluttered out of consciousness, the last thing she saw was a hat. A dark blue hat with a short black brim and a silver police medal.

PHIN

Somewhere in Mexico

He awoke in pain, dehydrated, and with an overwhelming urge to piss. Around him were the six empty beer cans, which he'd finished in rapid succession in order to get a quick buzz and dull the pain. Phin did get somewhat drunk, but it was a depressed, self-loathing inebriation that made him ache for Jack and Sam even more.

He pissed in his bucket, then spent twenty minutes tearing up a beer can to try and make a pick for his handcuffs. Unfortunately, rusty as they were, the padlocks were new and heavy duty. Thin aluminum, even when it was folded over and compressed using his teeth, wasn't strong enough to open the lock. It didn't work on his cell door, either.

Perhaps he could make some sort of knife or shiv, then stab the guard who wore his Tony Lama boots, giving him enough time to put together his DoubleTap 9mm. It only held two rounds, but if he took a machinegun from a guard he could...

Could escape two mounted M60s and several dozen guards, plus everyone in the arena seats who was armed? And then get out of the arena?

And go where?

Phin had no idea where he was. He could be a hundred miles from anyplace. Even if he managed to steal a car, how quickly would he be caught?

Phin put that out of his mind, continuing to twist and bend the can into something thin and pointy. The torch burn on his chest ached, probably infected. His head hurt, not just from the hangover, but from the machete blow he'd received. His stomach was also a big knot of pain. Though he'd been fed twice—and the food was actually delicious—the chili peppers had aggravated the sourness he'd been feeling since being captured. Phin's insides felt like a clenched fist.

"Put down the can, puto."

Phin looked up. It was a new guard, swarthy, stocky, his cattle prod drawn. He stood next to Phin's cell.

"I said put it down. You cannot get away. There are forty guards with automatic rifles. Beyond the arena are hundreds of land mines. And if you manage to escape, with no one in pursuit, there are kilometers of desert without any roads or shelters. You will die here, cabron. Make peace with that."

Phin decided he'd make peace in a different way, and launched himself at the guard with the bent can, aiming for the man's neck.

The cattle prod hit Phin in the stomach, the pain not unlike being shot. He fell onto his ass, and got another shock in the thigh that made him cry out, the prod juicing him until he managed to crabwalk out of range, retreating back into his cell and knocking over his piss bucket.

"Drop the can, estupido."

Phin dropped the can. His scream had awoken Kiler, who was watching while stroking himself inside his pants, a sweaty grimace on his face.

Phin's door opened. Again, he was led down the corridor, limping as he passed another armed guard.

It was night, but the klieg lights were so bright they hurt his eyes, and combined with the desert heat Phin felt his sweat bake off of him. The stands contained a few dozen people, some of them reading...

Programs? Had these assholes printed up brochures with matches and stats?

Phin squinted against the glare at a man in the front row. A man wearing a Hugo Boss suit.

"Got a grand on you, gringo!" Hugo yelled. "Don't let me down!"

Phin gave him the finger.

As a guard unlocked his shackles, Phin stared at the odds board.

1:1

They were giving him a 50/50 chance of surviving.

Phin looked at the unlucky bastard he had to fight, and saw a black guy glaring at him. Tall, lean, young. He was wearing his cotton pants low on his hips, gangbanger style. Rival dealer? Someone who wronged the cartel? Unlucky tourist? The kid had a height and reach advantage, along with the speed and endurance of youth.

Phin searched the man's face for compassion, humanity, and saw none. His opponent's eyes had that dead look, a prison stare devoid of compassion.

This wasn't some kid on vacation. This was a man who had killed before.

The loudspeaker crackled.

"Last call for bets, last call for bets. Number 16, with three wins, against Number 17, with one win. Even odds. The weapons for this match... spears."

An armed guard staked two spears into the ground, between Phin and his opponent. Apparently they would have to run for them. That was problematic; Phin's leg still ached from getting zapped with the cattle prod. He rubbed his upper thigh, and looked up at the balcony. Luther and Lucy had switched from purple capes to green, and Luther was shirtless beneath his. Even at a distance, Phin could see the gnarled scar tissue crisscrossing the lunatic's torso. Luther raised up his golden scepter, the skull on the end rubbing against the gong lightly, as one might caress a lover.

For a microsecond, Phin bathed in the hate he felt for those two psychopaths. He'd come to Mexico with no personal animus, no direct association, just a desire to preemptively protect his family. But Lucy and Luther had quickly risen to the top of his *people who must die* list.

Ranked just below the man he was about to fight to the death.

Phin focused on the spear, and when the gong rang he sprinted—

—and his leg gave out.

He fell to the ground, watching as #16 grabbed a spear in each hand and ran at him.

Things seemed to slow down, and Phin's entire world condensed to a tunnel-vision fixation on the spear tips as they drew closer. He turned onto his back, his arms extending as the weapons thrust downward, aimed at his face and chest.

His opponent was fast, and strong. Phin lashed out with his right hand, pushing away the spear as it sliced across his belly. His left hand caught the other and deflected it into the sandy ground next to Phin's ear. At the same time, Phin's right foot came up, kicking hard at #16's kidneys, his toe digging in.

As the black man staggered sideways, Phin held the spears and used his enemy's momentum to pull himself to his feet. He twisted his body, getting in close, and chopped #16 across the throat, putting all he had into the blow, hoping to break cartilage.

His adversary lowered his jaw just in time, Phin's hand bouncing off, and then he shoved Phin several feet backward. Phin regained his balance, his feet digging in, and attacked again.

Number 16 did something unexpected. Rather than jab with the spears, he swung them overhead, as if they were clubs. Phin managed to get his hands up, grabbing one, the other smacking down between his ring finger and pinky, snapping the pinky back.

As the pain from that and the slash on his chest began to register, Phin continued to drive himself forward, still gripping the one spear, tearing it from this opponent's hand. He continued to run past, taking the weapon with, then twisting around and stabbing.

The spear pierced #16's stomach, deep. Perhaps not a fatal wound in an urban area, with a hospital nearby. But in this hell hole, if the man didn't eventually bleed out, the infection would kill him.

Phin backed away as his opponent fell to his knees, clutching his belly wound. He stared at Phin with an expression of disbelief that slowly gave way to realization.

The man dropped his spear.

Phin kept his.

The crowd offered up some scattered boos.

"I…" the dying man said. "I don't wanna go out like this, man."

Phin looked up to the balcony, to Lucy and Luther.

"Goddammit… hurts." Number 16 stretched his hands out ahead of him. "Lookit all that blood. That's my blood."

Luther raised up his hand, and turned his thumb down.

The dying man let out a sob. "I done some shit. Bad shit. Unforgivable shit." He looked up at Phin. "You believe in hell, man?"

"No."

"No God? No heaven? No nothing?"

"This is it," Phin said. "Nothing comes after."

The man coughed, his lips scarlet. "Used to go to church, back in the day. Keep seeing all that fire and brimstone and shit waiting for me. Mama said ain't gonna amount to no good. Gonna go to hell."

"You're not going to hell," Phin told him. "You're getting out of hell."

Number 16 smiled. "Heh. Killed by a goddamn comedian. What's your name, funny man?"

"Phin."

The crowd began to chant. "Matarlo! Matarlo!"

"Name is Darnell. What they yelling?"

"They want me to finish you off."

"You gonna?"

Phin dropped his spear. "No." He pressed his hand to his own belly, which was bleeding heavily, then sank to his knees.

The gong rang, and three guards began to walk toward them. Their machineguns were raised.

Darnell spat blood into the sand, then laughed. "Stabbed a dude in the stomach, once. Knew it hurt this bad, woulda shot homeboy instead."

Two guards pointed their weapons at Phin, one placed the barrel of his against Darnell's temple.

"What a waste of a life," Darnell said. "I hope you're right, funny man, and there's no hell. If there is, be seeing you."

Phin made himself watch as the guard pulled the trigger. Darnell slumped over, eyes still open.

The gun was then turned on Phin.

In the balcony, Lucy whispered something to Luther.

Luther lifted a hand—

—extending a thumbs up.

Phin was yanked to his feet, to fight another day.

After being marched back to his cell, Phin was given a wrapped suture and several pills along with his six pack.

"Antibiotics," said the guard wearing Phin's boots.

The door was slammed. Phin crawled into the corner, his back against the bars.

"You're looking pretty bad," Kiler told him. "How about you give me that beer? You won't enjoy it anyway."

Phin popped the first beer, pouring it onto his stomach laceration.

"Aw, shit!" Kiler said. "That's just a fucking waste!"

The second beer, Phin pounded in just a few gulps. Then he stared at his dislocated pinky, jutting out at a right angle, and before his mind talked him out of it Phin grabbed the digit and shoved it back into place.

Phin's screaming was interrupted by his stomach turning over, expelling the beer he'd just drank onto the ground.

"That's two you wasted, you asshole!" Kiler rattled his bars. "Pass those other four over here."

Phin drank the third beer, managing to keep it down, and then unwrapped the suture and stared at his stomach. Stitching himself up proved harder than he expected. Not because of the pain, though it was substantial. But because it wasn't easy to get the needle through. Skin was tougher than he would have guessed, and there was much pulling and stretching. He finally managed to do a Frankenstein patch of eight large stitches, and then he sat back and took the antibiotics, which were in a plastic bottle along with a few Advil.

Kiler continued to antagonize him, but Phin tuned him out, closing his eyes, focusing on Jack and Sam because if he didn't he was sure he would start screaming and not be able to stop.

JACK

St. Louis

I should have flown.

Tequila slept for four hours. Katie put in some ear buds and avoided conversation altogether. And Herb the potbellied pig ate half of Harry's carpeting and two pillows, pooped it all out, and ate it again. He also kept nudging and snorting at my feet with his wet nose.

"Pigs root," Harry said. "They're naturally curious, and dig for the sake of digging. That's why I got him the rooting trough."

Apparently the rooting trough was a large tray of dirt that was supposed to satisfy Herb's digging instinct.

Herb ate all the dirt. Then he pooped it out and ate it again.

Watching the pig's dining routine, I vowed to never eat ham again. In fact, veganism was looking better and better. I'd never seen a carrot or a soybean eat its own dung.

As we approached the outskirts of St. Louis, Katie removed her headphones and made her way to the Crimebago's front seat. Harry referred to the area as the *cockpit*, for obvious rude reasons. Herb began to oink, nudging me with his wet nose, demanding to have his head scratched. I did so, while trying to listen to what Katie was saying.

"The Kansas City route is quicker. You should go west."

"GPS says Oklahoma City."

"I've gone both routes. KC also has a shooting range I like. It would be good to get in some practice."

"I'm pretty sure Oklahoma has shooting ranges."

"Look, McGlade, KC is closer, and if I don't get out of this RV and away from this pig I'm going to start screaming at the top of my lungs and not stop until my throat closes up."

"Kansas City it is."

Looking smug in victory, Katie came back into the cabin and sat across from me on the sofa. She was a few inches lower than me because Herb Bacondict had eaten her seat cushion.

"What do you shoot?" I asked before she could put her headphones back on.

Katie reached for her duffle bag, which was in an overhead compartment and out of the pig's snacking range, and set it on the floor. When Herb snuffled it, she gave him a firm slap on the thigh and said, "No!"

Herb oinked, then began to gnaw on the handle to the refrigerator.

Katie unzipped the bag and removed a walnut gun box. She handed it over. I opened the lid and whistled, staring at a .357 Colt King Cobra. Blue steel with black Pachmayr grips. I took it out of the form-fitting velvet and swung out the cylinder, staring at six rounds of Hydra-Shok expanding bullets.

"Hunting for bear?"

"When I shoot something, I want it to drop. Bear, mountain lion..." Her eyes crinkled. "Pig."

I glanced at Herb Bacondict, who had managed to pull open the refrigerator door, and had discovered a cardboard box of leftover pizza. Which he was eating, box and all.

"Shot a lot of pigs?" I asked.

"Only thing I've ever shot is paper targets. I actually picked that up after reading about you. Do you still carry that Colt Detective Special?"

I hid my wince. That was still a sore spot. "It was damaged a while back. I've got a Python now."

A corner of Katie's mouth turned up. "Revolvers never jam. Fewer working parts means fewer chances for the weapon to fail. You can't lose the magazine, you can cock it for an easier trigger pull, and you'll never leave the safety on, because it doesn't have a safety." She leaned closer to me. "You said that. To a reporter, in 1989. It was one of the first times you were in the newspaper."

I remembered the case, which was the first of my encounters with an elusive killer named Mr. K.

"You dig that up at the library?"

"No. I read the article when it came out."

Katie must have been older than she looked. Or a really precocious child. It had been in a feature done on female cops for USA Today, and they'd been particularly focused on what we carried.

"I'm surprised you remember it."

She shrugged. "I read everything I could when I was younger. That was my escape."

"Is that why you became a writer?"

"To escape? Or because I liked to read?"

"Either."

"No."

She didn't elaborate, reaching for the gun and box and tucking them away.

"So why do you write?"

"I like closure. Life is an ongoing story, and some parts of it are never resolved. Books have endings. I... I find comfort in the fact that things end."

I sensed there was more, but Katie seemed to be keeping her guard up.

"You told me this was personal for you," I said. "What is your interest in Luther Kite?"

Pain flashed across her face, and vanished just as quickly. She stayed silent.

"Family?" I prodded.

Katie nodded, just barely.

"When?"

"It's been a long time," she said after a dozen silent seconds. "A very long time. But some pain… it never goes away."

"I know what that's like," I said. "I've lost people. My fiancée. My ex-husband."

"I never talk about it." Katie put her bag back in the overhead. Herb the pig was noisily eating a plastic jar of mayonnaise. One of those big gallon jars found at Costco. I wondered why McGlade needed that much mayo, and then decided some things were best left unknown.

"Keeping things bottled up isn't healthy," I told Katie.

"He seems healthy," Katie pointed her chin at Tequila. "And he keeps everything bottled up."

"I'm an open book," Tequila said, surprising me by being awake.

"No secrets, huh?" Katie asked.

Tequila shook his head. "Jack's right. Keeping things bottled up is bad."

"Really?"

"Really," he answered.

"So tell me, then," Katie went on, "how many people have you killed?"

"Forty-eight."

Whoa. That was a lot higher than I would have guessed.

"And you've shared this with someone else?" she asked.

"Yes."

"Shrink? Priest?" Katie raised an eyebrow. "Girlfriend?"

"Dog," Tequila said.

For some reason, I hadn't pictured Tequila as a dog owner. "What kind?"

"Neo Mastiff. Her name is Rosalina." Tequila sat up and looked pointedly at me. "She's staying with a friend right now. My friend's name is Thelma Erno. E-R-N-O. She lives in Rogers Park."

"That your sweetheart?" Katie asked.

"We see each other sometimes. She tolerates the dog, but isn't a dog person."

"Does she know you killed forty-eight people?"

Tequila laid back down and closed his eyes. "No."

Katie folded her wiry arms across her chest. "I thought the point was to share things with one another."

"I do share things," Tequila said. "With my dog."

"The albino Smurf has the right idea," Harry said from the front seat. "Pets are the perfect sounding board. They're always there. They always listen. They never judge. For example, I told Herb Bacondict all about my addiction to clown porn."

"You've told everybody about your addiction to clown porn," I said. "I've seen you stop random strangers on the street to tell them about your addiction to clown porn."

"Clown porn?" Katie asked. "Like with face painting and rainbow wigs?"

"Rainbow wigs are pure sex," Harry said. "And any shoe size over 22 give me a rager."

"That's... disturbing," Katie said.

"Does anyone want to see the pics on my phone?"

We said *no* simultaneously.

"How about you, Grumpy?"

"No."

"How about your six little dwarf buddies? Would they like that?"

"Would you like two prosthetic hands?"

"See, that negative attitude is what I'm talking about, white Gary Coleman. I try to share something, and I'm met with disapproval and threats of bodily harm. And how did you even know it's a prosthetic? This thing is state of the art. They guaranteed me no one could tell the difference between my fake hand and a real hand."

"Real hands don't make a whirring, robotic noise when they open and close," I opined.

"Also, the shade is off," Tequila said.

Harry made a face. "Herb Bacondict doesn't judge me like you guys are doing now. You need to be more accepting of others, people. Take some lessons from the pig."

The pig was eating his own feces again.

"Pass," I said.

Katie put her ear buds back in and cranked up the music. Tequila's breathing slowed, indicating he'd gone back to sleep.

Herb Bacondict found a wrapped pound of butter in the fridge, and swallowed it in two large bites.

"That can't be healthy," I told the pig.

"Soo-wee!" Herb answered.

I couldn't tell if he agreed with me or not. Probably not, because the next thing he ate was a plastic bottle of mustard.

I glanced at Katie. Her eyes were closed, her face relaxed. She looked peaceful.

I believed her when she said the only things she'd ever shot were paper targets. But I wondered how long that would remain true if we found Luther Kite.

This was a woman with demons in her past.

But then, who didn't have demons? I had too many to count.

There's an old joke that life is 100% fatal, and no one gets out alive.

No one gets out unhurt, either. Everybody gets wounded. Physically, and emotionally.

Herb Bacondict snuffled my knees, and I rested my hand on his stubbly head and scratched behind his ears.

"We're all going to be hurt," I told him. "It's just a matter of time."

Then I leaned back and tried not to think about Phin.

And failed.

PHIN

Somewhere in Mexico

Hey! Hey, asshole!"

Phin opened his eyes. He'd been dreaming about Jack, slow dancing with her to an old Tom Waits song, and could still feel the warmth of her cheek against his, her scent clinging to him.

That was quickly replaced by the smell of body odor and human waste as the reality of his situation came crashing back at him.

"I'm talking to you, asshole."

Phin sat up on his bed roll and faced the cell opposite his. Glaring at him from behind the bars was a giant of a man, at least six and a half feet tall, three hundred pounds easy. His shirt was off, revealing a decade's worth of crude jailhouse tattoos, mostly of the white supremacist variety.

"I told you to give me your beer if you won," Kiler said. "You give me the beer, and when we face off I'll kill you quick. Now I'm gonna drag it out. Make you hurt for a long time."

Phin laid back down.

"Don't ignore me, asshole! You want me to fuck you before I kill you? I'll do it. Right in the middle of the arena, with everyone watching. What do you think your odds are against me? Ten to one? Twenty to one? I'm gonna make you my bitch."

Phin figured twenty to one was about right. Kiler was big enough to be a professional wrestler, and unlike the other dozen or so men who were locked up in this hellhole, he seemed to actually be enjoying himself. On his cheek, under his right eye, were nine tattooed tears. Jailhouse tats. Each one represented a man Kiler had killed.

Or *kiled*.

"What's your name, punk?" Kiler asked.

Phin knew better than to antagonize the gigantic psychopath that he'd eventually wind up having to fight, but his mood had been soured by being rudely awoken.

"Sheldon Liebowitz," Phin said.

"That some kinda Jew name? I hate Jews. Hate them even worse than the stinky spics in this dump. You a Jew?"

"Half Jewish, half African-American," Phin said. "My middle name is Tupac."

Kiler unleashed a tirade of hate speech, which wasn't as narrow-minded as Phin expected because his word usage was so limited.

When the large man finally calmed down, Phin said, "You spelled *killer* wrong on your stomach."

"What?"

Phin figured Kiler never knew that, because no one ever had the guts to tell him to his face.

"Killer is spelled with two Ls, dummy."

"No it ain't."

"Double L. They must have kicked you out of grammar school before you learned that."

"I wasn't kicked out," Kiler said. "I just didn't wanna go no more."

"You should have stayed. Because that's not all that's wrong. That swastika on your neck is facing the wrong way. The way you've got it says you hate Nazis."

Kiler's eyes widened. "Does not."

"You know how an upside down cross means you're a Satanist? A backwards swastika means you think all men are equal."

Kiler touched his neck. "That ain't true! Take it back!"

"You know it's true," Phin said. "You claim you hate Jews, but you told me yourself that you want to have sex with me. In front of the whole arena. You're obviously a Jew-lover. I bet you want to move to Israel."

Kiler stretched his enormous arms through the bars, his biceps so big they almost didn't fit, in an effort to reach Phin.

"Dead! You're dead, Jew boy!"

As Kiler screamed in rage, Phin closed his eyes and tried to focus on Jack's face. The tilt of her chin. The curve of her cheeks. The smile lines around her eyes. He remembered a night, not long after Samantha had been born, holding her at three in the morning to stop her from crying, Jack taking the baby from him just as Sam threw up all over her. Jack passed her back to Phin and she puked again. They both began laughing so hard they started to cry.

Phin had resolved himself to dying, years ago when he'd been diagnosed with pancreatic cancer. The cancer was now in remission, but Phin no longer had the ability to look death in the face and spit in its eye. He wanted to get old with the woman he loved. He wanted to see his daughter grow up. He'd gotten a second chance.

Now he wanted a third one.

The guard came in, short and Mexican and smelling of Old Spice, and read off a clipboard in Spanglish.

"Número diecisiete..."

Seventeen. That was Phin.

"Y doce."

Twelve.

Phin thought he knew who that was. Some college kid, built like a football player.

His cell door opened.

For some odd reason, Phin thought about the wedding ring he'd given his wife. The inscription inside the band.

For forever and beyond.

When Phin had written that, he'd meant that his love for Jack would outlive him.

Mexico was doing its damnedest to test that hypothesis.

"Ándale, puto!"

The leg shackles were removed, and then Phin was shoved roughly from behind. He still had his handcuffs on—heavy, rusty chains that had rubbed the skin on his wrists raw. As he was marched through the cell hallway, a machinegun at his back, the chains bumped against his broken ribs, causing a spike of pain with every step.

He was right. It was the football kid.

Phin beat him to death with an aluminum baseball bat, then tried and failed to find redemption in a six pack of warm beer as Kiler cursed at him.

YEARS AGO

LUCY

Indianapolis

The six-year old climbed to the top of the slide and looked to see if her parents were watching.

They weren't. Daddy was yelling at Mommy, waving his hands around and using bad words. Mommy had that mean look; the kind she had when Lucy spilled juice on the carpet.

They were fighting about Lucy. Mommy didn't like it that Daddy loved her more than he loved Mommy.

Lucy looked around the playground. There were some kids on the swings, and one on the green springy horse. No one was paying any attention to her.

She reached into her shorts and gently took out the frog she'd found by the pond. It wiggled, its long legs kicking out. The frog's skin was still moist, and it smelled funny.

"Do you want to watch me go down the slide, Mr. Frog?"

The frog didn't answer.

"How about we both go down?"

Lucy sat down, carefully cupped the animal in her hands, and anticlimactically slid to the ground. When she stood up, she checked to see if Mr. Frog was still safe.

He was.

"Was that fun, Mr. Frog? Want to do it again?"

The frog didn't seem to care one way or the other. Lucy wondered if he might want to do something else instead.

"Are you hungry, Mr. Frog? Want something to eat?"

Lucy walked over to the sandbox, looking for bugs. She couldn't find any. But she did find a bottle cap.

"Finish it, or you're getting a spanking," she ordered Mr. Frog.

Lucy used her thumb to push it all the way in, and the sharp edges came out of Mr. Frog's belly, which bled all over her hands.

The blood made Mr. Frog smell soooooo much better.

When the frog stopped moving, Lucy dug a hole in the sand and buried him.

"Now you're with your family," she said, pushing sand over Mr. Frog's body. The Lucy Garden Paradise Memorial Frog Cemetery contained six other frog corpses. But, unknown to Lucy, none of them were actually related. And one was actually a toad, not a frog.

But they all smelled good when they bled.

"Hello, Lucy."

Lucy looked up, and saw a woman standing next to her.

"Hello."

The woman was thin, and wore big sunglasses that covered most of her face.

"I saw what you did to that frog. How did it make you feel?"

"I dunno."

"Did it make you feel happy?"

Lucy didn't answer.

"Sometimes, when we hurt inside, we do things to feel better. Do you hurt inside, Lucy?"

Lucy shook her head.

"Never?"

"It hurts when I get spanked."

"Do you get spanked a lot?"

Lucy nodded.

"For doing bad things?"

"I spill my juice sometimes. And I put Jarvis in the oven. I got spanked for that."

"Jarvis is your cat?"

"Uh-huh."

"Did Jarvis die?"

"No. He just made a lot of noise and Mommy let him out and spanked me."

"Was the oven on?"

"No," Lucy said.

"Did you want to turn it on?"

"I couldn't reach the knob."

"You're not big enough, yet." The woman smiled. "But you will be, someday. You'll grow up big and strong and never let anyone hurt you ever again."

"What's your name?"

"I'm your mommy, Lucy."

That didn't make any sense. "You're not Mommy."

"I'm your real mommy. Those people adopted you when you were just a baby. I had to give you away. But one day we'll be together again. Would you like that?"

"You want to see Mr. Frog? I put him in a hole."

"I wish I could, sweetie. But I have to go. Maybe next time. When the time is right, I'll come for you, Lucy. I've been watching you for years. One day, we're going to be a family again."

Lucy began to dig up Mr. Frog. When she pulled him out of the sand, the woman was gone.

KATIE

Kansas City

It felt good to get away from the pig.

They'd rolled into KC after sunset. Katie, Jack, and Tequila had gotten rooms at a Holiday Inn Express on Rainbow Boulevard, while Harry McGlade and Herb Bacondict drove off in search of a place to park and spend the night. Which would be uncomfortable for McGlade, because Herb had eaten his mattress.

Tequila went straight to the hotel gym. Katie suggested to Jack that they take a walk, maybe find a bar, but the ex-cop preferred instead to stay in her room and scour the Internet for anything related to Luther Kite.

Which was fine with Katie. She'd been fruitlessly searching for Luther for a long time, and she'd sought out Jack Daniels because the woman had a knack for tracking down psychopaths. Let the cop do her thing.

Katie needed some alone time anyway. She grabbed her backpack and ventured out into the night.

After a sub sandwich at a local shop, Katie wound up at a nondescript neighborhood tavern called Mike Kelly's Westsider that didn't seem worth her time. She almost walked past, but the sounds of live music gave Katie hope the place would have a diverse crowd. Katie paid a five dollar cover and went in.

The band was a trio, and the lanky lead singer had longish, gray hair and a voice like butter. Katie found a stool at the bar, ordered a Maker's Mark neat, and sipped it while listening to a rock song about—of all things—the Dutch painter Jan Vermeer. It was an upbeat tune, there were a few people dancing, Katie found herself tapping her foot to the beat. When it was finished, the next song was something quieter, slower. Katie assumed it was a love song, until she started paying attention to the words.

"I scratch my name into your mirror," he crooned. "I burn my face into your eyes."

No. That wasn't love. That was something else. Something eerie.

She continued to listen, and realized the song was about a predator. Someone who had harmed another person so badly it caused a scar that could never heal, and an unwelcome bond between abuser and victim.

Katie raised the bourbon to her lips and clinked the glass against her teeth.

Her hand was shaking.

She managed to set it down without spilling any, threw a tenner on the bar, and went to the ladies' room, the lyric "Do not relax, you're not alone," following her inside.

At the sink she ran some cool water and wet her hands, then rubbed her face.

"Lock it down," she told herself.

But rather than lock it down, her stomach rolled and she threw up the bourbon. Katie was spitting the last of it into the drain just as a woman came in.

"Tough night, honey?" she asked, standing next to Katie and applying red lip gloss.

Katie appraised her. She was in her late forties or early fifties, hair teased beyond any measure of beauty, crammed into a skirt that screamed *bar skank*.

"I'm new in town." She put on what she knew was a pathetic smile. "I just really need to get fixed up. Any ideas?"

The woman stopped applying make-up long enough to lock eyes with Katie. *Fixed up* was a phrase that sounded innocent to the uninitiated, but was obvious to others. Depending on this lady's past, she might understand Katie's intent, or try to set her up with her second cousin.

"I don't do that anymore," the woman said.

Katie didn't have to fake desperation; her yearning was honest. "I heard about Troost Avenue. East of Troost. Can I go there?"

"You should stick with booze. They pour an honest shot here. Music is great. Cute thing like you should be able to find some sweetheart for the night."

"I don't need a sweetheart. I need this." Katie didn't try to control her shaking. "Please."

"Mess your life up with that shit," the woman said.

"It's my life." *And it's already messed up,* Katie thought.

The woman shrugged, as if deciding it wasn't her problem. "Whatever. Troost isn't good anymore. There's a pawn shop on Independence. You can score around there. But that's a bad area. Shouldn't go alone."

Katie mumbled a thank you and left the bathroom and the bar, music following her back out into the street. She headed west, found a fast food joint, and called a taxi from the toilet stall.

It took her eight minutes to change her clothes, twenty minutes to get to the east side of town, and two hours before she found what she was looking for.

Then things got really, really ugly.

DONALDSON

Baja

Four hours after leaving Phoenix, Donaldson was in Mexicali. That included crossing the border. As he expected, they green-lighted Donaldson through Customs without detaining him for inspection. His FMM visitor visa and vehicle permit cost about fifty bucks. Rather than risk using Irving's credit card, he paid with quarters and dimes stolen from the dead man's home.

It left him with a little over fourteen dollars left in the change jar. He turned onto Boulevard Lázaro Cárdenas and began to search for the proper store.

Donaldson was hungry, but he wasn't looking for food. During the long drive, he'd had a lot of time to think about how to find his Lucy. Baja was a big place. If she were there, hunting for her could take weeks, or even months, and might ultimately prove impossible. Like finding a needle in a haystack.

But there were ways to find that proverbial needle. The simplest solution was to have the needle come to you.

Donaldson parked at an OXXO, which seemed to be the Mexican convenience store equivalent of 7-Eleven, and hobbled inside, his pockets laden with coins. Inside he bought a lemon, a map of Mexicali, ten meters of heavy-duty clothesline, and a box of Gansitos snack cakes, which appeared to be chocolate-covered Twinkies with strawberry jelly inside.

The cost for everything; less than five US dollars.

166 · J.A. KONRATH

He gnawed on one of the Gansitos, getting used to Irving's teeth, plotting his next move, weighing pros and cons.

Would a tourist get more, or less, media attention?

The local authorities probably wouldn't announce that right away. Bad publicity.

Someone local would provoke a more immediate media response.

A man, or a woman?

Actually, it depended on their size. Donaldson was once a formidable predator, ready to take on all-comers. Nowadays, a strong breeze could kick his ass. Best bet was to look for someone small.

A child?

Donaldson had no specific preferences when it came to killing. He'd murdered people of all ages. But the populace tended to get disproportionally riled up when children died. Donaldson was seeking headlines, not a national manhunt.

The best bet would be to stick with what worked in Phoenix. Find someone at a disadvantage, like a drunk or an old person, and go from there.

He ate a second Gansitos, wondering why they weren't available in the US because the combination of crème filling, yellow cake, chocolate sprinkles, and strawberry jelly was a snack cake win. Donaldson retrieved some Xanax out of the pillowcase, popped two, and began to cruise the streets, searching for a suitable victim.

One hour and four Gansitos later, Donaldson felt terrific. His various pains had been dulled to manageable levels, the car was cool, his gut was full, and he'd found a skivvy bar on the edge of town called Quatro that was spitting drunks out into the parking lot every ten minutes or so. So far, they'd been in pairs or groups. But it was just a matter of time until some single person stumbled out, oblivious to his surroundings.

While waiting, Donaldson tied the clothesline to the undercarriage of the Caddy, doubled up the width of rope so it wouldn't snap, and put a perfect hangman's knot on the end.

If this worked, he wouldn't have to search Mexicali for Lucy. Donaldson would use her MO and drag someone to death, stopping occasionally to douse the person in lemon juice. News of the murder would spread, and his Lucy would know he was in town and she'd find him.

Donaldson put the noose in his pocket, sat in the car with the air on, and waited for his next victim, crouching like a spider in a—

There.

The man staggering out of the tavern appeared drunk as drunk can get. He was Mexican. He was alone. He moved like the ground beneath him was shifting. Donaldson rocked his bulk out of the Cadillac and as he unfolded the map he did a three-hundred and sixty degree sweep of the parking lot to make sure no one was watching.

"Can you help?" Donaldson asked. The map concealed the noose in his fist. "I'm looking for the Plaza de Toros Calafia."

The drunk turned on the heel of his overly ornate cowboy boot and made a face. "Que?"

"The Plaza de Toros," Donaldson said, reading off the ad on the back of the map. "Can you give me directions?"

"Eres muy feo."

"Where?" Donaldson was only a few steps away, and getting excited. As twisted and broken as his body was, he still felt the adrenaline spike, the dopamine dump, the natural high that always accompanied an atrocious act. Out of all the base instincts and emotions human beings were capable of, none were as viscerally satisfying as causing harm.

Donaldson lowered his head and shoved, hard as he could, knocking the intoxicated man onto the ground. As the guy flopped around, groaning gibberish, Donaldson looped the rope around his ankle and cinched it tight. Then he hurried back to the Caddy.

Time to paint the streets red.

He turned the engine over, threw the car into gear, and hit the gas, his whole body tingling with excitement.

Then there was an enormous *BOOM!* as the drunk's boot—still attached to the clothesline—came bursting through the back window.

Donaldson was smacked in the head so hard his face bounced off the steering wheel; an action which would have easily broken his nose if he still had one.

He managed to hit the brakes, screeching to a stop. Then he blinked, trying to regain the ability to focus, and gingerly touched the back of his skull. Along with the growing bump, he felt over a dozen lacerations; when the boot broke through, it peppered him with bits of glass, shotgun-style.

For a moment Donaldson was unsure what to do. The smart thing was to drive away, get patched up, then try again later. But a quick glance through the broken rear window proved the drunk guy was still on the ground, minus one boot but apparently unharmed.

Donaldson heaved himself out of the car, limped around to the back, and tugged the clothesline back through the window. Lurching toward his prey, he widened the noose, freeing the boot, and looped the rope over the man's neck and pulled it tight.

Since it was practically impossible to pull off a human head—Donaldson knew this having tried to do so several times—this should work perfectly. He hobbled back to the Cadillac, brushed broken glass off his seat, climbed in, and punched it.

The car accelerated, slowing as it took the weight of the Mexican, and then speeding up again.

"That's right!" Donaldson whooped, turning to take a look at the carnage. "How do you like pavement sledding, you drunk son of a—"

The *TWANG!* sounded like a perfect C chord strummed on a giant guitar. A millisecond later, the rope was catapulting back at Donaldson like a rubber band, flying through the broken rear window, and thwacking him in the left eye.

The pain was preternatural. Donaldson slammed on the brakes again, the Caddy fishtailing. When the car came to a stop, Donaldson's shaking hands probed his eye.

It felt like a warm hardboiled egg.

He adjusted the rearview mirror, chancing a look.

A demented, blood-soaked Cookie Monster stared back at him with a googly Ping-Pong eyeball.

Donaldson screamed, trying to shove his eye back into the socket, which cranked the agony up to eleven. When it wouldn't budge, he punched the dashboard until his hand bled, and then reassessed the injury.

On closer inspection, his eye wasn't actually sticking out. Instead, the rope had forced his upper eyelid behind his eyeball.

Having his optic nerve rubbed with sandpaper wouldn't have hurt as much.

Donaldson tried to stick a finger behind his eye to grab the eyelid, screaming as he did so,

Competing with the pain was rage. Donaldson opened the door, determined to beat the Mexican into a misshapen pulp. The man was sitting up, the rope no longer around his neck because it had been Donaldson's knot that failed, not the clothesline. That made Donaldson even angrier, and he searched the back seat for his crowbar, hefted it, and then set course to murder.

"Dónde está mi bota?" the Mexican asked, staring stupidly at his bare foot.

Donaldson could only point to a few times in his life where he wanted to kill someone as fiercely as he wanted to kill this man. He wanted to crack open his ribs, dig into his chest, and tear out this guy's beating heart and eat it right in front of him. He wanted to break the man's legs in so many places he could bend them backwards and make him choke on his own toes. He wanted to carve open his stomach and fill it with hot coals and then—

"Hey, check out Popeye!"

Four Americans had walked out of Quarto and were pointing at Donaldson and giggling. Two men, two women, each of them young and fit, all heading his direction.

"His head looks like my nutsack!"

"I think I'm going to puke."

"What a freak show. That should *not* be allowed out in public."

"Is that a mask? That's gotta be a mask."

Donaldson halted.

"Hey, scarface, how many ugly sticks did God break over your face to do that to you?"

Donaldson wasn't religious, but that was just plain mean. Stares and occasional comments were expected, given his appearance. But he knew the difference between disgust and aggression. Drunk, on vacation, looking to impress the girls; they were looking for a fight.

"He's staring at me, Brad. Make him stop staring."

Brad's hands balled into fists. "You staring at my girlfriend, creep?"

Donaldson considered the crowbar. In his earlier years, he would have thrown caution to the wind and had a go at beating them all to death. But Brad was pretty big. So was his buddy. And those women almost for sure worked out.

Donaldson already had enough failures for the day, and decided his best bet was to scurry off and lick his wounds in private.

"I asked you a question," Brad puffed out his chest and picked up his pace, closing the distance between them. "You staring at her?"

Donaldson backed away. "I was in an accident. I can't close my eye."

"Dónde está mi bota?" the drunk Mexican said, pointing.

Brand pointed, stereotypical ugly American striking the bully pose. "Did you steal this man's boot?"

Donaldson turned and hurried back to the car. He reached for—and missed—the door handle because his depth perception was shit with his injured eye. Feeling around until he found it, he managed to get inside and hit the lock just as Brad began banging on his window.

"Where you going, freak?"

"I need a doctor," Donaldson moaned.

"You need an ass kicking!"

Brad pounded harder. Donaldson chanced a look in the rearview, and saw Brad's musclehead friend coming up from behind.

Time to go.

Donaldson peeled out of the parking lot, wondering what the hell was wrong with people these days. He remembered when, decades ago, he could lure potential victims into helping him by pretending to be injured. He'd killed over a dozen unsuspecting good Samaritans by feigning a broken ankle, or a heart attack. But now, when he actually was injured for real, some ass-goblins were trying to injure him even more. It was like the collective compassion of the human race had taken a face-dive into the toilet.

He blamed violent video games.

Donaldson turned the Caddy east, keeping his good eye on the lookout for a hospital, hoping Mexico had as many as the United States did.

JACK

Have you heard of Emilio Cardova?"

"No." I was sitting in the desk chair in my hotel room, talking to Herb on my cell.

My friend, Herb. Not Harry's pet pig.

"The Cardova cartel is one of the largest in Mexico," Herb continued. "They have poppy farms as far south as Columbia. Specializing in syrup distro."

"Cough medicine with opiates."

"Right, but without the medicine. It's basically sugar water you can OD on. A few weeks ago, one of Cardova's men was arrested in La Joya, and tried to cut a deal. He said that Cardova had a secret compound where—get this—he's forcing prisoners to fight in gladiator games."

"Like the Roman Coliseum?"

"Supposedly worse. Fighting to the death while assholes bet on the outcome."

Nice. Humanity continued to thwart my efforts to have any faith in it whatsoever. "What's Luther Kite's link?"

"The suspect said that the arena was run by a scarred guy with long, black hair. They call him El Cometa."

I punched that in on my laptop and used Google Translate. "The Comet."

"*Cometa* also means something else in Spanish," Herb said. "It's another word for *kite*."

So Luther had made it to Mexico, and somehow wound up running death matches for a cartel.

"Where is the arena?" I asked.

"It's called La Juntita. Supposedly hidden somewhere in the Vizcaíno desert, but the guy couldn't point to it on a map. We're talking ten thousand square miles of wildlife refuge."

"Impossible to search."

"Or maybe the police know about it, but Cardova paid off the right people."

This was quickly devolving from very bad to much worse. "How about satellite images?"

"Suspect said the compound is well-camouflaged. Even if you knew where to look, you wouldn't see anything from above."

I closed my eyes. Violence was part of our genetic code. If there were only two people left on the planet, one would wind up victimizing the other. I'd known this for decades. But now that I had a child, my world-weary resignation had been superseded by paranoia. Paranoia that was constantly being reinforced by real life events.

I quit being a cop because I didn't want to deal with the violence anymore. I wanted a normal, boring, mundane, average, run-of-the-mill life, where the main worries were money and sex and health. How was I supposed to tell Samantha that her father went to murder a serial killer and wound up dying in a gladiator arena while men placed bets? That was so messed up it was almost funny.

"How are you holding up?" Herb asked, his voice soft.

"Fine."

"You sure?"

"This might sound awful, but I think I might be getting used to psychos targeting me and those I love."

"So you feel desensitized?"

"Heh, I wish I felt desensitized. Instead, I feel..."

How did I feel?

Cursed. I felt cursed. Condemned to walk the earth, fighting monsters. And I was pulling my friends and family into the chasm with me.

I sighed. "I'm just having a pity party, Herb."

"This isn't your fault, Jack."

"That's like saying it isn't the lightning rod's fault it keeps getting zapped."

"Phin chose to do this. It's on him."

"How is Luther Kite on him?"

"How is Luther Kite on you? He was never one of your cases. You were never after him. It's just some stupid quirk of fate. Shit happens. Don't let that define you."

"What if it defines me whether I want it to or not? What if I'm actually a magnet for psychos? Your wife doesn't want you to go anywhere near me."

"Thanks. Like I didn't already feel shitty about that."

"You wife isn't wrong, Herb. If I could have stopped Phin from doing this, I would have."

"She is wrong, Jack. For almost thirty years, Bernice has been worrying about me. Now her worries are about to end, and she doesn't know how to handle it. Be honest; has your life improved since you've retired?"

"My past won't allow it to improve."

"*You* won't allow it to improve. You haven't been living. You've been hiding. Not only from the world, but from yourself."

"What does that even mean?"

"It means that you need to be you, because you suck at being anyone else. Be Jack Daniels. Stop tippy-toeing around it. The only alternative is eating your gun and taking yourself out of the game."

"You suck at pep-talks, Herb."

"Suicidal thoughts go with the badge. Waller, the district shrink, thinks I'm trying to kill myself by eating junk food."

"Is she right?"

"No. I just like sugar. A lot. Hell, I'd *die* for sugar."

I changed the subject. "How did you find out about Kite and Cardova? That's pretty good police work for an old guy retiring next week."

"I called in a favor at Interpol."

"You don't know anyone at Interpol."

"Okay, you caught me. I worked with a pal in the gang unit who speaks Spanish, and we spent all day searching through Mexicali's version of a police blotter."

One of his last days on the Job, and he spent it helping me.

"Thank you, Herb."

"Least I can do. I'll keep at it, let you know if I find anything."

"I appreciate it."

"I'm serious about the *you being you* thing. You're one of the good guys. Denying your nature isn't going to get you anywhere."

Herb hung up, and I considered my next move. This information seemed important enough to share with Fleming and Chandler, who had access to resources above and beyond regular law enforcement. But Chandler hadn't given me a way to contact her. So I mimicked Harry's method and wrote a Reddit post using the keywords *White House, bugged, Daniels, McGlade, Fleming, and Chandler.*

Thirty seconds later, my cell rang.

"This is Jack."

"You and the idiot need to stop using the Internet like rank amateurs."

"Hi, Fleming. Good to hear from you." She didn't correct me and say she was Chandler, so I figured I'd guessed her name correctly.

"And don't use codenames on cell phones."

"You called me. Isn't your line encrypted?"

"Yes. But you should always act like every second of your life is being broadcast live on worldwide public television."

"That's... awful."

"Privacy is a myth. The faster you learn that, the better off you'll be."

That didn't seem like a decent way to live, but this wasn't the time to argue. "I have a lead. There's a drug lord named—"

"Don't say his name. We're already on it."

"How did you—"

"We're tapping your phone."

"Oh," I said. "Thanks."

"And your sugar-addicted partner is correct. Shit or get off the pot."

"Is that what he said?"

"He said be yourself or eat a gun. Do one or the other. You're not acting like the woman I met years ago at my apartment."

"Wait… this is Chandler?"

She sighed. "Again with the codenames."

"You and your sister really sound alike."

"This small talk thing; I'm not big on it."

"Not sure how I can respond to that without it sounding like small talk."

"If this arena exists and doesn't show up on satellite photos, we can try using infrared. I also have some other ideas how to find it."

"How do we know if my husband is—"

"My sister located his cell phone. It was in the trunk of a rental car. Car was returned earlier today."

"By Phin?"

Chandler paused, then said. "No. By someone else. We're working on figuring out who. Now that we know who is involved, we know who to ask."

"So you think he's there?"

"Assuming this place exists, we'll find it. And assuming he's there, we'll find him. Assuming he's still alive. See you in two days."

"How do I contact you if—"

"You don't."

She hung up.

If I'd felt bad earlier, I felt a lot worse having talked to Herb and Chandler. My paranoia and worry meters each hit the red zone.

I checked the time on my cell, wondering if it was too late to call my daughter. It was.

Calling her was probably a bad idea, anyway. Some psycho could be listening and trace it to my mother and child. A premise that would seem utterly ridiculous, except that it wasn't. Bad people from my past have repeatedly targeted my family, and my family had suffered terrible tragedies simply because they were unlucky enough to be my family.

Though Herb mentioned that suicidal thoughts went with the badge, I hadn't ever seriously considered ending my own life.

But to save my daughter? I'd end my own life without a second thought if it kept her safe.

Since I was already feeling so darn good about myself, I went over to the mini bar to get my drink on. But it wasn't a mini bar, it was just an empty mini fridge, sadly lacking in liquor.

Wishing I'd taken Katie up on her offer of bar hopping, I texted her to see if she was around. After waiting more than a minute for a response that never came, I called Tequila's room.

"Yeah?"

"It's Jack. I'm thinking about going out for a beer."

"Yeah?"

"Thought you might want to join me."

"Yeah?"

"Yeah."

"No."

"No?"

"I'm watching *Toy Story 2*."

"Really? That doesn't seem like it would be your thing."

"Pixar tickles my childhood sense of whimsy."

"Indeed," I said.

"Have you seen it?"

"No."

"It just started. To infinity and beyond."

"Excuse me?"

"That's what Buzz Lightyear says. To infinity and beyond."

I stared at my wedding band. On the inside, Phin had inscribed; *For forever and beyond.*

I wondered if he'd gotten that from the movie.

I wondered if I'd ever have the chance to ask him.

Tequila hung up. That meant I could either find a watering hole on my own, or call up McGlade.

I found a watering hole on my own. On the recommendation of the cab driver, I wound up at The Standard Pour Tavern and I found a tiny round table for one facing a TV that was playing—go figure—*Toy Story 2*, but with the volume down so I couldn't hear what was happening.

A waiter came over, and I dropped forty bucks on a bottle of local brew called Boulevard Bourbon Barrel Quad. A lot of money for a beer, but it was twenty-five ounces and almost 12% ABV, and I figured that would be all I needed to get me through the evening.

Muffled music and applause filtered in through the wall from the bar next door. They sounded like they were having more fun than I was; getting slowly tanked, avoiding thoughts of my husband and daughter, and trying to lip-read computer animated characters.

The quad got me where I wanted to go, but then *Toy Story 2* ended and something much less colorful came on, and I was stuck there, alone with my thoughts.

Phin was either okay, or he wasn't. Nothing I could do there.

Sam was the happiest toddler ever, but the world was a big, bad place that tried to kill her mother on a regular basis, and chances were high some of that would spill over onto her.

Herb (my friend, not Harry's pig) was probably right that I needed to act more like me, but that was hypocritical advice because I was convinced he would adjust to retirement about as well as I have.

Luther Kite was never supposed to be my problem, but that didn't matter; we were headed for a confrontation.

I had decent people on my team. Chandler, Fleming, and Tequila were the kinds of allies that you'd be scared shitless of if they were enemies. Val was my only female friend, and as competent a cop as I'd been in my prime. Harry was Harry, but as irritating as he could be he'd saved my ass more than once, and I could count on him. Katie was...

Katie was what?

Smart. Competent. Focused. Driven.

Damaged.

To some degree, we're all damaged. Life dishes out more shit to some than to others, and some can cope with it better than others, but no one gets out unscarred.

Katie had been scarred. I'd interviewed far too many victims of violent crimes to not see it in her. The way she talked. The way she moved. The questions she asked, and the answers she gave.

This Luther Kite expedition was more than just book research to her. It was personal. And that made Katie dangerous.

The beer was kicking in big-time, and against my better judgment I called McGlade.

"You in danger, or drunk?" Harry asked.

"What is that supposed to mean?"

"You only call me outside of work when your life is being threatened, or you've had too much to drink."

"Don't be ridiculous. You're my brother, Harry." I frowned. "Sort of."

"Ahh. Drunk. You want to party with me and Bacondict? We ate a bunch of pot cookies two hours ago and they're starting to kick in. We're going to listen to Pink Floyd's *Animals*. You'd think his favorite song on the album is *Pigs*, right? Because he's a pig. Well... guess what? It is! Isn't that hysterical?"

"Hysterical," I said, even though it wasn't hysterical. "I'm calling about Katie. I think she's hiding something."

"Really? Ya think? No duh, Einsteinpants. That's why we brought her along. You ought to be a detective, Jack Daniels. Your name is Jack Daniels. Like the whiskey. Isn't that hysterical?"

"Hysterical," I said, even though it wasn't hysterical.

"You know, if they ever do a spin-off of my TV series, starring you as the main character, they should name it after a drink. What do you think about the name *Whiskey Sour*?"

"Not much."

"I bet it could find an audience. You're one of those strong, angsty, neurotic chicks that people like for some reason. Hey! Maybe a reality show. They could follow you around with cameras, catch you brooding over all the mistakes you've made. Good TV. It would be hysterical. Isn't it hysterical?"

We seemed to be caught in some terrible loop.

"Harry..."

"Wait a sec... Herb wants to talk to you. Hold on." There was a rustling sound, and at a distance away from the phone Harry said, "It's Jack, she wants to talk to you. Go on, answer it. You're being rude, Herb. Just talk to her, say hi. Fine, be a dick." Another rustle. "He stepped out for a minute," Harry said.

"McGlade, I called to talk about Katie."

He didn't reply.

"Harry?"

"What? Who is this?"

"It's Jack."

"Heh. I was just thinking about you."

"How many pot cookies did you eat?"

"All of them. Wait... who is this?"

"It's Jack."

"Jackie! You should come over, party with us. Herb and I had some edibles. Wait! I hear something outside," he whispered. "I think it's the cops. The pigs. Heh! Pigs! Herb Bacondict is a pig. You know that song *Pigs*, by Floyd? He loves it! Wait... who is this?"

"I think Cheech & Chong did this bit."

"I love Cheech & Chong!"

I hung up, reminded why I never called Harry outside of work or when my life was in danger. But I did glean one nugget from the conversation. McGlade didn't trust Katie, either.

I flipped through my contacts on my phone, looking for some-one to drunk text or dial, and frowned at how few friends I had.

Happily, my phone rang, so apparently someone in the world loved me. I checked the number.

Katie.

"You got my message?" I asked. "I'm drinking a giant beer at this bar called—"

"Jack, I'm in trouble." She sounded dazed, perhaps hurt.

"What's wrong?"

"I need you to get over here right now."

"What happened, Katie? Where are you?"

"I just got picked up," she said, starting to cry. "I'm in jail."

YEARS AGO

LUCY

Indianapolis

It was total, utter, complete, 100% bullshit.

Lucy hated her bitch of a mother. She rode Lucy's ass about everything. Her grades. Her eating habits. Her hygiene. Her room. Her bedtime. Her clothes. Her friends (actually, her lack of friends.)

Things had gotten worse since Daddy died. And if the bitch knew about the special kind of love she and Daddy had, it would have pissed her mother off even more.

"Just let me borrow the car," Lucy said, trying to sound calm and in control. "Please."

"Borrow the car? You're eleven years old!"

"I'm fifteen! And I—" Lucy cut herself off. It would probably be best if Mom didn't know about the fake driver's permit Lucy made on the Xerox machine at the library. "I'm old enough to take care of myself," she said instead.

Mom put her hands on her hips; her power-pose. "You're failing two classes, you dress like a slob, and you are not old enough to take care of yourself and definitely not driving anywhere!"

Jeez, scream much? "So you drive me," Lucy said, cucumber cool.

"You have school tomorrow!"

"It's a writing convention. It's educational."

"It's six hundred miles away. You'd miss a full week of classes. And a bunch of creepy horror and murder writers getting drunk and rambling on about where they get their inspiration isn't educational."

Lucy crossed her arms over her chest. "It beats the shit out of school."

"Language! That's why I don't like you reading those kinds of books. They're morbid and low class and don't teach good values."

"Andrew Z. Thomas is guest of honor. He's the best writer *ever.*"

"I don't care if he's the second coming of our Lord Jesus Christ. You're not going."

"Daddy would let me go."

"No, he most definitely wouldn't."

"Daddy loved me more than you."

"Don't talk like that."

"He used to tell me how pretty I am. And how you're ugly and mean."

"What a horrible thing to say! Go to your room!"

Lucy considered the straight razor she carried in the back pocket of her jeans. The whole, beautiful scene played out in her imagination.

Mom says, "What do you think you're doing with that razor, young lady?"

"I'll show you," Lucy tells her, forcing the blade between her mother's lips and carving out her ugly tongue and then holding it overhead like a trophy.

Then, as her mom cries for mercy, Lucy slashes her. Over and over. Back and forth, conducting a symphony of blood and screams, until Mom finally apologizes for being a gigantic asshole for her whole life and begs Lucy's forgiveness.

"I'll never forgive you, Mom," Lucy tells her. "I'm not going to miss you, and neither will anyone else. I'll bury you in the Lucy Garden Paradise Memorial Frog Cemetery, where you'll rot in eternity with forty-seven frogs, thirteen mice, eight birds, fifteen cats, nine dogs, and a hamster named Steve."

And then she'll die, sobbing in unbearable physical and emotional pain.

"*Fuck you, Mom. Don't expect me to visit your grave.*"

"Are you listening to me, Lucy? I said, go to your room!"

Lucy didn't bother arguing, and skulked off into her bedroom. But that didn't mean she was actually listening to her mother. Instead of pouting like the sullen teen she pretended to be, Lucy began to pack. Clothes. Books. Toiletries. She was sick of living there. All the rules. All the bitching. It was time to get the hell out. To make her own life.

She waited until she heard the bathtub faucet turn on—Mom always took a bottle of wine into the bath after they fought—and then she grabbed the bitch's car keys and got on the road.

Such a wonderful concept, being on the road.

Lucy had a feeling she was going to like it. A lot.

PHIN

Somewhere in Mexico

He was shivering.

The cell hadn't cooled off. Which meant a fever.

Phin ran his fingers across his sweaty forehead, feeling the heat, then began to probe his assorted wounds to gauge tenderness. When he pressed the slash in his stomach he'd stitched up, it felt like he was being branded.

He pulled away his filthy shirt and chanced a look.

Not only could he see the infection, swollen and ugly and red and leaking clear fluid, but he could also smell it. Like bad meat left out in the sun.

Phin checked his plastic water cup. Empty. He found a beer can with a few sips of warm Tecate still left, and poured it onto the gash.

The pain was so acute he groaned.

"That looks bad, Jew Boy," Kiler said. "Blood poisoning. Maybe you'll get lucky and die before I have the chance to kill you."

Phin's knowledge of infection was limited. But he knew that the mentally deficient racist was probably right. Some disease-causing agent had entered Phin's body, and if it multiplied and spread into his bloodstream, that would lead to sepsis and death.

Whatever antibiotics they'd given him hadn't worked. He was no doubt producing antibodies, but the fever meant the bacteria was spreading faster than he could mount an internal defense.

Phin weighed his options.

Choice A was dying.

Choice B was somehow reducing the bacteria load in his body.

He placed his hands over his wound, his breath coming in shallow gasps. This was going to hurt. It was going to hurt a whole lot.

Phin pictured his wife's face, clenched his jaw, and screamed through his teeth as he began to squeeze out the pus.

JACK

Kansas City

The uniform sitting across from me was named Rinkovec. I'd sobered up quite a bit during the taxi ride to the police station, and the ninety minutes in the waiting room, and I was drinking some vending machine coffee that was actually pretty good.

"Thanks for agreeing to talk to me," I said.

"I've seen the TV show. You aren't that fat in person."

The actress that played my character on the television series based on McGlade's exploits was eighty pounds overweight.

"Thanks. Has Katie confessed to anything?"

"Not yet."

"Has she said anything at all?"

"No."

I leaned forward. I knew this game, because I'd been playing it since before Officer Rinkovec was born. He and his partner thought Katie was a junkie. Since more than ninety percent of suspects talk to police and inadvertently incriminate themselves, they assumed Katie would do the same. But, apparently, Katie buttoned up. Now Officer Rinkovec would have to convince a state's attorney and a judge that the search was legal.

The secret of interrogation was to get people to answer questions. It was human nature to want to explain yourself, even if you admit to guilt in the process.

Cops were human, too.

"Have you arrested her?" I asked.

"Not yet."

"And what are the proposed charges?"

He leaned back in his chair, lacing his fingers behind his head. "Drug possession. Class C felony."

On his desk, between us, was a hypodermic needle in a puncture-proof evidence bag.

"Did Katie tell you what that is?"

"No."

"So it could be insulin."

He smiled. "We both know it isn't insulin."

The man was gabby, and confident. But he should have known better than to talk to the police.

"Did she consent to the search?"

His smile went away. And that told me all I needed to know.

"So what was your probable cause?"

He shrugged. "She was disoriented. Looked out of it."

"Do you want to explain how a disoriented woman constitutes suspicious behavior?"

"She appeared to be under the influence of a controlled substance."

"Is she high now?"

He shrugged his shoulders.

"If you're holding her, and she's under the influence of an illegal drug and anything happens..."

He'd taken the bait, and just realized he'd incriminated himself. Bad enough that he searched Katie illegally, and didn't get a confession. Now he admitted to me that he thought she was high, but didn't get her medical help.

"We're just passing through your fine city," I said. "Katie has been through a lot, lately. I really appreciate you picking her up for her own safety. I'd like to take her back to our hotel, and we'll be on our way by later this morning."

He didn't say anything.

"If you'd like me to," I went on, "I could also thank your Captain. He might be a little irritated by a phone call at four in the morning, but when I explain that you were helping out a disoriented woman, I'm sure he'll agree with the state's attorney, the judge, and Internal Affairs that you made the right call."

If Officer Rinkovec liked me when I arrived, he didn't anymore.

"I don't think we'll need to involve him," he said. "I'll have your friend brought to the waiting room, and you both can get on your way."

I stood up. "Thank you, officer."

We didn't shake hands.

Ten minutes later, Katie and I were in a taxi heading back to the Holiday Inn, and twenty minutes after that, in the hotel lobby.

"Thank you," she said while we waited for our elevator. Her first words to me since her phone call.

"What was it?" I asked.

She looked at the carpeting. "H."

"You're an addict?"

"I was."

"Was?"

"I haven't used in a long time." She rolled up her sleeves, showed me some faded track marks on her arms.

"If you're clean, why buy again?"

"You'll think it's stupid."

I waited. The elevator came. We each pressed our floor number.

"I went to this bar. Heard this song. Brought back some bad memories."

"You're right," I told her. "I think that's stupid. And you're not coming with us."

"Because I made a mistake."

"Because I won't allow an addict to watch my back."

I got out on the third floor. Katie followed me.

"I know you've been through some things, Jack. But that doesn't mean you're allowed to judge me."

"I'm not judging you. I just don't trust you."

I inserted the key into my door.

"I can smell the booze on your breath," Katie said, raising her voice. "Does that help you cope with the past? Barry Fuller? Mr. K? Charles and Alex Kork?"

"Good luck with your book, Katie."

I went into my room, closed and locked the door, and listened until I heard her walk away.

LUCY

Somewhere in Mexico

It was total, utter, complete, 100% bullshit.

K wasn't acting like a friend, or a mentor.

He was acting like her mother. Or some creepy, deranged uncle.

"The Hanover guy is hiding something, K. I *know* it. C'mon. Let's take him to the playroom. Please?"

Lucy hated saying please. She also hated having to ask.

"He's popular with the gamblers," K said. "Emilio wouldn't like it."

"So you do whatever Emilio wants? Are you his little bitch, now?"

K didn't even look at her, continuing to stare off into empty space. "We've already got his next fight scheduled. Pick another prisoner to play with."

"But I want Han-overrrr," Lucy said, extending it into a whine. "I've been thinking about your hotplate idea. I've been *fantasizing* about it, K. We can make him hold his foot on it. His tongue. His junk. He'll tell us his entire life story, and then start making up shit he thinks we want to hear. Don't you want to do that Hitchcock thing?"

K glanced at her, his zombie gaze without the barest hint of interest. "Pick another prisoner to play with."

Lucy raised an eyebrow (actually, she raised the scar tissue where her eyebrow used to be). "Are you high, K?"

"I'm… medicated."

"How much of that lean have you had?"

K didn't answer.

"Can I take a few men, go into town?" she asked. "Maybe find some new blood for the games? Wouldn't it be fun to see two elderly nuns in a knife fight?"

"We have enough prisoners."

"Okay, then let me go and see a movie, then."

"You've got a thing for Mr. Hanover. He's fighting later."

"K, I feel all cooped up. This is the longest I've stayed in one place since I was a little kid. I need a change of scenery, you know what I'm sayin'?"

"No," K said.

"You're not letting me leave?"

"This is where we belong, Lucy. We're… different. It's dangerous for people like us, out there." K pointed a misshapen finger at the throne room window. "They want to hurt us. But here, we're safe. Here, we're rulers. Here, we're feared."

K finally had a bit of life in his eyes, but it didn't arouse Lucy. It scared her.

"You know I love it here, K. But I don't want to feel like I have no choice. I know you're the one who made the deal with Emilio, but we came here together. I should have a say."

"You're my queen, Lucy. A queen's place is by her king's side." K's gnarled mouth twisted into a grin. "Forever."

"Of course, Your Majesty," Lucy said, bowing as deeply as she could. "I'm going to the bathroom. I'll see you again when the games start."

K went back to staring into empty space. Lucy backed up out of the throne room, limped down the hallway, and began to consider how to escape.

The compound was guarded 24/7. No way to get in or out without K's or Emilio's permission. And even if she could steal a car and slip past the men outside, K would go after her. Without any money, and with her disfigured appearance, she wouldn't be able to get far, or hide for very long.

As she'd feared, this place had become her prison. The only way Lucy would be able to leave was if she was in charge. And Lucy could only see one way that would happen.

She had to somehow get rid of Luther Kite.

DONALDSON

Donaldson couldn't find a hospital. He tried to stop for directions, but none of these assholes spoke American, and the majority ran away when they took a good look at his face.

In an effort to do something to better his situation, Donaldson stopped at another OXXO.

The needle nose pliers set him back two dollars and forty cents. Donaldson took four Xanax and four Tylenol-3, waited until he began to get drowsy, and slipped the tips of the pliers between his eyeball and eye socket and wiggled them around, feeling for his inverted eyelid.

When he felt something fleshy, he squeezed the grips and clamped down, concentrating on lightly tugging the lid back into the proper place. The pills dulled his pain considerably. In fact, they did too good a job, and Donaldson yanked harder than intended.

His eyelid tore off with the ease of tissue paper.

As the blood began to squirt, Donaldson stared at his severed eyelid, still clamped in the jaws of the pliers, and wondered what he was supposed to do next.

Go to a doctor, probably.

KATIE

Kansas City

Rather than call a taxi, Katie used the Uber app and got a ride back to the east side. She asked the driver to wait for her, walked into the alley, and retrieved a few of the items she'd thrown into the garbage can.

On the way back to the hotel, she thought about Jack Daniels. Renting a car and tailing the Crimebago wouldn't be terribly difficult—it was bright red for crissakes—but there was a possibility she could lose them at the border.

Plus, the moment Jack found Luther, Katie wanted to be there.

That meant convincing Jack that she was worth keeping around. Which shouldn't be that hard.

There were still some things about Luther Kite that Katie hadn't told Jack.

Things Jack would want to know before she went hunting.

Things that could well mean the difference between life, and death.

PHIN

Somewhere in Mexico

Banging on the bars awoke him.

Phin opened his eyes, saw the guard standing next to his cell. It was the one who'd stolen his Tony Lama boots.

"Despertarse, puto. Time to go fight for your life."

Phin stared at his hands, crusty with his own fluids. Then he looked at the wound on his stomach and almost vomited. It reminded Phin—in the most horrible way possible—of the mess Samantha used to make when she used to eat spaghetti.

"Y número diez."

Diez.

Ten.

Kiler.

The racist began to whoop and holler, rattling his chains. "You think your gut hurts now, Jew boy? I'm gonna reach in there, pull out your insides, and fucking strangle you with them!"

Phin closed his eyes, pictured his baby and her mother one last time, and in his mind he apologized to them both.

I'm so sorry, my beautiful ladies. I tried my best.

Then Phineas Troutt stood up and marched into the arena to face a messy, terrible death.

DONALDSON

He didn't go to a doctor. At this point, he didn't think the injury could get any worse, or any better.

Instead, he marched back inside the OXXO and spent four dollars on eye drops, duct tape, and plastic cling wrap. Back in the car, Donaldson tore off a rectangle of plastic, squirted it with Visine, and pressed it to his naked eyeball.

It hurt. A lot.

Donaldson took two more painkillers, then taped the plastic wrap to his face, making a kind of half-assed eyepatch goggle.

As blood mixed with the Visine, his vision turned pink.

He took two more Xanax, then passed out, thinking that when he awoke he should definitely go to a doctor.

JACK

Kansas City

I'd barely managed to slip off to sleep when someone knocked on my door.

I picked up my Colt, and approached the door from the side, then stood next to the jamb. I could have peered through the peephole, but I'd seen too many movies where the person got shot in the head doing that. So instead I opted for asking who it was.

"I could still shoot you through the wall," Tequila said. "A .45 can penetrate wood and plaster even easier than the aluminum door."

I opened it. Tequila was wearing a black tee shirt and pants, which was more than I had on. I was in one of Phin's old Alice Cooper tees, over black boyshorts.

"So how am I supposed to avoid being shot by a visitor?" I asked.

"Don't answer the door," he said. "Ever."

I tried to gauge if he was being serious, and decided he probably was.

"I was going to grab some breakfast. Interested?"

"Are you sure you want to risk it? I've heard breakfast is the most dangerous meal of the day."

"You'll be with me. I'll keep you safe."

"Just got up. I'll meet you down in five."

I'd already showered last night to get the pig smell off of me, so I put my hair in a ponytail, brushed my teeth, put on jeans, and checked out the continental breakfast.

Tequila was at the egg bin, filling up a second plate with food. His first plate was piled high with over a dozen sausage patties.

"Hungry?" I asked.

"Protein," he said.

I grabbed a Greek yogurt and scooped in some granola, then poured a large black coffee and met him at a table. Tequila ate like he was working out; doing reps with a focused, pleasureless sense of purpose. I enjoyed my food, but the coffee was meh. I set it aside and went with earl grey tea, two bags to compensate for the lower caffeine content. When I returned to our table, Tequila was working his way through a bowl of raisin bran, no milk.

"Carbohydrates," he said.

"It's this pithy conversation that makes me glad we're eating together."

"I'm not good at small talk. Or any talk."

"Conversation isn't too hard. It's just listening, responding, and offering your own thoughts."

He drank his entire glass of orange juice and wiped off his mouth with the back of his hand, and for a moment it looked like he was going to respond. But instead he got up and went for more sausage.

"I spoke with Fleming this morning," he said when he got back. Apparently they had a history. "I've got an idea to infiltrate Cardova's compound."

He shared it with me.

"Are you sure you want to do that?" I asked when he was finished. "That sounds ridiculously dangerous."

"If Phin is there, it might be the only way to get a message to him."

"I could do it."

Tequila stared at me like I was an auction item he was thinking about bidding on.

"If this goes sour," he said, "it's probably best that Samantha still has one parent alive."

Ouch. But he made sense.

"Do you like kids?" I asked. I'd met Tequila over twenty years ago, but only seen him sporadically during the intervening years. He'd never met my daughter. Or my husband.

"I don't know any," he said.

"Ever want to have children?"

He shook his head. "I shouldn't reproduce."

"Why not?"

"Most people shouldn't reproduce. Me included."

"Ever want to get married?"

"No."

He was right. He was terrible at small talk.

"Katie won't be joining us for the rest of the trip," I said, finishing my tea.

"Good. She's trouble."

"She's going to try to follow us."

"I could stop her."

"She's determined."

"Determination doesn't count for much when you have two broken legs."

I leaned back, studying the man. "I can never tell when you're kidding."

"Humor is an evolutionary trait, meant to put people at ease. Men use it with other men to bond, and with women to get them into bed." He finished his last sausage. "I don't bond. And I don't need humor to sleep with a woman."

"So you weren't joking. You'd break both of her legs."

He shrugged. "One leg would probably be enough."

I ate more yogurt. "I've never known someone like you before. And I can't even say that I know you."

"You know me. What you see is what you get."

"You don't love anyone."

"Just my dog. Rosalina. And that's more of a fondness than love."

"You have no compunction about using violence."

"It's a tool."

"Have you hurt innocent people?"

"Never innocent. But I've hurt guilty people more than they might have deserved."

"Have you ever lost a fight?"

"Everyone loses fights, Jack."

"When?"

"There was this one time, I was fighting eight guys—"

I laughed. Tequila didn't react. He wasn't kidding.

"Okay, we'll continue under the assumption that you're a sociopath," I said, "and you lack the ability to empathize. So why did you decide to come along on this trip? Because you like excitement?"

"Not particularly."

"Because you're hoping for the chance to hurt some people?"

"Is that what you think?" Tequila asked.

"I don't know what to think. That's why I asked."

He nodded. "I'm not a sadist. I don't enjoy hurting people. I'll do it if I think the situation justifies it."

"Like breaking thumbs over a gambling debt."

"They should have paid their marker."

"Killing people."

"I've never done that." Then he added, "For money."

"Taking on a serial killer running a gladiator ring funded by a drug cartel."

"I'm doing that because I like you."

"That's the reason?"

"I don't like many people."

I shook my head. "There has to be more than that. People have friends, but they don't risk their lives for them."

"You do," Tequila said.

I frowned. "Lately, it's been my friends taking the risk."

"One of the reasons I like you, Jack, is because you represent something I admire."

"What's that?"

"You're one of the good guys."

"You're here helping me. So you're one of the good guys, too."

"No, I'm not. I've never self-sacrificed. I've never put my life on the line for a greater cause. Or to save other people. You have." Tequila leaned back, lacing his fingers behind his head. "What does that feel like?"

I thought before I answered. "Necessary," I said.

"I haven't felt necessary for a long time." Tequila's face softened, making him appear much younger, and he looked away from me and off into space. "I think I'd like to try it again someday."

I took a last bite of yogurt and pushed the bowl away.

"See?" I said. "We just had a conversation."

"I'd rather risk my life for someone else," Tequila said.

"It gets easier."

"What does? Conversation, or risking your life?"

"Both."

He nodded, then pushed away from the table. "I'm going to get in a post breakfast workout. Join me?"

"I'm going to talk to Katie. See if I can persuade her to go home without you having to break her legs."

"If you can't, I'll be in the gym. Just come get me and I'll take care of her."

Once again, I couldn't tell if he was kidding or not.

DONALDSON

Somewhere in Mexico

A knock on the glass startled him, and he jerked his head up and saw a man at the driver's side window. Younger guy with a cheesy teenstache.

The clerk from the OXXO.

Then the pain hit. As bad as anything Donaldson had ever experienced, like he was being stabbed in the brain with a red hot, salt-covered fork. He checked the rearview, and saw his makeshift eye patch had fallen off and his eyeball had dried up to the point where it was wrinkled like a large, pink raisin.

Another knock. "You've got to move your car, man. This lot is for customers only."

Donaldson thought about arguing that he was, indeed, a customer. Then he thought about going to a doctor. Then he took more pills.

Even if he could find a doctor—and Donaldson was beginning to doubt this backwards-ass country had any medical facilities at all—he didn't know what they could possibly do for him. His eyelid was gone. His eyeball was desiccated. His ID was phony, and linked to a man he'd murdered. The only money he had left was a handful of change.

"Don't need no doctor," Donaldson mumbled to himself.

He had made it this far on his own, and he decided to see the situation through to the end.

Ten minutes later, the pain had ebbed and he was back in the OXXO, spending his next to last dollar.

For a corkscrew.

PHIN

The shackles came off, and a feverish Phineas Trout was left standing in the arena, staring at the crowd of lunatics placing bets on human lives, relatively certain they would be the last thing he ever saw.

He shivered, partly from illness, partly from fear, and against his better judgment he glanced at the board posting his odds.

Fifteen to one, against.

Kiler was brought out, whooping like the maniac he was. When his chains were removed, he pointed at Phin and waggled his tongue, his free hand rubbing his crotch.

"Last call for bets, last call for bets. Number 10, with eight wins, against Number 17, with three. Height, weight, and age advantage to number 10. The weapons for this match... axes."

The guard wearing Phin's boots dropped a fire axe at Phin's feet.

Phin wasn't much for reflection, but in that moment he found himself thinking about his life. He'd been born and raised in the Chicago suburbs, average in every way. Not a happy childhood, but nothing he couldn't get over. Mediocre grades, enough athletic skills to get a partial soccer scholarship at a decent school. There had been buddies, and women, and co-workers in various careers, but nothing noteworthy or permanent. Nothing ever defined Phin, or challenged him.

Until the cancer diagnosis. Then he said fuck it and dropped out of the rat race, living hand to mouth, getting paid however he could. That included a variety of illegal activities, in order to ameliorate the pain of dying with drugs and whores.

That's when he met Jack. He'd been preying on a street gang, robbing their pushers, and they'd gotten angry enough to run him down and try to murder him. But Phin had been on a coke bender, and hadn't felt like getting killed, and managed to beat the shit out of a bunch of them before Jack rolled up and arrested him, probably saving his life.

He was instantly smitten.

Jack was all the things he wanted to be. She had purpose. Direction. Honor. Bravery. Life to her was something that challenged you, not something you tolerated.

They didn't date. She was a cop. He was a thug. Capulets and Montagues, Sharks and Jets, oil and water. But they did become friends, and when the opportunity arose to be more than that, Phin pursued it with everything he had.

And, son of a bitch, it somehow worked out. Phin found love. He found purpose. He finally became the person he wanted to be.

That was about to end, in a gladiator arena in some Mexican desert, facing a white supremacist psychopath in an axe fight to the death.

Not the way he'd ever expected to go out.

He bent down, almost falling over because of the pain in his gut, and managed to pick up the axe. Two feet long, about seven pounds, blade on one side of the head, a pick on the other. Caked with grime and sand and the blood of the dead.

Then he stared at Kiler.

That man was a monster. In both body and mind.

Maybe, if Phin had been healthy, he could have put up at least a little bit of fight. Gone toe-to-toe for a minute or two.

But in his current condition, Phin knew he wouldn't be able to block a single swing.

Kiler, an ugly grin on his ugly face, marched toward Phin with the axe.

Phin looked at the crowd.

Looked at the guards.

Looked at Luther and Lucy on their balcony.

Looked at his own shaking hands.

And knew what he had to do.

He dropped the axe and ran back toward the entrance, where the guard that had led him into the arena was standing. As the guard raised his machinegun, Phin dropped down to his knees and touched the ground at the man's feet, assuming a position of prayer and subservience.

"Por favor," Phin begged. "Amigo, por favor."

The crowd began to laugh. The guard joined in.

Kiler advanced, axe raised.

Phin put all of his remaining strength into the move.

First, he grabbed the guard by his boot heels.

Next, he yanked as hard as he could, pulling the man's feet out from under him.

Finally, Phin's hands twisted both of the heels on his Tony Lama boots, removing the body and the barrel of his concealed DoubleTap pistol.

In a move he'd practiced a hundred times, Phin fit the parts together, two rounds of 9mm ammo already loaded in the double barrel, and twisting onto his shoulder, pointing the weapon at Kiler.

The first shot hit the giant in the throat, the gun kicking hard in Phin's hand. Kiler bent forward, clutching his bleeding neck, and Phin fired his last round, right into Kiler's open mouth.

Whatever the racist's last thought was, Phin blew it out the back of his head.

He immediately dropped the DoubleTap, raising his hands above his head as the guards swarmed around him and the beating began.

Just as he was starting to black out, he saw Luther stand up...

...extend his hand...

...and turn his thumb down.

LUCY

"Don't kill him," Lucy said, turning to K and touching his bony arm.

"He cheated."

"Hanover isn't who he says he is. Those were his boots that guard was wearing. What kind of man has a gun hidden in his boots? He could be a cop. CIA. Interpol. If you kill him, you could be compromising Emilio's whole operation."

K stared at her.

"Let me take him to the playroom," Lucy said. "I can make him talk. After we know who he is, you can do what you want to with him."

"People lost money on this match."

"Call it a disqualification. All bets are off. We have to know who this guy is, K."

His eyes still on Lucy, K switched his hand gesture from thumbs-down to thumbs-up.

Lucy grinned her lopsided grin. "Can I bang the gong?"

He nodded. She took his staff and rapped the fake skull against the brass, the sound ringing out across the arena.

The guards ceased their assault on Hanover and stood at attention. K made a hand gesture, and they dragged the unconscious man out of the arena.

"You'd better find out something," K said.

Lucy narrowed her eye. That was the second time in as many days that K had threatened her.

She valued her freedom. But more than that, Lucy valued her life.

And she wasn't going to let some broken crackpot overlord in some petty desert fiefdom take away either.

"I think you'll be surprised at what I'm able to do," Lucy told him.

Unpleasantly surprised.

DONALDSON

Mistakes were made.

Donaldson checked his reflection in the rearview mirror. His ruined eye still had the corkscrew in it, and it hung to cheek-level because Donaldson had forgotten to take the optic nerve into account. It stretched like pink chewing gum, keeping his eye attached to his brain.

And it was strong. Yanking wasn't getting him anywhere.

Donaldson's stomach lurched and he dry-heaved, having thrown up the last of the Gansitos moments after beginning the self-surgery.

The worst part was; not only could he still feel the corkscrew twisted into his eyeball, he was also able to see through it a little bit, and stared at a blurred, foggy image of his lower lip.

What he needed to do was pull as hard as he could, and hope he didn't tear out his frontal lobe.

Donaldson sucked in as deep a breath as he could...

Gripped the corkscrew tight...

And noticed the needle nose pliers on the passenger seat.

The pliers had a wire cutter in the jaws.

He blew out the breath he'd been holding. Cutting seemed like a much better way to sever the optic nerve than yanking.

As it turned out, that assumption was incorrect. The cheap wire cutters were dull, and didn't work well on tissue.

It took Donaldson ten minutes of squeezing and twisting to detach his eye. The process might have gone quicker, but he kept passing out from the agony.

Live and learn. If it happened again, he'd yank.

Or maybe go to a doctor.

With one dollar and seventeen cents left of his life savings, Donaldson limped back into the OXXO to get a needle and thread.

The needle and thread was $1.50.

"Give me a break, man," Donaldson told the clerk. "I need to sew my eye socket shut."

"Tiene que ir a un medico."

"Same to you, asshole."

He settled for a ninety-nine cent bottle of superglue.

Back in the car, he liberally applied glue to his bleeding, empty eye socket, then pinched it closed until it dried, sealing the wound.

Donaldson was pleased with himself for all of three seconds. That was when he discovered his fingers were stuck to his face.

JACK

The text from McGlade said he was parked in front. I texted Tequila, tipped the maid, and met Harry outside of the hotel with my bag. I knocked on the Crimebago side door, and Herb Bacondict answered.

"Swaaaaa," he said, sniffing at me with his round, moist snout.

"He answers the door?"

McGlade appeared behind him. "I taught him to let himself out so he stops shitting in the RV. Pigs are smarter than dogs. Next I'm going to teach him how to bark and fetch."

"Why don't you just get a dog?"

Harry's face scrunched up. "Huh. Never thought of that."

Herb moved aside, allowing me to enter.

"What the hell happened?" I asked, looking around. The seats were all torn to bits, the carpeting in shreds, curtains pulled down and torn up. It looked like a tornado hit.

"Funny story," Harry said. "So Herb Bacondict and I were under our bro blanket—"

"Your what?"

"Our bro blanket. It's a blanket, that bros share."

"And what do bros do under the bro blanket?"

"We bro-out."

"Of course you do." No point in questioning him further. It wasn't like things would get less stupid.

"So we were broing-out under the bro blanket, riding the pot cookie wave, and then Herb got a hog-sized case of the munchies and pretty much ate every piece of fabric in the Crimebago."

"Why didn't you stop him?"

"I was laughing too hard."

"Of course you were."

"I peed myself," Harry said. "Twice."

"It's great we can be open like this."

"I know, right? Then Herb ate my Chewboxers."

"Your what?"

"My Chewbacca boxer shorts. Chewboxers. I soaked Chewie's bowcaster so I took them off, and Herb ate them. It was hysterical."

"You need to look up *shame* in the dictionary, and then find yourself some."

"I'm not a role model, Jack. I'm a cautionary tale. Which is a lot more fun."

"Mmm-hmm," I said, ignoring him by this point. "We can't drive to Mexico in this."

"I've already got it covered. After a quick clean up I can refurnish, then we're on the road again."

"It will take days to get all of this repaired, McGlade. Maybe weeks."

"I was just going to stop at Target. A few beanbags, a couple of mattresses, a new bro blanket…"

I shook my head, emphatically. "No way."

"We need a new bro blanket. We can't bro-snuggle out in the open. Society isn't mature enough to accept a man-hog brolationship."

"I'm not traveling in this—quite literal—pig sty. Tequila and I are going to the airport. We'll meet you in Mexicali."

"What about Katie?"

"She's out."

"Maybe you guys need some broette time."

"Good idea," I said. "We'll pick up a broette hammock and have a nice, long swing."

"They sell those? Awesomepants!" Harry narrowed his eyes. "Wait, are you being sarcastic? I can't tell. I'm still pretty high."

"See you in Mexico," I said, opening one of the overhead compartments and adding my Colt Python to the duffle bag of firearms I'd brought along. "Don't let Herb eat any of my guns."

"I'll put them in the trap."

"And don't let Katie come with you. She was arrested last night, buying heroin."

McGlade didn't appear to be listening, his attention focused on tapping his cell phone. "How many *Ms* are in *hammock*?"

"Don't let Katie come with, McGlade. She's a heroin addict."

"Yeah yeah, Katie, heroin, arrested, got it. I can't find any bro hammocks on Google. I found *ham hocks*. Yikes." He put his fake hand over Herb's eyes. "Don't look, bro hog. It could be someone you know. And they look… *delicious.*"

I left the Crimebago, finding Tequila standing in the parking lot.

"We're flying," I told him. "Drop your weapons off inside and watch out for McGlade. He's stoned and feeling bromantic."

Tequila stepped inside, and I heard Harry exclaim, "Buddy! The ladies have bowed out, so it's a three-way Brofest all the way to Baja!"

Tequila came back out within eight seconds. "Cab?"

"Calling one now."

We walked back to the hotel lobby, and Katie was sitting there, reading a local newspaper. She saw us come in, tucked the paper under her arm, picked up her bag, and approached.

"Any chance you've changed your mind, Jack?" she asked.

"No."

"What if I had some information about Luther Kite that you don't know? Information that can help find him?"

"If it leads to his arrest, I'll put in a good word so you get the first prison interview."

"I'd rather come along."

"No."

"I know why Kite is in Mexico."

I kept my face neutral. Tequila had wandered over to the front desk, and began helping himself to a complimentary bowl of apples.

"Years ago, he traveled with another killer named Orson," Katie said. "They wandered over North America. Killing. Stealing. Even picking up occasional jobs. My research led me to believe they wound up in Baja for a bit, doing freelance interrogation work for some of the crime bosses."

"Cab's here," Tequila said, his mouth full.

Katie pleaded with her eyes. I felt my resolve weakening, and glanced at Tequila. He shook his head.

"I've been clean for thirty years," she said.

"No such thing as an ex-junkie." Tequila glanced at me and mimed breaking something in half.

I shook my head. "Katie, this isn't personal. I really do wish you the best. And I hope you get the help you need. I mean that. Goodbye."

I turned to leave. Katie said, "This isn't over, Jack."

I kept walking, Tequila at my side.

"You're going to think about this moment later," Katie said after us. "And wish you'd made a different call."

"Take me ten seconds, tops, to break both her legs," Tequila said out of the corner of his mouth.

"I thought you weren't a sadist."

"I'm not. I'm a survivor. And there's something off about her."

I didn't tell Tequila, but I felt it, too.

The more distance we could put between us and Katie Glente, the better.

LUCY

After the guards brought an unconscious Hanover into the play-room and shackled his arms and legs to the rack, Lucy held a bottle of ammonia under his nose until he began to thrash his head back and forth.

"Who are you?" she asked him.

He passed out again. She considered tightening the chains. People were more eager to answer questions when their shoulders and hips were dislocated. But then she noticed the odor. It was one of the death stenches that yucked her out.

Rot.

She traced it to Hanover's blood-caked shirt, and peeled it back.

Ugh. How could he stand to smell himself?

Lucy put on one of the ill-fitting rubber gloves she kept in the playroom for occasions such as this, and gave the infected wound a poke.

Hanover yelped.

"You awake, tough guy?" She jabbed him again, making sure her face was turned away from the stench. "I have some things to ask you."

Lucy stuck her finger under one of his swollen stitches, and he went all fainty again.

More ammonia. More fluttering eyelids. This guy didn't even know where he was.

"Who are you?" she asked.

"I came..."

"Yeah?"

"Kill... Luther..."

Lucy sighed, hard as her lungs allowed. "I know that. Luther and I dragged someone you know to death, blah blah blah. I'm not buying. What's the real reason?"

"Kill... Luther Kite... pro..."

"Pro? Pro what? Pro basketball? Pro-choice? Prohibition?"

"Pro... tect... fam..."

He zoned out again. Freakin' irritating.

"Fam? What's fam?"

Lucy stuck her finger in up to the first knuckle and his whole body jerked.

"Family!"

Protect family? That wasn't the revenge scenario he'd spun when they'd first met.

Vengeance was a decent motivator. But it didn't have the same oomph as trying to save the ones you loved. People were willing to die for that shit.

Lucy had seen it, firsthand. Parents willing to fight harder for their children than they would for their own lives. That could have explained Hanover's continued success in the arena. Maybe he wasn't a cop with specialized training or some law enforcement agenda. Maybe he was just doing this for his family.

"So it isn't revenge?" she clarified.

A head shake.

"It's to save people you care about."

A nod.

Finger still inside him, Lucy leaned over until she was close to his ear. "If you were alone with Luther, could you kill him?"

Nod.

"Would you try to do it even if it killed you?"

Emphatic nod.

Interesting.

"Mr. Hanover, I do believe it may be worth keeping you around a little while longer."

Lucy removed her finger, then gave him a friendly slap on the belly, prompting a gorgeous, full-body scream. Then she trotted off, to go root through the garbage bin.

There would be maggots there. And that was exactly what Mr. Hanover needed to help him focus.

DONALDSON

Fingers glued to his empty eye socket, barely conscious because of all the pills he'd taken, Donaldson drove down Boulevard Lázaro Cárdenas at ten miles per hour below the speed limit, looking for someone to drag to death. His only criteria was that the person be sleeping soundly, or small enough to handle.

It had taken him almost an hour to tie a slipknot on the end of the clothesline still attached to the bumper, partly because he could only use one hand, partly because his fluffy-blurry-woozy-codeine-alprazolam-zolpidem-fentanyl drug haze made Donaldson repeatedly forget what he was doing, along with where he was, his own name, and why for some crazy reason his hand was stuck to his face.

It had been a process.

Then came a seemingly endless search for a victim. Groups of men. Groups of women. Couples. Tall guys. Big ladies. Some clown dressed up as a clown. A giant fish (though that last one might have been a hallucination.)

After hours of scoping out unsuitable targets, he finally spotted a decent possibility on the street, walking alone.

A kid.

Donaldson wasn't good with ages—this little snot couldn't have been more than eight or nine—but he was small, and he seemed oblivious to his surroundings, focusing intently on a cup-and-ball, which had to be the stupidest toy ever made. A wooden cup on a stick, attached to a sizeable wooden ball on a string. Swing the ball and catch it in the cup. Then repeat over and over and over and over again until the realization of how horrible life is finally set in.

Welcome to the constant, ongoing disappointment known as existence, *kid. I almost envy the fact that you're about to die.*

Almost.

Donaldson pulled onto the street in front of the boy, then awkwardly put the car into park. After much fumbling, including a fifteen second period where Donaldson was immobile because his sleeve had gotten caught on the gearshift, he finally managed to open the door and step outside. Balancing his hip against the side of the hot car, he reached over to the passenger seat and grabbed his last Gansitos cake.

"Hey, little boy… you want a snack?"

The boy stopped and stared.

Donaldson took a wobbly step forward.

"C'mon, you little punk piece of shit. Take the snack cake from the nice man who wants to drag you to death behind his car."

The boy reached out his hand.

"That's right, dummy. Your mother never warned you about strangers, and now you're about to become a newspaper headline. Stupid Boy Dies Horrible—"

The wooden ball hit Donaldson on the head with the force of a brick. As the world lost all focus, the child twirled the ball over his head like a medieval mace, then struck Donaldson in the knee.

Donaldson crumpled like a demoed building. The kid bent over, and swiped the Gansitos cake Donaldson had dropped.

Then the little bastard hopped into Donaldson's Cadillac and drove off.

JACK

Kansas City

Flight delays were an interesting study of human nature.

This was the computer/satellite/GPS age, where we can see almost fourteen billion years into deep space. There was no possible way an airline didn't know the exact time one of their planes would be ready to take off.

The airlines knew. But they didn't share the info with their passengers.

Because of human nature. If Tequila and I had been told our flight to Mexicali would be delayed by nine hours, we wouldn't have waited around the airport. We would have rented a car, or checked into a hotel, or even killed time at the airport bar.

But instead, the airline lied. It knew exactly how long takeoff was being pushed back, but it only revealed that information a tiny piece at a time.

Post an hour delay, people are irritated, but delays are expected.

Push it back another half hour, no big deal.

Forty more minutes? Already been waiting for ninety, so at this point it doesn't matter.

And so on. And so on. Until you realize you've wasted nine hours of your life sitting in an airport.

Human beings are incapable of making big decisions when they are being crippled by numerous little decisions. It was why people stayed employed at soul-crushing jobs, because they only had to handle it on a day by day basis, rather than think of it as a forty year wasted chunk of their lives.

I was as guilty as anyone else. I sat there, enduring the delays, much like I'd spent over two decades chasing murderers. It was bearable, because I was spoon-fed it over a long period of time. But looking back on it as a whole, it was easy to count the regrets.

Which I had plenty of time to do, waiting for that goddamn plane. And it wasn't as if Tequila was the perfect guy to get delayed with, skilled as he was in the art of conversation. He killed the time with an endless, annoying routine.

Do push-ups.

Eat.

Nap.

Repeat twenty times.

As breakfast turned to lunch turned to dinner and the flight kept being pushed back by infuriatingly small increments, I got an UNKNOWN call on my cell.

"This is Jack," I answered.

"Your flight will be delayed for two and a half more hours," Chandler said. Or maybe it was Fleming.

I almost asked how she knew where I was and what I was doing, but I would have just sounded naïve. All sufficiently advanced technology appeared as magic to luddites.

"I'm chasing lost time. Already put in six hours. If I quit now, those hours would be wasted."

"That mentality is how Las Vegas stays wealthy," she said. "We found the arena."

"It's true?"

"Unfortunately, yes. I've seen some… *unfortunate* aspects of human nature. This one is near the top of the list."

"And is Lu—" I stopped myself from saying his name. "Is the man my husband was chasing at the arena?"

My phone buzzed. I held it at arm's length and watched a grainy, blurred picture show up on my texting screen. But the details were good enough to reveal a desiccated, black-haired maniac in a purple robe, sitting next to an equally scarred and hideous woman.

Luther and Lucy, looking as if they were presiding over a Mardis Gras parade.

"And my husband?" I asked.

A pause. Then, "Yes. He's there."

"You're sure?"

Another pic appeared on my phone. This one with better resolution.

A man on the ground, bloody, being beaten by six guards.

Even steeling myself for the worst, it felt like being slapped.

"That was taken eighteen hours ago. A moment earlier, he shot a man in the arena. Satellite caught him being dragged back inside the compound. No sight of him since."

"So we don't know if he's still..."

"The subject matter aside, this is a gambling facility. These prisoners are assets, and they represent significant investments with dollar values attached. Odds are they haven't killed him."

I couldn't think of anything to say.

"Jack... this place has a lot more security than we thought."

"How much?"

"It's going to be comparable to breaking into a military base."

"That bad?"

"Breaking in a military base during wartime. It's doable, but we're going to need all hands on deck. You have to keep your head in the game, Jack, and compartmentalize your personal feelings. If you have a breakdown in the field, it could compromise the mission." She added, "And the personnel."

"Who is this? Chandler or Fleming?"

"Again with the codenames?"

"Who?"

"It's Chandler."

"Remember when your sister was being held at that black site?"

A short pause, and then, "Yes."

"How did you do it?" I asked, my hand starting to shake. "How could you function knowing what they were doing to her? How did you compartmentalize your feelings?"

"I didn't," Chandler said. "But I'd had enough training that I could fake it."

I thought about Phin, swallowing the sob that was creeping up. "I can do that."

"We'll call you when your flight arrives. "

She hung up.

Tequila was doing push-ups. Again. He halted long enough to raise an eyebrow at me.

"Looks like your plan is a go," I said. "Can I ask a question?"

"You want to ask how I compartmentalize my feelings," Tequila said.

"And you're going to tell me you don't have to, because you don't have feelings."

"No." Tequila hopped to his feet, then set his bulk in the seat next to mine. "Emotions are like injuries. You can learn to separate them from yourself. Sort of like they're a mosquito, buzzing around, that you can ignore."

"How can you ignore part of yourself?"

"Give me your hand."

I did. Tequila's hands were as hard and stiff as two by fours.

"Tell me when this hurts," he said, gripping my index and middle finger and crushing them together.

My first reaction was to yelp and try to pull away. But my digits might as well have been trapped in a vice.

"You feel the pain."

"Yeah."

"It's just pain. It's not killing you. You're not being injured. You're not in danger. It's a sensation that we've learned to associate with negative emotions. But it's like walking into a room with a bad odor. After a few minutes, you get used to it and can't smell it anymore. That's why garbage men aren't constantly throwing up."

"This still hurts." I was beginning to sweat. It felt like my knuckles were ready to pop.

"Of course it does. I'm squeezing your nerve endings."

"So how am I not supposed to think about it?"

"That doesn't work. The trick isn't to ignore it. The trick is to put it in a place where you can still cope and it doesn't hinder you. This is a physical sensation. It's automatic, and you can't block it. But the emotional response to it is learned behavior."

"So I have to pretend it isn't happening?"

"You're not listening," Tequila said, increasing the pressure. "Have you ever put off some chore? Like you have to do the dishes? You can't completely ignore them, because you know they have to get done and they're in the back of your mind. But you can prioritize other things before you get to the dishes. Reading a book. Going for a run. Getting some work done. The dishes still need attention, but you're doing other things. What do you have to do right now?"

"I have to rescue my husband."

Tequila moved closer. "And what things do you have to do before that?"

"Catch this flight. Meet my people. Take inventory. Plan the raid."

"Can you picture the flight?"

I could. "Crowded. Cramped. Long. Boring."

"Can you picture your people?"

"Me, you, Val, Chandler, Fleming, Harry." I rolled my eyes. "Herb Bacondict."

"Do you still feel the pain in your fingers?"

"Yes."

"Does it still hurt?"

"Yes."

"But you can still think and focus on other things," Tequila said. "And you can also compartmentalize pain."

"I don't feel like I'm compartmentalizing anything."

Tequila looked down. I followed his gaze and saw he had his hand on my waist, his fingers pinching an inch of my leftover pregnancy flab.

When I saw it, the pain came with it.

"I've been pinching you the whole time," Tequila said. "The only thing that gives the pain power over you is when you focus on it. It's your choice whether to submit to the pain, or put it off like chores or a buzzing insect. The pain won't go away. But your reaction to it can change. You just need practice."

Tequila let go of me, then dropped and began doing more push-ups. I lifted up my shirt, saw the bruise already starting to form on my side.

I'd just learned something important. But I didn't know if I could learn to do the same thing with emotional pain.

Only one way to find out.

I pinched the same spot Tequila did, until tears almost came. Then I thought about my husband, having to fight in an arena, being beaten, all alone with no hope.

I started to cry.

So I pinched harder, and did it again.

And again.

And again.

And by the time our flight finally arrived, I had no idea where the two and a half hours had gone.

DONALDSON

Having his car get stolen by a child was bad enough. But the little bastard had also done a real number on Donaldson's head and knee. One, or both, may have been fractured.

He limped up the street until his leg wouldn't work anymore, and then passed out on the curb.

When he awoke, someone had stolen his last forty-six cents.

And his dentures.

His car was gone, all of his medication was gone, all of his Gansitos were gone, the clothesline was gone...

Not that he'd be able to drag someone to death without a vehicle. Manually pulling someone behind on a rope would be more like walking a dog on a leash. He doubted that would get Lucy's attention.

Fingers still glued to his face, Donaldson managed to get up onto his feet, with no idea what he was supposed to do next.

He was in pain, and sick. Besides the whole eye incident, which happily he couldn't entirely remember, he was also withdrawing from all the pills he'd been popping like candy. Cold turkey was a nasty bitch, and the shiver-shake-vomit boogie his body danced to was even more unbearable in the hundred degree heat.

Donaldson managed to find a public bathroom, drank from the sink, threw up, and drank again. Then he considered his options.

He was in too bad a shape to go on even the lamest of crime sprees. But he needed food. So he dug a greasy piece of cardboard and a few cigarette butts out of the garbage, and asked passersby how to spell *help* in Spanish.

"How do I write *help*?"

"Help, please?"

"Can you tell me how to write *help* here?"

"Will one of you assholes spell *help* for me?"

"Feo!" a woman said as she hurried past.

Donaldson wrote FEO on his cardboard using the ash from the butts. Then he found a sliver of shade next to a fountain and sat there, begging for change, as people strolled by, pointing and making faces.

After six hours he was dehydrated, sunburned, feeling even sicker, and had made twenty-three pesos. About a buck and a quarter US.

Maybe enough for something to eat.

Maybe. Donaldson wouldn't be able to find out. Because as he was standing up, some kid ran past and stole his cup.

PHIN

When consciousness returned, Phin found he was on a cot, his hands cuffed over his head and threaded through a heavy, iron U-bolt attached to the wall.

He had no idea where he was or how he got there. Phin gave his head a quick shake, trying to clear mental cobwebs, force alertness. Then he looked around.

This wasn't his underground cage. Instead of bars, the walls were adobe brick, with a small, square window. And while the room was about the size of a prison cell, it had more of an old house feel to it. Or a mission. Phin heard Mexico was littered with abandoned missions and churches.

Had he somehow been rescued?

Memories came back in fits and starts.

Shooting Kiler in the arena.

Being beaten by the guards.

Lucy.

Phin recalled some situation with Lucy. She was asking questions. Hurting him. But he couldn't remember what had happened, and wondered if it had just been a fever dream.

That reminded Phin of the infection in his chest. He looked down, saw his bloody #17 shirt had been replaced by a clear, plastic bandage.

No, not a bandage. Tape. Packing tape.

While the wound didn't ache like it had previously, Phin felt an unpleasant tickling sensation.

Squinting, Phin noticing something else odd about his make-shift dressing.

It was moving.

The tape seemed to undulate, as if something underneath was wiggling.

Panic stitched through him, and Phin stretched, trying to detach the tape from his sweaty skin. A corner lifted up, and something small and pink squeezed out and slid down his ribs.

As Phin stared, the pink thing began to squirm, and he realized what it was.

His chest wound was infested with maggots.

JACK

Thirty seconds after we landed, I got a text that read HOTEL LUCERNA.

Mexico was hot. Like sticking-your-head-in-an-oven hot. While we waited for a taxi, Tequila did push-ups, and I poked at the bruise on my side, wondering if I was learning a life lesson or indulging in some self-destructive masochism. Perhaps both.

When the cab spit us out at the Hotel, another text flashed on my screen. POOL.

Chandler and Fleming were at a patio table, under a large sun umbrella. Though identical, they didn't look very much alike at first glance. Chandler's hair was now black, cut in a pixie. She wore a black bikini under a black mesh cover up, and her body was tanned and trim. Fleming's hair was long, red, and in a ponytail, she had on a floppy hat to protect her pale skin, and her high-tech wheelchair was familiar to me. The last time I'd seen it was in the Northwoods of Wisconsin.

Tequila went up to Fleming, scooped her up out of the chair, and they kissed, hard.

"Nice to see you again, too," Fleming said, blushing.

"I'd like to take you to your room."

"You always did get right to the point." Fleming glanced our way. "You guys be okay without me for half an hour?"

"An hour," Tequila said, his eyes not leaving her.

"An hour." Fleming ran her fingers across his biceps. "Maybe ninety minutes."

"What about Bradley?" Chandler asked.

Tequila raised an eyebrow. "Bradley?"

"Guy I'm living with," Fleming said. "My boyfriend."

Tequila shrugged. "He can join us."

"He's not here. But we have an understanding." She turned to glare at her sister. "Like you and Heath do."

Something passed between them, a thinly veiled look, and then Fleming said, "Good to see you, Jack."

I nodded as Tequila carried her off, then sat in a padded chair across from Chandler, who had a computer tablet in front of her.

"That's new," I said, eyeing Fleming's empty, electronic chair.

"A gift from McGlade."

Made sense. Harry must have appropriated it.

Chandler punched in a passcode too quickly for me to see, and an aerial view of the desert came up on her screen.

"Your husband is being kept at an old mission, seven hundred kilometers south of here in the Vizcaíno desert."

"I don't see anything."

"Their satellite camouflage is good. They even have the carport and landing strip disguised."

"How did you find it?"

"We picked up one of Cardova's men. He gave us the general vicinity. Then Fleming tagged land and air traffic, zeroed in, and thermal imaging gave us the layout. We've counted forty armed men—"

"Forty?"

"Those are just Cardova's. A lot of the visitors who bet on the matches are also armed, or travel with bodyguards. Plus there are servants. We haven't been able to pinpoint the number of prisoners, but from the IR activity we've logged, there are at least thirty, with new blood coming in once a week. I've been studying the layout, trying to devise a plan to get in and out. Checkpoint is too heavily guarded, and there are regular patrols on the east, and west. But the path from the north is open. Here's why."

Chandler zoomed in, to what looked like a hole in the ground.

"I don't know what that is."

"That's a pockmark made by a landmine. A VS-50 or a PMN. We figure this whole area, from here to here, is mined."

I frowned. This was way beyond my realm of experience. I was a retired homicide cop, not James Bond or Rambo.

"Do you know where they're keeping Phin?"

"No."

"Do you have a plan?"

"No. We don't have enough manpower, or any air support. Infiltration is risky. Extraction is riskier, especially if your husband's mobility is compromised."

"Can we sneak in somehow? Wear disguises?"

"Good call. We'll dress up as tree surgeons, and smuggle Phin out in a fake cactus."

"Seriously?"

"No. Don't be stupid."

I rubbed my eyes. I was tired, and scared, and worried, and not in the mood for Chandler's glib badass act. But I couldn't do this without her, so I shut the hell up.

"Jack, I don't think you actually understand what this entails. I can do my best to minimize our risk, but it's going to be impossible to get in and out cleanly. People are going to die."

"Could we grab Cardova? Force him to let Phin go?"

"Cardova has better security than the President."

My shoulders slumped. "So it's hopeless."

"I have an associate named Heath. He's meeting us later. He'll have some equipment that might be useful. But the chances of us pulling this off aren't good."

I searched her face, trying to find any sort of compassion. "What if he was your husband, Chandler?"

"Honestly?"

"Yes."

She leaned back in her chair. "I don't think anyone I married would want me risking my life to save him. And I would feel the same way. If I knew he was in a hellhole like this, no possibility of escape… I'd send in drones to bomb it into oblivion."

"You'd kill him?"

"I'd end his misery, and stop it from happening to anyone else. You don't send in the living to recover the dead. And any poor bastard trapped here," she tapped the screen, "is as good as dead."

PHIN

brought some fresh maggots," Lucy said, holding up a jar and giving it a little shake.

Phin didn't say anything, but he watched her intently as she peeled off his chest tape. Lucy sniffed.

"Much better," she said. "K—Luther—he taught me this trick. They eat all the dead tissue, and clean out the wound so it can heal. K discovered it accidentally. He was seeing how long he could keep this guy alive, and flies laid eggs in his wounds, and—ta-da!—the guy lived longer. Doctors actually do this, too. It's called *debriding*."

Lucy dumped more maggots on, then replaced the makeshift bandage.

"Does it hurt?" she asked.

Phin didn't answer. It didn't hurt, but it was disconcerting, and itchy.

"Not in a talking mood. Mr. Hanover? I can make you talk, you know. But if we're going to be working together, I'd prefer the lines of communication to not be forced. You told me you wanted to protect your family. Tell me about them."

He didn't respond. Lucy rolled her eye. "You don't have to tell me their names, dummy. But tell me what you're willing to do for them. You said you'd die to protect them. If you want me to trust you, you need to convince me."

Phin considered it. Then he said, "I have a son. He's almost three."

"And your wife?"

"She's a writer. True crime. She's doing a book about Luther, and she was getting too close to him. He sent her a warning."

"What kind of warning?"

Phin recalled a chapter from one of Katie's books. "He mailed her something."

"What?"

"Somebody's skin. Packed with dry ice."

"Oooh, creepy. And when was this?" Lucy seemed particularly interested, and Phin knew why. She'd been Luther's companion for the last few years, and would have noticed if he'd mailed anything.

"It was a long time ago," Phin said.

"Good answer. So why did you wait so long to come after K?"

"I couldn't find him. He disappeared for a while."

"Another good answer. See how well this communication is working, Mr. Hanover? You've almost convinced me that you're telling the truth, and if I give you the chance you'll kill Luther Kite. That's what you want to do. Right?"

Phin nodded.

"Good. You told me your wife is a writer. So what's her name?"

Phin didn't answer.

"You worried I'm going to hurt her or your son? I don't care about them, or you. But I love to read, and I want to confirm that you're telling me the truth."

This was tricky. If he mentioned Katie, then Lucy could ask Luther about her, and deny Phin's story.

"I don't want him to know," Phin said.

"I'll be cautious."

When Phin didn't respond, Lucy said, "Or… we could go back to the playroom, I could make you tell me. Trust me, this way is easier."

Phin had backed himself into a corner. He didn't see how he had any choice.

"Glente," he said. "Her name is Katie Glente."

She removed her ear buds, and took her passport out as they got ready to cross the border at Calexico. Herb Bacondict snuffled her face, and she gave the pig a pat on his hairy head.

"Herb, do you have your Breeding Swine Health Certificate?" McGlade called back from the driver's seat.

"Do you expect him to answer?" Katie asked.

"I'm not sure. I'm really, really caffeinated."

They'd driven practically nonstop from Kansas City, and Mc-Glade had only let Katie take the wheel for a four hour stretch, and for brief two minute interludes when he got up to use the bathroom.

"How much of that energy drink have you had?" she asked.

"I finished it."

"You finished a whole case?"

"You helped."

"I only had one."

"Well, you missed out. I don't know what Taurine actually is, but my piss was neon green and shot out in spurts, like a sprinkler. Are we still being followed by those bigfoot UFOs?"

"No," Katie said, deadpan. "The dinosaur ate them."

"The one on roller skates? Or the motorcycle?"

"Don't be stupid, Harry."

"You're right. The roller skater could never catch a UFO. Unless they were... rocket skates! Were they rocket skates?"

"You sure go to lengths to amuse yourself, don't you?"

"You may notice the pig in the beanbag sitting next to you. So, yes."

Katie glanced out the window. "How long will it take to cross the border?"

"Assuming no problems, maybe an hour. I just texted Jack. My suggestion; let me break it to her that you came along. She doesn't like surprises. You need to ease her into them. It's like climbing into a hot tub, but the hot tub vocally disapproves and acts bitchy."

"No problem."

Convincing McGlade to bring her along had taken very little effort, but Katie still needed Jack to find Luther. It would be easier to be with Jack when that happened, rather than follow her around.

They got in one of the inspection lanes and slowed down.

"Time to hide the guns," Harry said. "You have anything to put in the trap?"

Katie opened up her duffle, removing her Colt and the X26 Taser with extra cartridges.

"How about knives?" she asked, thinking of her Schempp.

"Stash it. Can't hurt."

McGlade flipped a few switches on his dashboard, including the defrost, rear cabin lights, and cruise control, and then pushed the button on his seat forward. The floor next to Herb opened on hydraulic cylinders, revealing a smuggler's box. Katie placed her weapons atop Jack's bag, already stored away.

She also put a padded envelope in the compartment; one of the items she'd recovered from the alley in Kansas City.

"So how many times have you gotten past the border in this vehicle?" Katie asked.

"Never tried it."

"Seriously?" She stared down at her packet.

"Shouldn't be an issue, even if they search, they won't find the compartment. Besides, they're primarily looking for drugs, not weapons." He locked eyes with her in the rearview mirror. "You didn't put any drugs in there, did you?"

"No."

"They have dogs, Katie. I'm not holding. I don't want to risk it, even though I've got a medical marijuana card for Mittelschmerz."

"What's Mittelschmerz?"

"Painful ovulation."

"How'd you scam that?"

"I'm rich. And a smart ass. Did you hide drugs in there?"

"No."

"Even if it's pills, Katie. Those dogs are supernatural. They can smell a termite with salami farts from a hundred yards away."

"No drugs, McGlade."

Harry closed the trap door. It seated in seamlessly, blending into the floor without leaving an outline. Herb looked at her and snorted.

It'll be fine, Katie told herself. *As long as we don't draw any special attention to ourselves, we'll be okay.*

Then McGlade started singing scat music, and Herb began to oink along.

"Zaba doobie yabba doo da doobie yabba doo bad dee dee dooba dooda deebie deebie da!"

"Oink oink!"

"Zooba dee opp opp deebie dooda doobie dabba deepie doopy da!"

"Oink oink!"

Katie took out her phone and Googled *Mexican prison*, so at least she'd know what to expect when they locked her up for life.

She frowned at the search results. They didn't look very nice.

When they finally pulled up for inspection, and the pig did a dead-on Ned Beatty impression, and Harry joined in, Katie emotionally prepared herself to be hauled away. The quest she'd been on almost her entire adult life was at an end, and she'd failed.

If only things had gone differently in Kansas City.

If only she hadn't decided to ride with that idiot, Harry McGlade.

If only—

"Welcome to Mexicali!" Harry said, starting up the RV as the border patrol waved him through. "We need to find some energy drinks."

She blew out a breath, grinned, and shook her head.

Un-fucking-believable.

JACK

The Crimebago Deux was parked in a convenience store lot on Boulevard Lázaro Cárdenas, sticking out like a giant red sore thumb. The taxi let me out across the street. I tipped the driver, gave the rest of my change to some poor, badly disfigured man panhandling, and walked to the RV.

I knocked on the door, and Herb Bacondict answered

"Hello, Herb."

The pig pressed its wet nose against my face and snorted.

I climbed aboard, and saw Harry sitting on a beanbag, wearing a large red Mexican hat. Several other beanbags and body pillows were strewn around the cabin, along with a few folding lawn chairs. Herb plopped down next to Harry and oinked.

"Congrats," I said. "You turned a hundred thousand dollar vehicle into a freshman dorm."

"Hiya, Jackie. Want a gas station churro?"

He reached over and opened up the fridge. Every shelf was filled with churros.

"You think you have enough?" I asked.

"You can never have enough churros, Jack."

I gave Herb a pat on the head, looked for a place to sit, and saw a pair of ear buds on the counter.

"Goddammit, McGlade, you brought her along."

"I had no choice, Jack. She promised me sex."

"So you did it for sex?"

"No. I did it for the *promise* of sex. I never got any sex."

"Where is she now?"

"I told her to wait in the store until you calmed down because you were gonna throw one of your *why did you do that McGlade?* fits without any appreciation for the fact that once again I'm putting my ass on the line to do you a favor that you'll never, ever pay back."

I considered my responses, and then my phone buzzed. I smiled, and texted back my location.

"So where are Moodypants and Wheels?"

"At a hotel. You gave her that wheelchair?"

He shrugged. "Seemed like the nice thing to do. Former owner didn't need it anymore. Is Cuervo Junior with them?"

"He and Fleming are... getting reacquainted."

"Seriously? That guy gets more ass than a bar stool. You think it's because he's got those rock hard abs?"

I considered Tequila's abs. "Might have something to do with it. Any problems at the border?"

"Smooth as cake. Did the Jason Bourne twins come up with a plan?"

"It's going to be harder than we thought. Let's get the guns ready."

McGlade did his super-secret-press-seventy-buttons thing to open his smuggler trap, and when the top raised I found myself staring at my bag, Katie's Colt, a stun gun, and something in a padded envelope.

"Harry, is this envelope yours?"

"Is it filled with clown porn?"

"For some reason I'm reluctant to check."

He came back from the cockpit. "Did I ever tell you my clown porn name is Mr. Scrotals?"

I pointed into the trap. "Is that filled with Mr. Scrotals selfies?"

"Never seen it before. But I've got some selfies on my phone."

"Pass."

"Mr. Scrotals is a bad clown. He needs a spanking."

"He needs a muzzle."

I squatted down and picked up the envelope, giving it a light squeeze. There was something firm and rectangular inside.

"This isn't yours?" I asked.

"Never seen it beforepants. Must be Katie's."

I tore it open, not sure of what I was about to discover. It turned out to be a digital camera.

"Jack…" Harry said, shaking his head, "that's not yours and might be filled with private, intimate pictures." He took it from my hands. "Me first."

After a few seconds of button mashing, McGlade frowned. "No battery."

"Do you have any batteries?" This was more than just curiosity. It was cop instinct. Something was up with Katie, and she'd deemed this camera important enough to hide from the Border Patrol Officers.

"No. It's one of those weird-shaped rechargeable batteries."

I put the camera in my pocket, and then hauled up the gun bag.

Harry and I spent five minutes checking the extra magazines and adjusting the Hensoldt scopes on my two Heckler & Koch PSG1 semi-automatic sniper rifles. I'd also brought a Mossberg 500 tactical shotgun, and three 9mm Glock 17s with side holsters.

When someone knocked on the Crimebago door, I had a feeling who it was going to be.

What I didn't expect was for her to be on crutches. But it didn't make me any less happy to see her.

"Val Ryker! Welcome to the Crimebago Deux," Harry had somehow come up behind her on the street. "Can I help you up?"

"Why do I think you're just looking for an excuse to grope me inappropriately?"

"You mean there's some situation where I could grope you and it wouldn't be inappropriate?"

She handed McGlade her crutches, and I helped her aboard. Then we embraced.

"Thanks for coming, Val."

"Glad I could finally return a favor." She gave Herb Bacondict a pat on the head like having a hog in an RV was normal.

"You... doing okay?" I asked, giving her a once over. She was about my size, a little younger, wearing jeans and a Packer tee, standing slightly askew.

"I bet it was Lump," Harry said, climbing in and tossing her crutches on the floor. "Did he confuse the front door and the back door again?"

Val had learned to ignore Harry years ago. "How is your cute firefighter fella?" I asked. She'd been with David Lund for longer than I'd been with Phin.

"Still cute. Still fighting fires."

"Has he seen a specialist about the whole micropenis thing?" Harry asked.

"Am I the first one here?" Val asked. "Other than the smelly pig?"

"Don't listen to her, Herb," Harry said, covering his ears. "You smell fine."

"I wasn't referring to him." She offered McGlade a fake smile. "Oooh. Burnpants."

"Chandler is doing recon," I said. "Fleming and Tequila..."

"Are also doing recon," Harry said, "on each other."

"How was your flight?" I asked.

"Shitty. I had to lie to Lund so he didn't insist on coming with. I said you and Phin are having problems so I was going to Mexico with you."

"Not exactly a lie."

"When I landed, I had eight messages from him. He knows something's up."

My cell rang, and I excused myself. It was Herb.

"Jack, where are you?"

"I'm in Mexicali, Herb. What's up?"

"Where exactly? My plane just landed."

I wasn't sure I heard that correctly. "You're here?"

"Mexico is really strict on firearms, so I couldn't bring mine. I hope you have extras."

My eyes began to well up, and I wiped them with the back of my hand. "I think we can find something suitable for you, partner. We'll be right there to pick you up."

DONALDSON

That was Jack Daniels. He was sure of it.

And she gave me three bucks and change.

Donaldson hadn't seen Jack in a long time. Before he'd been disfigured. So it made sense that she didn't recognize him.

But he'd never forget that bitch.

He could only think of one reason why she'd be in Mexico. She was after Luther Kite and Lucy, just like he was.

So how could he follow her?

Donaldson had no car, was in excruciating pain, and his fingers were still glued to his eye socket.

He watched Jack get into the big red recreational vehicle, and had a ridiculous idea.

The RV had a ladder on the back, leading to the roof. At the front of the roof was a wind deflector; a large v-shaped wedge that made the vehicle more streamlined so it used less gas.

Donaldson had driven trucks. Wind deflectors were hollow, to save on weight. They also made a good place to store dead bodies, provided the corpse was properly secured. If he could climb the ladder, traverse the roof without making any noise, and then hide inside the deflector, he could tag along with Jack to her destination.

It was difficult, risky, and really stupid. But Donaldson didn't have any other options. At the rate he was going, he'd starve to death in Mexico before ever finding his Lucy.

But there was no way he'd be able to climb up there with one hand. No possible way.

He tugged on his arm, grunting in pain, the scabby skin around his socket stretching until Donaldson's world went squiggly.

No good. He had to try something else.

With great difficulty, Donaldson got to his feet and scanned the street, looking for inspiration to strike. He was actually considering stepping into traffic, because the force of being hit by a car would probably be enough to remove his hand from his face, and that's when he noticed the red and white candy cane pole outside of a shop, glinting in the Mexican heat.

The universal symbol of barbers.

He stumbled over to the barber shop, garnering the expected looks of shock when he walked inside and everyone stopped what they were doing to stare at the freak. While they gawked, he quickly located an errant pair of scissors on a nearby tray and snatched them up. The nearest hairdresser began to protest in Spanish, but stopped his approach when Donaldson raised the scissors and giggled manically.

He wasn't about to mess with his eyelid again. Especially when it had been such a hassle to get shut.

But fingers? Who needed fingers?

The sharp implement made quick but bloody work of his fingertips, hacking them off in only a few forceful snips, and then his hand was free.

Donaldson shoved the scissors into his pocket, grabbed a towel, and got the hell out of there.

As expected, no one followed the crazy, disfigured, bleeding man out into the street.

Walking so erratically he almost fell, Donaldson dribbled the rest of the superglue onto his new wounds, pressed the towel against the stumps, and then stumbled toward the motorhome. He climbed the ladder with caution, but caution probably wasn't needed.

Donaldson felt indestructible.

Donaldson *was* indestructible.

Nothing could stop him. Not injury. Not pain. Not lack of drugs. And definitely not some old, obsolete bitch cop.

Destiny was calling, and Donaldson was its willing servant.

Quietly climbing across the roof, he made it to the wind deflector, hid inside, and gummed the towel to his face so he didn't make a sound, because something was threatening to come out of his mouth and Donaldson had no idea if it would be laughter, sobs, vomit, screams, or some combination of all four.

LUCY

"Death is the end of everything. And it closes in on us."

K was acting crazy.

Again.

Maybe it was the drugs. Maybe it was PTSD. Maybe he'd finally just gone mad like one of those stupid kings from the Shakespeare plays he was getting more and more obsessed with. The other day she'd found him reading King Lear, and he was literally *leering* at it.

"I don't like it when you get weird like this, K."

"For the poor wren, the most diminutive of birds, will fight, her young ones in her nest, against the owl."

"You're not making sense."

"Birds of a feather, Lucy." K stared into space. "And the flock is coming."

"Maybe we should get the flock out of here," Lucy said.

K didn't react.

"I said—"

"Don't repeat yourself, Lucy. Once is enough."

For a millisecond, Lucy considered jumping him. They were equally weak, equally disfigured. She carried a razor, he carried a knife. But K was bigger, and had more fingers. Lucy might get a slash or two in, but then the guards would come, and K would likely do something to her out of spite, like skin Lucy's legs and make her crawl across an acre of rock salt.

He was unduly vindictive in that way. Probably best to keep a lid on her temper.

"Hanover told me who his wife is."

"Hanover?"

"The prisoner. Number 17. The one who came here to kill you. Remember?"

K didn't respond.

"His wife is a true crime writer. I downloaded a few of her ebooks. She writes about serial killers."

"Does she now?"

"Her name is Katie."

"Katie?"

K did that stare-off-into-nothing thing, but with more intensity than usual. As if he was trying to remember something.

"What is her last name?" K asked.

Lucy considered her answer. If she told the truth, and K remembered who the woman was, he might take Mr. Hanover away from her and ruin her murder plot. But her gut told her it wouldn't matter. And Lucy always did get a thrill out of almost getting caught.

She went with her gut.

"Glente. Katie Glente."

No reaction at all from K. Lucy found it marvelous. Stupid Mr. Hanover came out here to protect his family, and Luther Kite didn't even know who they were. Both were absolute idiots.

"A ministering angel," K whispered.

Lucy sighed, raising her voice. "Prophetic words, my king. I must now hither to yon water closet and replace my stoma bag."

"See you at the games, Lucy."

K grinned in a creepy way, and she bowed and got out of there.

Things were getting worse. K's threats were becoming more frequent, he was acting more and more nutzoid. The Luther Kite she used to know had his shit together. He'd probably always been insane. At least he had since his youth, when a combination of tragedy, abuse, and genetics forged him into a man. But this new, Shakespeare quoting person was insane in a different kind of way.

Not calculating and remorseless, or even risk-taking and narcissistic. K was more along the lines of sitting naked in a corner and cackling while playing with his toes.

She needed to take him out before his crazy wound up hurting or killing her.

Lucy passed the throne room guard—K's paranoia had grown to where he wouldn't even go to the can without an armed guard—and then made her way down the stairs, thinking about Hanover.

Sometimes you just needed a Kamikaze. Lucy wasn't willing to die in order to murder Luther Kite. But Hanover claimed he was ready, willing, and able.

Lucy had her doubts. When she and K had first come to Mexico, and he'd talked his former employer, Emilio Cardova, into funding this gladiator arena in the middle of nowhere, she'd done her research on ancient Rome, the Coliseum, the grand bloody spectacle that had never been matched before or since. Supposedly, some of the condemned had even saluted Emperor Claudius even though he'd sentenced them to die.

Lucy doubted that ever happened. It certainly hadn't happened since they'd been at La Juntita. People would beg for mercy. They'd try to escape. A few even committed suicide in the arena. But Lucy had seen precious little heroism, and zero self-sacrifice.

Maybe Hanover really did have what it takes, and he'd kill Luther Kite even if it meant he'd be boiled in hot oil. Maybe he really did care that much about protecting his family. Lucy had seen many die, but never with anything she'd describe as bravery. Talking about something and actually doing it were two different things.

Because of this, she couldn't trust Hanover.

Not without testing him first.

Lucy made her way to the playroom, and noted one of K's guards was following her. Keeping his distance, but not letting her out of sight. Not entirely unexpected. K was paranoid, perhaps to the point of schizophrenia, but Lucy actually *was* plotting against him.

Still, K disappointed her. The Luther Kite of old times wouldn't have had men spy on her. If he had doubts about Lucy he would have dealt with her face-to-face, and it would have ended with one of them dying horribly.

That's what D would do.

The more time Lucy spent around K, the more she missed Donaldson. That man was as sick and twisted as they came, but somehow amid all the violence and mutual depravity and exchanged pain, he and Lucy had bonded.

She missed the old bastard.

But D was gone. And Lucy was stuck here, at La Juntita, to deal with K.

La Juntita. Juntita wasn't even a word. Lucy had looked it up, thinking it was Spanish or Latin. But it was gibberish. As nonsensical as Luther had become.

She needed out.

In the playroom, Lucy picked up the hot plate, waved at the guard, and then plugged it into the kitchen extension cord. She carried it to Hanover's room, which had no working electrical outlets. The cord was barely long enough to reach. Lucy set it near the foot of the bed.

"Making me soup?" Hanover asked.

"Testing your commitment. I gotta be sure you're going to be able to go through with the plan. Repeat it back to me."

"You take me into the torture room—"

"The playroom. We call it the playroom."

"The playroom, and chain me to the rack, but I've got a key to the shackles. I uncuff myself, grab the knife that you placed behind my back, and stab Luther to death."

"Go for the throat," Lucy said, imagining it. "Or the eye."

"I'll go for the throat or the eye."

"And then what?"

"That's it. He's dead."

Yeah. That was where things got dubious. "I'm going to have to yell for the guards, or else they'll think I was involved. They'll come in. You're not getting out of this alive."

"I know."

"Your death could be long and terrible."

"I know."

"You seem pretty calm about it. I've seen lots of people die. They usually aren't calm."

"I've been through the stages of death before," he said. "Bargaining isn't going to mean anything here, so I went straight to acceptance."

"Maybe. Unless you're working out some sort of different plan," Lucy said. "Get you're hands free. Take me as a hostage. Try to escape."

"Where could I go?"

"Survival instinct is a tough thing to squash, Mr. Hanover. I have to make sure you're going to go through with the plan, not deviate from it."

"How can I prove it to you?"

Lucy lifted up the hot plate, the spiral heating element glowing bright orange. "If you burn the bottoms of your feet off, you won't be able to run away."

JACK

I gave Herb Benedict a hug, and for the first time since forever I felt like everything was going to turn out okay.

"You didn't have to come," I said.

"Yes, I did. Of course I did. Bernice will get over it. You okay?"

I pulled away, met his eyes. "This one is going to be a bad one, Herb."

"Let me guess. Odds against us. Going up against an overwhelming evil. No chance at all we're going to survive."

"That's about right."

He winked. "Wouldn't have it any other way."

We got on the Crimebago Deux, and Herb shook Val's hand. "Good to see you, Val. We should all get together sometime when someone's life isn't on the line."

"Where's the fun in that?" Val asked.

"This is Katie Glente," I said. She and I hadn't shared any positive communication since she came back from the store. I asked her what was on the camera. She refused to tell me. I told her I was keeping it. She shrugged, found her ear buds where she'd left them, and tuned me out until we'd arrived at the airport.

"Ms. Glente," Herb said, shaking her hand.

"It's a pleasure, Lieutenant Benedict, to meet the best Homicide cop to ever work in Chicago."

Katie shot a glance at me. My turn to act like a petulant teen who didn't care.

"Herb!" Harry threw his arms open and came hurrying out of the front seat. "My God, it's so good to see you! I think you've lost weight!"

Herb stared, looking astonished, as McGlade hurried right past him and threw his arms around the pig.

The pig said, "Snort."

Harry said, "Herb Benedict, meet Herb Bacondict. I'm sure you'll agree the resemblance is uncanny."

"I hate to say I've missed you, McGlade. And I won't, because it's just plain untrue."

Harry pointed a finger in Herb's face. "Don't eat my pig. But if you're hungry—and seriously, when aren't you?—there is a fridge full of churros."

"You're lying."

"I'm not."

"I don't like to be teased about churros, McGlade. They're one of my three favorite Mexican donuts, along with buñuelos and sopapillas."

"Check for yourself, oh weighty connoisseur of carbohydrates."

Herb opened the refrigerator.

I've never seen anyone's eyes get that big.

There was a soft squealing sound, and honestly I wasn't sure which Herb made it.

Both Herbs began working their way through the fried Mexican treats, and Katie went back to her music. Harry drove to the hotel, where we picked up Chandler, Fleming, and Tequila. McGlade offered to get the ramp, but Tequila was able to lift Fleming, and her chair, up into the motorhome with a quick, clean jerk.

Val offered Fleming and Tequila cordial greetings, but became several degrees cooler when it came to Chandler.

"Val," Chandler said. "Been a while. How's work?"

"Steady."

"How's Lund?"

"Great. We're living together. Engaged."

"He's a good man," Chandler said. "He deserves you."

"Thanks. How's your work? Still killing people for money?"

Chandler shrugged. "Sometimes I do it for free."

"Tell me if they start wrestling," Harry called back from the cockpit. "That would be hot."

Tequila stepped between them, offering his hand to Herb. "I didn't recognize you at first."

Herb shook it. "I put on a few since we've last met."

"A few?" snorted Harry. "You're twice the man you once were. It's like you went back in time and ate your younger self."

"You haven't changed at all," Herb said, ignoring Harry.

Tequila shrugged. "Grayer. Older. Slower."

"He hasn't slowed down one bit," Fleming said. "And why is there a hog in the RV?"

"That's Herb," Harry said. "He's Jack's old partner."

Herb patted Herb on the head. "Harry is desperate for attention. Look at me, everyone! I bought another really stupid pet!"

"Herb Bacondict is not stupid," McGlade said. "I taught him to fetch. And I'm teaching him to roll over. You're just jealous because he looks better in a tie than you do."

Not sure how I missed it, but the pig was, indeed, wearing a man's tie.

And, awful as it sounded, he did look pretty good in it.

"As amusing as all of this is," Fleming said, "We've got a nine hour drive to La Juntita, and we still need to meet Heath for supplies. If we want to get there predawn, before the guests arrive and the gladiator games begin, we need to leave right now."

"So you guys figured out a plan?" I asked.

Fleming nodded. "Not a good plan. But if it works... it'll be a real blast."

PHIN

You want me to put my foot on that," Phin said, staring at the glowing burner on the floor next to the bed. "On purpose."

"It will prove your commitment. And it will ensure you don't try to run off."

Phin hadn't intended to run off. He'd already come to terms with the fact that he was never leaving this place. If Lucy gave him a chance to get rid of Luther Kite, he was willing to take it, even if he died.

Though the maggot debridement was working well, and his fever was almost gone because Lucy had hooked up an IV full of antibiotics at his insistence, Phin wasn't keen on touching his bare foot to a hot plate.

"For how long?" he asked.

"Ten seconds."

Phin didn't think he'd be able to do it.

"Think of your wife and son," Lucy said. "Or would you prefer I tell Luther about them?"

He realized he'd trapped himself. Luther had probably never heard of Katie Glente. Then Lucy would realize he lied. And this crazy woman's anger would result in a lot worse than a burned foot.

I can do this.

I've dealt with worse.

This is for Jack and Sam.

Just a bit more pain, then I can do what I came here to do.

Phineas held his breath—

—swung his foot off the bed—

—stretched for the hot plate—

—and was too far away.

"Is that as far as you can go?" Lucy asked. She lifted the plate up, getting it close enough for Phin to feel the heat.

The cord stretched, and it got closer…

And closer…

And then it went slack.

The hot surface bounced off of Phin's foot for a microsecond, then Lucy dropped the burner to the floor.

"Shit," she said. "Extension cord pulled out."

"Uncuff my hands," Phin suggested. "Then I can move closer."

"You're a funny one. I'll go find another cord."

"I'll be here. Hurry back."

As soon as she left, Phin began to twist and pull on his shackles, determined to get the hell out of there before that little psycho returned, even if he had to yank off his hands to do so.

DONALDSON

First, it was sweltering under the wind deflector.

Then, when the RV hit the highway, the sound was deafening.

Then, when the sun went down, it was freezing.

Mexico was awful.

But his suffering, all of it, was worthwhile if it meant he could be with his Lucy again.

JACK

Three hours into the drive, I got up to go to the bathroom, knowing Val was already in there. I waited for her to get out.

"Can we chat for a bit?" I asked her. "Alone?"

"Are you going to ask me about the crutches?"

"No. I figured if you wanted to tell me about that, you would." Plus, I'd already heard about Val's condition a while ago, via Harry. "I want to talk about Dixon Hess."

My friend winced. "What about him?"

"You know what it's like to have someone target the people you love."

"Yes."

"Would you have died to protect them? From Hess?"

"In a heartbeat." Val squinted at me. "Where are you going with this?"

I tried to compose my thoughts in a way that made sense, which proved difficult because I wasn't even sure what I was shooting for. "Being a cop has put a lot of my friends and family in danger. There doesn't seem to be an end to it. So many people have gotten hurt, or killed, because of bad guys I spent decades trying to stop."

"That was good work, Jack. Worthwhile. You've saved countless lives."

"And what was the trade off? You ever hear that old moral dilemma? You have the power to save ten strangers, or one person you love. Who do you save?"

"The person you love."

I nodded.

"But you can do both," Val said. "You can protect society from the worst offenders, and also protect your family."

"Like I protected Phin?" I made a face. "You know my history, Val. This is the sixth or seventh time something like this has happened. See? I've lost count. When I retired, I thought this would stop. But it hasn't. How long before some maniac from my past comes looking for Samantha?"

Val folded her arms over her chest. "So what's your solution here? You're going to commit hari-kari in front of Luther Kite so he leaves your family alone? You know that won't work. Monsters like Kite, and Hess, they're always going to be around, preying on people. We can't ignore them. We can't hide from them. The only way to deal with them is to fight."

My shoulders slumped. "Pull up one weed, two more spring up."

"The answer isn't to stop weeding. You stop weeding, the weeds take over and the whole garden dies."

I knew Val understood my point, and agreed with me. She was just being stubborn.

"If someone went after your niece, Grace. And you could stop it by dying, you'd do it."

"Jack, I know the amount of stress you're under. Believe me, I know it as much as anyone. But you aren't thinking clearly here."

"Can you answer my question?"

"It's a shitty question. That's junior college philosophy class nonsense, not real life."

"But you'd die for her."

"Now you're scaring me."

I let out a deep breath. "You're right. I'm stressed out."

"When was the last time you slept?"

"What day is it?"

Val touched my upper arm. "When this is over, bring Phin and Sam up to Lake Loyal. We'll drink some beer, ride some horses, have a cookout."

"Sounds nice."

"It *is* nice. Life is nice. It's easy to forget that when you're dealing with nutjobs."

Tequila walked up to us, Fleming in his arms. Val and I let them pass, and they went into the bathroom.

"He took her to the toilet," Val said. "That's sweet."

A rhythmic, pounding sound commenced, followed by female moans.

"That's sweet, too," I offered.

We left them to do their thing. I found an empty beanbag, and eased down into it. Herb Bacondict clopped over to me and put his fat face on my knees.

"Roll over," I told him.

He didn't move.

"Gotta use your cop voice," Harry said. "Herb! Roll over!"

The pig dropped down to a prone position, and then ripped churro ass.

"No one light a match!" McGlade yelled. "That's methane! The whole motorhome could blow!"

No one lit a match. But several people did put their hands over their noses. Val was not among them.

"Horses are worse," she said, shrugging.

I got up and leaned over Chandler, who was on her tablet. I glanced at Katie, whose eyes were closed. She was still listening to music. Everyone else was watching McGlade's flat screen TV, some series about monsters invading a town.

"Can I get data off a digital camera if it doesn't have a battery?" I asked Chandler, keeping my voice down.

"Does it have an SD card?" Chandler answered without looking at me.

"I don't know."

"Can you check?"

"Not at the moment."

Chandler glanced at me, then followed my gaze to Katie.

"Something wrong there," Chandler said.

"Drugs."

"Something more than drugs. You know how Val tactfully mentioned that I kill people?"

"Yeah."

Chandler pointed her chin at Katie. "I'll bet you even money she has, too."

LUCY

A cord, a cord, my kingdom for a cord.
   Ah, shitballs... now I'm doing that lame-ass Shakespeare thing.

Lucy couldn't find another extension cord anywhere she looked. She'd gone through the mission, room by room, had asked every guard she'd met, and had even ventured into the underground holding cells.

It was as if the universe conspired against her.

Infuriating, because the concept was so perfect. Forcing Hanover to burn his own feet would show his determination and his resignation to his fate, it would prevent him from coming after Lucy when K was dead, and it would be funny as hell to watch. All wins.

But for lack of a cord...

Maybe there was a way to do it without the grill. Heat up a piece of iron? They still had those iron boots that hot lead could be poured into.

She frowned at the idea. That lacked the delectable irony of Hanover torturing himself for what he thought was the greater good. There was something almost poetic about the hot plate idea. Cell coverage was sometimes spotty at La Juntita, but along with several Katie Glente books, Lucy had been able to download that Alfred Hitchcock story with the electric grill, *The Agreement*. She'd read it with slowly boiling excitement, grinning as it got worse and worse, and laughing at the twist ending that had been sooo perfect.

Maybe she would read it to Hanover, after he'd cooked himself. A cherry on top of the pain sundae.

Lucy already planned to hit him with a one-two punch after K died. The first; that Luther had no idea who his wife and son were, so this had all been for nothing. The second; that Lucy was going to kill his family anyway.

That would be even funnier than watching him keep his feet on a burner for ten seconds. She basked in the absurdity of it. What kind of idiot would do something like that for their family?

Family, Lucy knew, was nothing more than a group of incompetent strangers that you were forced to live with. Love was bullshit. Caring was a way to manipulate others so you could get your way.

When she'd been young, Lucy thought that love was Daddy visiting her room at night, giving her toys in exchange for touching her.

That hadn't been love. That had been abuse. Daddy had taught her that the strong should take advantage of the weak, and it was a lesson that Lucy had taken to heart.

Did Hanover do that to his child? Creep into his room at night with a toy truck or a stuffed bear and a jar of Vaseline, exchanging gifts for sick secrets?

Probably. All people were abusers. The American nuclear family was nothing more than a breeding ground for victimizers and their victims.

Lucy knew the truth, and anyone who said otherwise was a liar. No good came from caring about someone else. People hurt you when you were with them. And they continued to hurt you when they were gone.

Lucy would teach Mr. Hanover that lesson. Even if it took days.

But first, she needed to find a damn extension cord. It would have been so much easier if Hanover was in the playroom, which had plenty of electrical outlets.

Oh, snap.

Why didn't I think of that earlier?

Put him in the playroom. Duh.

Lucy allowed herself to feel stupid for a few seconds, and then her mood brightened as she went to fetch some guards.

It was time for Hanover to prove how much he thought he loved his family.

JACK

When we met with Chandler's contact fifty miles outside the Vizcaíno desert, practically everyone was asleep. Katie, both Herbs, Tequila and Fleming, Val. I'd had an insomnia problem for decades, and sleep was my constant enemy. Chandler seemed equally antsy, tapping her foot in spurts, flexing and stretching various body parts in some kind of isometric exercise.

McGlade stopped the RV when Chandler told him to, and then she put on some night vision goggles and hopped outside.

I stared through the open side-panel door, but all I could see was the black Mexican desert and a million billion stars in an equally black sky.

I heard faint conversation. A man with a Mexican accent. Then a slap.

I took out my gun, stepped out into the night. Noises, coming from the rear. Clanking, a rattling of chains.

"Chandler?" I whispered.

Chandler materialized out of the darkness like a magic trick.

"It's okay. Heath is almost done hooking up the equipment to the trailer hitch."

"Did he bring gas?" McGlade, from the front seat. "I'm on my reserve tank."

"I have gas," someone said, walking up to Chandler's side. A man in his thirties, Latino, handsome, wearing fatigues and a black leather eyepatch. "Where on this giant American global warming abomination is the gas cap?"

"I'll do it," Harry said. "I need to drain the lizard."

"I see a pig in the vehicle," said the man I assumed was Heath. "Is there also a lizard?"

"Yeah, and it's huge." Harry climbed out and walked past. "Keep a safe distance away."

Chandler folded her arms across her chest. "Jack, this is Heathcliff. Heath, Jack Daniels."

He bowed, clasping my hand and gently touching his lips to my knuckles. "I am honored, and enchanted, to be in the presence of someone so lovely, yet so obviously competent."

"If you have muck boots," Chandler said, "now is a good time to put them on."

I gave Heath a quick once-over. He had a stance, a bearing, that was recognizable. "You're an operative. Like Chandler."

"There is no one like Chandler," Heath said. "*Mi bonita* is like the rare *Cosmos atrosanguineus* flower. Only one exists, and can only be replicated by clones."

Chandler scowled. "I'm a septuplet. Not a clone."

"Perhaps. But none of your sisters can compare to your passion and beauty."

"You're begging to get slapped again."

Heath winked at me. "Her foreplay, it is rough. But it makes the coupling so much sweeter."

Their flirting reminded me of my husband, so I climbed back in the RV to get away from it.

"Who's here?" Val asked, opening her eyes.

"Pepé Le Pew," I told her.

Chandler came inside, followed by Heath. He smiled at Val. "Chandler, please do me the kindness of introducing this lovely creature."

Neither Chandler, nor Val, said anything.

"I see," Heath said. "So sad for anger to exist between two such beauties. Is it jealously?"

I needed to diffuse this before someone got slugged. "Heath, this is Val. Val, Heath."

Heath kissed Val's hand, and Chandler made a big deal out of not noticing.

"Val, I can see by your lovely ring, you are engaged. Is this what causes your friction with Chandler? You have shared the same man?"

"Chandler and I have a history."

"The problem," Chandler said, "is that I live in this century, and Val lives in a little house on the prairie."

"Having morals and values isn't restricted to any given time period, Chandler."

Heath shook his head, sadly. "Please, lovelies, no more bickering. This is all so snarled and complicated and *telenovela*. The only solution I see is to make love to you, Val, so we're all on even footing."

"Do I have any say in this?" Val asked.

"You do not. But I shall take extra care to put your needs before mine."

"How often does his Don Juan act work?" Val asked Chandler.

"He overrates his abilities," Chandler said. "About everything."

"Bonita, tell me you are not still sore about that tiny little incident in Abidjan."

"We're surrounded by gunman," Chandler jerked her thumb at Heath, "and Lothario here takes off running."

Heath appeared surprised. "That was my staunch, unrepentant feminist streak, *mi amor*. I knew a woman as capable as yourself would find your way out of that situation, and did not need a man to rescue you."

"You were supposed to cover our six, and you fled like *un conejo asustado*."

"Untrue. I did not flee like a frightened rabbit." He puffed out his chest. "I fled like a proud, determined jaguar, who used his large brain to realize he was very outnumbered." Heath shrugged. "I was simply following my training. *Make sure you are safe before you attempt to save others*. You remember that lesson. Besides, you survived."

"I was shot twice."

"And who was there to share his compression bandages with you?"

"I took them from your pack after I broke your nose."

"Not true!" Heath turned to Val. "My nose was bleeding, but was not broken. Much to the relief of *muchachas* everywhere."

"I think I like your boyfriend," Val said.

"Help yourself. Just don't count on him when the shit goes down."

"Isn't that what we're doing now?" I asked. "Counting on him if the shit goes down?"

"I am only being paid today to provide the explosives," Heath said. "Not for my mercenary abilities."

"What are the explosives for?" I asked, feeling very out of the loop.

"For the good of humanity," Chandler said. "Even if we get your husband out of that place, they'll keep bringing people back. La Juntita has to be closed, permanently."

"And how much do these explosives cost?" I asked.

"Chandler has already arranged for payment," Heath said.

"How much?"

"For the explosives and other equipment?" Heath held up one finger.

"One thousand?" I turned to Chandler. "Let me cover that."

"One hundred thousand," Chandler said.

"You guys are kidding." I looked around, but no one was grinning. "Right?"

"Explosives cost money, and I brought a lot with me. Plus vests and assorted gear. But I am not making a dime off of this illegal munitions transaction. This only covers my expenses. There are dealers to pay. Officials to bribe. Transportation fees."

"How much would it cost to have you help us?" I asked.

Heath laughed. "How much to go on this suicide mission? Are you an honest police officer, may I ask?"

"Yes."

"Then you cannot afford me. But *bonita…*" he stared at Chandler and winked. "I would provide the equipment, and my services, for just two hours in the bedroom with you."

"I'll give you forty minutes in the shitter," Chandler said.

"One hour."

"Forty-five minutes."

"This hardly seems fair, since you enjoy it just as much as I do."

She glanced at his lap. "I'm not the one trying to hide his hard-on."

"Fifty minutes. My refractory time is not what it once was."

"No butt stuff."

"Deal."

A partially hunched-over Heath stood up and led Chandler into the bathroom.

"I'm beginning to feel really undersexed," Val said.

"You can come up to the cockpit," McGlade said, climbing in through the side door. "I'll show you why it's called a cockpit."

"How about right here?" Val said. "Right in front of everyone?"

McGlade's face lit up, then sunk when he realized she was teasing. "You're mean. We're going on some crazy *Dirty Dozen* suicide mission, and everyone is getting laid in my motorhome but me." He pointed to the bathroom. "They've got the right idea. Validating life with sex, before going into battle. But rather than consider that I might actually be a human being with real needs, you belittle me, make fun of me, and remind me that I don't have a significant other like both of you do. That I'm just a sad, lonely, unloved fool."

Wow. Where'd that come from?

Val blinked. "Jeez, Harry. I'm sorry. That was insensitive. You're actually a pretty decent guy, and in your own way you're also, dare I say, a little charismatic."

"Really?" he said.

Val nodded. Harry looked at me.

"I guess a woman could do worse," I said truthfully.

"Lots of terrible men in the world," Val said. "You're probably in the top fifty percent."

"Wow. If I knew I actually had a shot, I wouldn't have jerked off when I was outside. But I guess I could pop some Viagra and throw you one if you give me about ten minutes. Would you mind wearing a red clown nose?"

Val politely refused his offer, and Harry went back to the driver's seat.

Herb opened his eyes. "Did I miss anything?"

I ticked off my fingers. "The explosives are here, make love before war, and cherish your partner because some people don't have one."

He smiled. "Then you should be extra grateful, Jack. You've got three partners. Phin is your husband, you're in business with McGlade, and you and I will always have one another's back."

"Count me as a fourth partner," Val said. "Everyone in this motorhome is here for you, Jack."

That didn't make me feel good. It made me feel quite the opposite. Here was a group of people willing to lay down their lives for me.

And I was a self-interested Judas goat, leading them all to the slaughter.

PHIN

He wasn't making any headway with the handcuffs other than rubbing more skin off his wrists, but it didn't matter because Lucy and four guards marched him back into the playroom, and once again chained him to the rack, giving it enough of a crank to make Phin's broken ribs wake up.

"What about that handcuff key and that stashed knife?" he asked.

"We have time," Lucy told him. "The hot plate, first. Be right back."

JACK

W e've got an hour before dawn." Chandler pointed at her tablet. "Everyone maintain radio silence unless it's essential. We're approaching from the north, through the minefield. Jack and Herb, use your metal detectors. Don't step anywhere until you clear it first. Heath, Tequila, and I will be behind you with the wheelbarrows. Heath and I are going to set up explosives at key points around the two main structures. We'll each have a radio detonator, but all of the blasting caps will be wired together, and we only have one receiver, which we're going to place here, at the eastside base of the arena. Everyone is armed?"

I had my Colt, and an extra Glock. Val and Herb had my other Glocks, and Herb had the Mossberg shotgun. Harry, Katie, Chandler, Fleming, Heath, and Tequila had whatever they brought with. We all had Kevlar vests and helmets, compasses, and binoculars. It felt like we were going to war.

Which, I suppose, we were.

"Fleming, there's a ridge here, a hundred and ten meters to the south. You'll provide cover from there. Can you make it?"

Fleming patted her armrest. "Mecanum wheels and two horsepower. This chair can handle any terrain."

"Val, that leaves you here in the RV. Your best vantage point is the roof. Will that be a problem?"

"I'll manage."

"Jack, Harry, Herb, you're breaching the mission building. Doors here, here, and here. Most of the guards will be asleep, and we don't want to wake them, or any servants. Tequila, as soon as we pass the minefield, you're on your own. You have the printout?"

He nodded.

"What can I do?" Katie asked.

"Stick with Jack and follow her orders. To the letter. If you take one misstep… Fleming, what's your longest confirmed kill?"

"One point eight kilometers," Fleming shouldered the H&K rifle. "From the ridge to the arena is easier than shooting turds while sitting on the toilet."

"I won't take any missteps," Katie said.

"We have four mission objectives. Find Phin. Free the prisoners. Find Kite. Blow the place."

"You don't blow it until I give the signal," I told Chandler. "You said there are more than only guards inside. There are servants. They should have a chance to get away."

Chandler nodded. "You make the call. But you *will* make the call. That hellhole is going bye-bye, and I'm the one who paid for this operation."

Heath tapped his chest. "*Bonita*, you hurt me in *mi corazón*."

"Okay, people, outside. Com and starlight checks."

As they began to head for the exit, I said, "Wait."

Everyone stopped. All eyes were on me.

"I'm not one for speeches," I said. Then I locked eyes with each of them in turn.

Fleming wasn't exactly a friend, but she was a damn fine person to know. More compassionate than Chandler. More competent than I'd ever be, even in that wheelchair.

Heath, who I'd only just met, but was putting his ass on the line.

Chandler, who I'd traded so many professional favors with that maybe we actually were friends. I was so lucky to have her on my side.

The same with Tequila. The guy was impenetrable, but we'd gone through a lot together, and his loyalty was unwavering.

Val, the younger sister I'd never had. Coming to help even as she battled her own demons.

And my brothers, Herb and Harry. I didn't know what I'd done to deserve them. In McGlade's case, I'd probably done something bad. But they were as much a part of my family as Phin and Sam, and once again they were risking their lives for me.

What do you say to that?

"And I'm not one for sentiment," I continued. "But thank you. All of you. I know the sacrifice you're making. And I won't ever forget it."

No one said anything. Then Harry spoke up.

"Jack's right. She sucks at speeches. But to anyone who gets out of this alive, drinks are on me."

The joke hung there like a crooked painting.

McGlade took another swing at it. "Wow, cheer up, people. Chances are the majority of us will probably survive."

Again, no one laughed.

"I was in a gay relationship once," he said, "but I got hurt in the end."

Silence.

"Damn," Harry said. "Tough crowd."

People filed out of the motorhome, McGlade last. He gave Herb Bacondict a pat on the head. "You're sitting this one out, buddy. My pets never seem to make it through these things."

Herb pissed all over the floor. McGlade closed the side door and said to me, "Don't tell him, but as soon as we get back to Chicago, it's straight to the butcher."

"Not cool, Harry."

"You know what's not cool? Fifteen thousand dollars of damage to the Crimebago Deux that insurance refuses to cover because I don't have a rider for domesticated swine. The only way I'm letting him in my condo is as single portions, wrapped in tinfoil."

The desert smelled like I imagined it would; like lonely wind and dry plants and dusty sand that coated nostrils and lips. It was chilly, and eerily quiet.

We did sound checks with our ear bud radios; one of Fleming's toys. They were so tiny I was afraid I'd lose mine. Chandler gave us the basics on how to use the night vision goggles and the metal detectors. To keep our approach silent, Herb and I each had a second ear bud that plugged directly into the headphone jacks. So I was effectively deaf to sounds of the environment, and could only hear my team, or the electronic whine of metal being sensed.

Val rested her crutches against the back of the RV, made sure her rifle was slung correctly, and casted a glance my way.

"Be careful," she said, her words hitting my ear receiver a second after I saw her lips move.

"You, too."

Tequila gave Fleming a peck on the cheek, and then she motored off into the green-tinted night. Then he, Chandler, and Heath loaded wheelbarrows with high explosives, and as a group we moved north.

I had a surreal moment. I was a city cop from the Midwest, and I'd done some scary things and been in some dangerous situations, but here I was in Mexico wearing Starlight goggles and holding a metal detector about to navigate through a minefield.

"Keep it low and horizontal, almost touching the ground," Chandler said. "Long, slow sweeps, a full one-hundred and eighty degrees. If I'm right, you'll start getting signals in—"

The *WHEEEE!* of the detector startled me so badly I almost dropped it. I took a few heartbeats to regain composure, and bent down, spray painting a reflective white X over the spot. Then I moved left, around the mine, and continued forward.

"Stay close to her, Herb. We don't want gaps between you."

The second mine I found didn't frighten me as much.

By the fifth, I felt like I might actually survive.

"Slow it down, Jack," Chandler said. "This isn't a race. We've still got more than fifty meters to cross."

The breeze was cold, but after ten minutes I was soaked with sweat. Most of my attention was focused on finding mines, but a detached part of my mind wondered what the hell had happened to the human race. Mankind was hardly the only species that murdered its own kind. Lions slaughter cubs from other prides. Chimpanzees fight wars. Dolphins kill for sport. But only man planted bombs in the ground to indiscriminately kill strangers.

I was fifty years old. That was five decades of knowledge and experience. And all of that could disappear in an instant because some asshole built a bomb that killed when you stepped on it, and some other asshole bought a bunch and buried them all in a field.

As a cop, I'd seen and contemplated death. But if you really wanted to question the meaning of life, walk through a minefield. It really messed with your head.

"I stepped on something, and heard a click," Herb said.

Everyone froze. I felt myself become dizzy.

"Don't move," Chandler told him. "Jack, can you get over to him?"

I carefully worked my way around the last X I'd painted, staying away from the edges, and made it to Herb. He smelled like raw, sweaty fear.

Or maybe I was smelling myself.

"Hey, buddy," I said.

"Hey, buddy." He chuckled. "This kinda sucks."

"You're not going to die here, Herb."

"You sure about that?"

I nodded.

"Jack," Chandler told me, "move your detector over Herb's foot."

I did. When I heard the whir of metal, I almost lost it.

"Hear something?" Chandler asked.

"Yeah."

"Does it sound like a mine?"

"I can't tell."

"Some shoes have a steel shank in the sole. Do yours, Herb?"

"How would I know that? I got them for thirty bucks at Sears."

"Is there any clothing you don't buy at Sears?" Harry asked. "You dress like the cast of *Barney Miller*."

"McGlade, shut up. Jack, move the detector over to Herb's other foot, see if the sound is the same."

I listened to Chandler. "I heard something."

"Does it sound similar?"

"I think so."

"Herb, I'm pretty sure it's your shoe, and you just stepped on a rock. But we're going to get a few meters ahead of you, just in case. Jack, lead on."

"I'm not leaving him."

"Jack, I've got a wheelbarrow full of plastic explosive and blasting caps. I'm not the person to fuck around with right now."

Herb nodded. "Go. It's probably my shoe."

I gave him a harsh stare.

"Get out of here." Herb smiled, then winked at me. "I gotta do this one solo, partner."

Slowly, reluctantly, I continued to go north, marking mines until the whole caravan was ten meters away from Herb.

"Are we clear yet?" I asked.

"Keep going until we're all out. If the mine goes off, we're going to have to deal with forty armed guards."

I pressed onward. When we reached the north face of the bull-fighting ring, everyone stopped.

"Okay, Herb," Chandler said. "You can take a step now."

"If you blow up, I'll name another pet after you," McGlade said. "Maybe one of those really fat elephant seals that grunts."

There was no reply.

"Herb?" I said.

Silence.

"Herb?" I raised my voice, wondering if my ear radio was working.

"Chandler was right. It was a rock. Catch up to you guys in a minute."

I sank into a pool of beautiful relief. Then I looked at my team.

Chandler was headed east. Heath was going west.

And Tequila was already gone, his wheelbarrow abandoned.

DONALDSON

After they parked, Donaldson waited for them to leave. His intent was to go inside the RV, find a weapon more suitable than his stolen scissors, and tail the group to Lucy.

But all of Jack's friends hadn't left.

Some girl had stayed behind.

And that same girl was on the roof of the motorhome, facing away from Donaldson.

She had a gun. But that was okay.

Donaldson was indestructible.

He crawled toward her, clenching the scissors in his fist.

The girl's gun was big.

And Donaldson wanted it.

LUCY

The hot plate was gone.

Lucy was sure she'd left it in Hanover's room. But when she returned, after moving him to the playroom, no hot plate.

Could she have gotten the rooms mixed up? They all did look the same.

She checked every room on the first floor. Couldn't find it.

Checked with K. He didn't have it, either, and Lucy left when he started quoting goddamn Shakespeare.

It wasn't in the kitchen, or the pantry, or the dining area. She wondered if one of those idiot guards took it. So Lucy located a high-beam flashlight, then wandered outside to search.

JACK

We left the metal detectors next to the third wheelbarrow, and the four of us walked around the outside of the arena.

"Six guards," Chandler whispered in my ear piece. "A pair on the east side of the stadium, smoking. Two on the south side of the house. And two more at a shed, on the northwest side. They're cooking something on a hot plate."

I shivered, my nervous sweat chilled by the cool desert air.

Herb, Harry, and I had done raids before, and I knew the hand signals to direct Herb to move around the house clockwise, and Harry counterclockwise.

"What?" Harry said.

"Go that way," I pointed.

"Then just say *go that way* and cut the commando BS. I thought you were waving away mosquitos."

"Go!"

He went.

"*Levanta tus manos!*" my ear bud crackled. "Get your hands up!"

I heard shouting, in Spanish and English. Then Chandler's voice.

"They have Tequila."

I dropped down, and turned to tell Katie to do the same.

But she was gone.

KATIE

She was close. So close she couldn't stop from trembling.

Years, she'd searched. For most of her life.

And her journey was finally nearing an end.

Katie tucked away the camera she'd easily picked out of Jack's pocket, gripped the Colt King Cobra hard as she could to make sure she didn't drop it, and sprinted toward the mission building as soon as the patrolling guard turned the corner.

She had already fulfilled one decades old promise she'd made to herself.

Now Katie was about to make two more come true.

PHIN

Lucy had been away for so long, Phin had allowed himself to hope that perhaps he'd gotten some kind of reprieve.

Then she returned. With the electric burner.

So much for hope.

"Sorry to keep you waiting," she said, plugging it into the wall. "Some of the men took it to heat up a can of tamales."

Lucy placed it next to his foot, close enough that the heat was uncomfortable.

"So, here's the game. You touch your right foot to the hot plate and hold it there for ten seconds. I'll count out loud."

"And what happens after ten seconds?"

"Then we do it with your left foot."

Phin squirmed. The heating element was already so close, it had begun to burn him. There was no possible way he'd be able to hold his bare flesh to that without jerking away.

"And what if I don't do it?"

"Then I'll do it to you anyway. But that will show me that I can't trust you, and I'll crank up the rack until your tendons and ligaments detach. I'll make sure you don't die, though. I'll keep you alive so you can watch what I do to your wife and son when I have them brought here."

A scream began to well up in Phin, and he didn't think he'd be able to stop it.

"It's okay to make noise," Lucy said. "I actually like it."

The two guards came in. "El Cometa needs you in the throne room."

Lucy's scarred face twisted into something that Phin guessed was a pout. "I'm in the middle of something."

"An intruder was caught, trying to break in."

Lucy let out an overly dramatic, teenage-girlish sigh. "I guess we'll continue this later."

She turned to leave.

"Lucy!" Phin said, shaking in pain, "Fire hazard!"

Lucy paused, looked at the burner just inches from his feet, reached for it—

—and switched it off.

She left. But Phin no longer hoped for a reprieve.

He was going to die. And die in agony.

But, if he proved himself, maybe he would get a shot at killing Kite.

Phin clung to that.

JACK

Lights were coming on everywhere, and I pulled off my night vision goggles before I was blinded.

"I lost Katie. Does anyone have eyes on her, or Tequila?" I asked. "Tequila, are you there?"

"Copy," said Fleming. "They took Tequila inside. Cracked him in the head first. Might have disabled his com. Over."

"Herb? You see Katie?"

"No. But more guards are coming out of the mission. I count five."

"Harry?"

"I was pissing. You guys try to piss with night vision goggles on? It looks exactly like Mountain Dew."

"Chandler?"

"Copy. Rigging explosives, haven't seen them."

"Copy that. Same here," Heath added.

"How about you, Val? Do you see Katie?"

No answer.

"Val? You there?"

My stomach sank. Where the heck was Val?

DONALDSON

The girl wasn't struggling very much at all.

Even more proof that I have super powers, Donaldson thought. *I snuck up without her hearing me, grabbed her with little effort, and now I'm flying.*

Wait... why am I—

The girl had flipped him off the edge of the RV, and he hit the ground so hard he bounced.

Donaldson's wind blew out of him, and as he desperately tried to suck in some oxygen there was a huge *BANG!* next to his head.

The girl on the roof is shooting at me.

He managed to get onto one knee, blindly reaching for the motorhome's side door handle as another shot passed between his open legs. If Donaldson still had something there, it would have been blown off.

Pulling hard, the door swung open, and Donaldson planned to take cover when a demon appeared in the doorway and squealed at him.

Donaldson fell backward, managed to turn onto all fours, and then began to crawl as fast as he could toward the lights in the distance.

JACK

Who fired the shots?" Chandler said.

I looked back in the direction of the Crimebago Deux. "They came from beyond the minefield. Either Fleming or Val."

"Copy that," Fleming said. "It came from Val's twenty, over."

"Was she the one shooting?" I asked. "Or..."

Or was she the one shot?

Could some patrol, or guard, have gotten to Val without any of us noticing?

"That was me," Val said. "I'm okay."

I blew a stiff breath out between my teeth.

"There was a man on the roof of Harry's RV. He attacked me. Knocked off my goggles. He took off in your direction. I don't see him."

"More guards coming," McGlade said. "I count ten."

"Another eight on my side," Herb said.

"Copy. I'm going back for the last wheelbarrow," Chandler told us. "Lay down suppressing fire. Keep them off of me and Heath."

And then everyone began shooting.

LUCY

The guards led her into the dining room. There was a muscular man on his knees, hands cuffed behind him, bleeding from the side of his head. Luther was standing over him with his Spyderco Harpy in one hand. In his other was a piece of paper. He held it out for Lucy to see.

It was a computer printout of a man's face.

Mr. Hanover.

"It was in his pocket," Luther said. "That, and two guns, are all he had on him."

Lucy's mind whirled with scenarios. Had Hanover been lying? Was he actually a cop? How did this affect her murder plot?

Outside, there was gunfire.

"Is this a raid?" Lucy wasn't sure who she was asking, K or the man.

"We're prepared for a raid." K brought his curved blade up to the man's ear. "How many of your men are out there?"

The man stared impassively. He didn't say anything. He didn't so much as flinch.

Not even when K cut off his ear.

Lucy had never seen anything like that. Not ever. K was holding this guy's severed ear, and the dude didn't even blink.

K took a step back. "Well may it sort that this portentous figure comes armed through our watch," he whispered.

More gun shots. Closer. The five guards in the room raised their weapons.

Lucy didn't know what to do. She realized she was frightened. Of whoever was outside. Of K. Of Hanover, who she realized must have lied to her. Of this kneeling man who didn't react to pain.

"He is an omen, Lucy. As harbingers preceding still the fates."

"Will you fucking stop it with the fucking Shakespeare!" she screamed. "Make him say something!"

"Who are you?" K said, holding his knife to the man's throat.

The man didn't speak. Didn't move.

K lowered his crooked body, peering into the man's face, cocking his head. "It doesn't matter what I do to him. He isn't going to talk. This man is empty inside. You can see it in his eyes. It's like... gazing into a mirror."

Lucy considered the straight razor in her back pocket. Killing the prisoner was an option. Maybe K was right, and he'd never talk. But if he did, and Lucy's deal with Hanover was somehow revealed, she would die a horrible death.

The other option was killing K. The guards were covering the doors, and no one was looking her way. Lucy could slit K's throat, and try to escape amidst the chaos.

"Three of you, bring him to the arena," K said. "Keep your guns on him. If he tries anything, shoot him until you run out of bullets."

They led the man away, and K turned to Lucy. "You have Hanover in the playroom."

She nodded, slowly dropping her hand to be closer to her razor.

"Bring him to the arena. These men may not talk. But we'll see if they'll fight."

Huh? "K... that makes no sense."

"This man was carrying Hanover's picture. Is he a friend? Is he an enemy? This is how to find out."

"We don't even know what's going on out there. It could be cops."

"Or a rival cartel. Or prisoners trying to escape. Or the men, shooting at shadows. For all I know, princess, it could be friends of yours, here to rescue you. I know you want to leave. You could have gotten a message out a dozen different ways. You could have sent your mind waves out to the machines in the sky."

She shrank back. "Mind waves?"

"They record our thoughts. Don't pretend you don't know. The spiders who crawl in your brain when you sleep. The cameras, everywhere."

And it was now official. K had turned the corner into paranoid ranting madman crazytown.

She nodded, trying to appear as sincere as possible. "You're right, K. We need to fix this. I'll bring Hanover to the arena right now. We'll find out everything."

Lucy hurried out of there, fast as her skeletal legs could carry her twisted frame, the guards trailing her as she entered the playroom. When she unshackled Hanover's hands, Lucy whispered, "You have to kill Luther."

"When?"

"He wants you to fight in the arena one more time. Kill your opponent, and I'll make sure you have a shot at Kite."

They marched Hanover out at gunpoint, and Lucy wondered where she might be able to find a gun. If K was coming for her, she wasn't going down without a fight.

JACK

Chaos.

I'd been in a few shootouts, but this was different. I didn't know who was firing, where they were, where to fire back, or what to do next. I'd known a few vets, heard them talk about the confusion, the insanity, of war, and at that moment I fully understood what they meant.

My back was against the arena, bullets flying everywhere, dozens of guns firing from so many directions I couldn't pinpoint any of them, four people at once yelling in my earpiece, and I had no idea how to react.

Then someone's voice rose above all the others. Chandler, saying, "Take cover!"

What cover? There was no cover. I was in the middle of a shooting gallery, and too frightened and disoriented to know my left from my right.

I looked around, spotted a storage shed fifty meters to the east, realized that if I stopped to think about it for too long I'd freeze, so I just ran.

I'd never felt so exposed. Every step I took, every millisecond that passed, I expected a bullet to cut me down. I didn't know where it would come from, or where it would hit me, but there was no way anyone could survive a situation like this, out in the open with dozens of people shooting, no reason or sense or order to any of it.

And then, somehow, I was at the shed. I got behind the far wall, crouched down, my Glock at the ready. Somewhere during my sprint I'd dropped my night vision goggles. But it didn't matter, because as I stared into the darkness, watching muzzle flashes wink like fireflies, the gigantic lights of the arena blazed on and illuminated the whole area, bright as the noonday sun.

I saw Herb, pinned down.

Harry, pinned down.

Chandler, pinned down.

No sign of Heath. No sign of Katie. No sign of Tequila.

And then, cutting through the cacophony of gunfire, I heard the roar of an engine, coming from the bullfighting ring.

PHIN

After the guard started the chainsaw, he dropped it in the sand at Phin's feet.

Another guard did the same, next to Phin's opponent. Then all of Luther's armed men backed off of the field.

Last call for bets, last call for bets...

The stands were empty, except for men stationed at the two mounted M60 machineguns with their bulletproof shields. Luther and Lucy were in the balcony, clad in purple robes.

Phin looked at the man he was about to fight. He'd never seen him before. New guy. Short, but with a muscular build. Blood soaked his head, and shirt, indicating an injury.

Even so, Phin knew his odds were the worst he'd ever faced. He wasn't even sure how he could still stand up. He still had a low fever. His injuries were so numerous, he couldn't even count them all. He was exhausted.

All around, gunfire crackled. Phin had no idea what it meant. He couldn't say he cared much, either. Even the best case scenario; the government had sent in armed forces to liberate the prisoners, didn't mean much to Phin, because he was going to be sliced in half within the next thirty seconds.

The real tragedy here was he had never gotten a chance to get his hands around Luther's scrawny, diseased throat.

The gong sounded.

Neither combatant moved.

A few seconds passed, and Luther gave some sort of hand signal. The M60 on Phin's left fired into the arena, punching 7.65mm wounds into the sand between the men, the sound so loud Phin flinched.

"You have five seconds," Luther yelled. "Four... Three... Two..."

The short guy picked up his chainsaw and began to approach Phin. As he came into sharper focus, Phin realized how muscular he actually was. He looked like one of those He-Man dolls Phin had played with as a child.

He-Man shouted something at him, which Phin couldn't hear above the roar of the chainsaw engines. His opponent looked very determined, and tougher than a box of nails.

Okay, then.

This is how it ends.

Last fight.

Last stand.

Last breath.

Last call.

Phin bent down, picked up the chainsaw, and said, "Let's do this."

He put his finger on the trigger, revving the saw, and then thrust it forward, putting his weight behind the attack. He-Man parried, spinning blade hitting spinning blade with a force that made Phin's whole body shake. Phin ducked down and turned, letting centripetal force carry the saw in an arc, going for He-Man's knees.

The short guy jumped over it, *actually flipped sideways in mid-air*, and landed lightly on his feet, his weapon still pointed Phin's way.

Impressed as Phin was, he continued to advance, sweeping the chainsaw sideways, missing, but twisting his body around and following up with a spin kick at the man's head.

Phin was fast. This guy was faster. He ducked Phin's kick, so quick it looked like he'd disappeared, and came up on Phin's other side, giving him a firm tap in the kidney and yelling something.

Phin doubled over, and He-Man shoved him backward, hard. Phin's ass hit the sand, and he brought up the chainsaw to block the death blow he knew was coming.

The death blow didn't come.

Phin guessed what was happening. This guy didn't know how these battles worked. He was as reluctant to kill Phin as Phin had been reluctant to kill every opponent he'd fought in these insane gladiator games.

But He-Man didn't understand the rules. Only one of them would survive this. And if this guy—who was stronger, faster, and a much better fighter than Phin was—wanted to show him mercy, Phin would gladly accept that gift.

Phin dropped a shoulder, and mindful of the saw blade, he used momentum to roll up to his feet.

He-Man dropped his chainsaw and raised both hands.

Phin hesitated.

Then he thought of Luther Kite. If he won this, he could get a chance at Kite.

Was it okay to kill one defenseless man, if it saved countless others? If it saved Jack and Sam?

No. It wasn't okay.

But Phin was going to do it anyway.

He lunged.

JACK

I watched as they dragged Harry inside the mission.

Herb was captured a few moments later.

Gunfire continued to ring out from all directions.

"They've got Herb and Harry," I said, pushing my earpiece in deeper. "Who's still out there?"

"I don't have a shot from here," Val said. "I can try driving the RV closer."

"Copy that, hold your position." I couldn't tell if it was Chandler or Fleming talking.

"I can get closer."

"You can hold your goddamn position. You and Fleming are the only reasons we're not all dead yet. Fleming, what's your count?"

"Five down. Four more incoming."

"Copy. Val, do you see the men at the top of the arena? They're manning those mounted M6os."

"I can see them."

"Take them out."

"Kill them?"

"No, take them out for coffee. Hell yes, kill them!"

I held my binocs to my face, zooming in on the man standing behind the biggest machinegun I'd ever seen.

"I can't hit him," Val said.

"Goddammit, Val, if you're pulling some pacifist shit in the middle of a firefight—"

"She's telling the truth, Chandler." It was Fleming. Obviously. "The gunners are behind polycarb. I've already tried. Our rounds won't penetrate."

Polycarbonate. Bulletproof glass.

"Jack, you've got men coming at you," Val said.

I looked, and saw ten guys running my way.

"Copy that," Fleming said. "I don't have a shot."

"Val?"

One went down, clutching his leg.

The rest of them ran toward the only shelter around. The shed I was hiding behind.

I had all of three seconds to make my decision.

"Hold fire!" I yelled. Both at my teammates, and at the approaching guards.

Then I dropped my guns, put my hands over my head, and surrendered.

PHIN

The short guy sidestepped the thrust, spinning like a matador, and backhanded Phin in the jaw.

Phin narrowed his eyes. Being punched was one thing. But a backhand was so...

Condescending.

Phin was really starting to dislike this cocky little bastard.

He came at him swinging, and He-Man cartwheeled out of the way. He tried to rush him, and He-Man did a back handspring.

This guy was harder to hit than a speed bag. So Phin did something he wouldn't expect.

He threw the chainsaw.

The man's face registered surprise, and as he ducked the spinning blade Phin let fly with a roundhouse that actually connected with his side.

It was like hitting a tree.

He-Man popped the jab, catching Phin in the shoulder, and Phin followed with an elbow that glanced off of his jaw.

The short guy said something, just as Phin was in the middle of a kick. His foot bounced harmlessly off the man's chest, and Phin didn't hear what he said. He followed with an uppercut, and then He-Man tied him up in some complicated arm lock and pulled Phin to the ground.

"Jack Daniels."

Phin began to thrash, and then the guy's huge leg was wrapped around his neck, threatening to snap off Phin's head.

"I'm here with Jack Daniels. This is a rescue."

Phin didn't stop fighting. "You asshole. Why did you let her come here?"

"It's Jack. How was I supposed to stop her?"

Phin let his body go slack, and he was struck by a wave of realization. "You're a gymnast."

"Yeah."

"Is your name Tequila?"

"Yeah."

"Nice to finally meet. Jack has said nice things."

"Keep struggling, so they don't catch on."

Phin was then on his side, his arms pinned behind him. Even if he had been struggling, he didn't think he could have prevented the move.

"So what's the plan?" he asked.

"Plan A was for me to break you out of your holding cell. But you weren't there."

"Plan B?"

"Let myself get captured and find you that way. I swallowed some lock picks."

"Was there a Plan C?"

"Radio for backup. Including Jack, we've got five others helping."

"Have you done that yet?"

"The radio was in my ear."

Tequila's ear was gone, only a clotted hole remained.

"This was a shit plan," Phin said.

Tequila rolled again, forcing Phin onto his back. "I'm going to pretend to snap your neck, then get up and rush Kite's balcony. When I draw their fire, you grab a saw and head for the guard to my left. Then get out the way you came in."

"How are you going to get out?"

"I'm not," Tequila said.

"I don't understand."

"I've done some bad things. This is a chance to do a good thing. Go to your wife."

Phin wasn't sure what to say. He had to settle for, "Thank you."

Tequila released him. "I have a dog. Rosalina. Jack knows where she is."

Phin nodded.

Tequila torqued his body, and Phin went limp.

After getting up, Tequila broke into a sprint. He made it ten steps before the machineguns began to fire, chewing up the sand around his feet.

Luther and Lucy backed up, out of view.

Phin sprang to his feet, grabbed the saw, and beelined for the guard, catching the unaware man in the shoulder, then tearing the machinegun from his hands and spinning to help Tequila.

Tequila was turning and flipping across the arena, hand springs and cartwheels and twists and jumps and bullet after bullet tore through his body. When he reached the end of the arena, he launched himself into the air and managed to catch one hand on the lip of the balcony as Lucy and Luther retreated in apparent surprise and fear.

Tequila hung there for a moment. There was so much blood coming out of him he looked like a sponge being squeezed.

And then the M6os cut him down, and his lifeless body kissed the arena floor, and Phin said a silent goodbye to the bravest person he'd ever met.

Then he went to go find Jack.

JACK

We were on our knees, hands cuffed behind our backs, rope binding our wrists to our ankles, Harry on my right and Herb on my left, lined up along a wall in a room filled with instruments of torture. We'd been stripped of our gear, belts, and shoes. Harry's eye was swollen, and Herb had dried blood on his chin from a rifle butt to the nose.

Two armed guards stood at the door. I couldn't hear gunfire anymore, and wondered if the room was soundproof.

But there could have been another reason for the lack of sound. Maybe my friends had retreated.

Or been killed.

"Can't you pull your fake hand off?" Herb whispered to Harry.

"It's grafted to my nerves with bioelectric sensors, or some shit like that. I don't pay a lot of attention when I see my orthotic surgeon. That guy can *talk*."

"But if you pull hard enough—"

"Yes, Jumbo, I can pull it off. Then I'll quickly untie all of us with my stump before those guards ten feet away from us notice anything funny."

"I'm sorry I got you both into this," I said.

"It's not your fault, Jack."

Harry snorted. "Bullshit. It's totally her fault. You're a cop, Herb. I was a cop. How many lunatics from our pasts come calling on us? Answer: zero. Jack attracts psychopaths like dog shit attracts flies. No offense, Jack."

"None taken." We were in far too much trouble for me to be offended by anything.

"Let me tell you," Harry went on, "this is not my preferred method of dying. I always thought it would be something else."

"How did you think you'd die?" Herb asked.

"A stroke in the middle of skydive sex."

"There's an image I don't want in my head," Herb said.

"That hurts, Herb. Because I wanted it to be with you. I've always wanted to tag that pale, flabby ass. Also, in this fantasy, you don't have a parachute."

"You're so sweet."

"You're so fat."

"How about you, Jack?" Herb asked.

"I'd been hoping for old age," I said. "After my daughter had grown up."

"Lame," Harry said. "Skydiving sex is cooler. What's your death fantasy, el chubbo? Drown in a giant vat of pudding?"

"Honestly? I was always stuck on that selfless hero ending. Getting my ticket punched just as I was saving someone's life. You know, like pushing a child out of the water just as I'm eaten by a Great White shark."

"Have to be a damn big shark," Harry said. "Like the biggest shark ever."

The door opened, and the guards walked out. I craned my neck to see who it was, hoping for the slight chance it was Chandler, or Val.

It was Luther Kite.

He wore a purple cloak, like a king might wear, but it was ratty and old and looked like a cheap costume. His black hair was greasy, patchy, and his pale complexion and scarred face made him look zombie-ish.

Behind him, Lucy. Short, disfigured, her gnarled skin stretched tight across her skull and giving her the appearance of a very ugly doll.

"And the winner of the most hideous person in the world is…" McGlade said, "an unexpected tie!"

Luther lurched over to us, studying each in turn. Then he asked, "Who are you people?"

PHIN

He went through the entryway, the AK-47 he'd taken from the guard at the ready, staying low in case he met resistance.

He met none. No one was guarding the underground prisoners.

Phin checked the wall, where he'd seen the keys for the shackles and cages. The key ring was hanging there like it had been waiting for him.

He began to open up cells.

LUCY

That arena match had been something.

Lucy had almost taken the opportunity to kill K while it was going on, but when the fight began, she'd been transfixed.

Hanover had performed adequately. Too bad he got his neck broke. Woulda been fun to have tried the electric burner thing with him. But that short guy... he'd been amazing. Leaping and spinning around like it was the Olympics.

A shame he was dead. He'd been a lot of fun to watch.

They were rushed to safety by guards as pops of gunfire continued to erupt all across the compound. But whatever attack they'd been under was sure to end soon. A sentry informed K that three intruders had been captured and taken to the playroom.

Time to finally find out what was going on.

The prisoners were on their knees, hogtied. Lucy didn't recognize either of the men. But the woman...

"Who are you people?" K asked.

The man on the left who'd called them hideous began to laugh. "Seriously? He doesn't even know who we are? Skydiving sex! I traded skydiving sex for this!"

Lucy slapped the guy, shutting him up, then looked closer at the woman.

"You're that cop. Jack Daniels."

The woman said nothing.

Lucy turned to K. "Remember? From Michigan?"

K came closer, peering at Jack. "I do. Good to see you again, Jack. Did the sky machines tell you where I was?"

JACK

In my capacity as a law enforcement officer, I'd unfortunately encountered many examples of mental illness.

The Diagnostic and Statistical Manual of Mental Disorders, known as the DSM-V, catalogued all of them according to type and severity.

The correct medical term for Luther Kite's disability was *in-fucking-sane.*

I gazed hard into the monster's eyes and said, "Yes, Luther. The sky machines told me."

He flinched like I'd smacked him. I ran with it.

"They've been whispering to me, Luther. They know all about you, and sent me here to help."

"How?" he whispered.

"I can turn the machines off."

"She's fucking with your head, K. She came here with her friends to kill you. To kill us."

He brought his face close enough to mine that I could smell his breath. It stank, strangely, of rotten lemons.

"Did you come here to kill us, Jack Daniels?"

I refused to blink. "I came here to free you, Luther Kite. I know how you have suffered. The robots have sent me signals."

Lucy tugged his arm. "You can't believe this shit, K."

"But she knows about the robots."

"She's making that up. Trying to confuse you. Next she's going to start quoting fucking Shakespeare."

Shakespeare? I knew a little Shakespeare.

"He's mad that trusts in the tameness of a wolf," I said. "Lucy is lying to you, Luther."

"Just kill the bitch, K."

"The lady doth protest too much," I warned him.

"My kingdom for a horse!" said Harry.

"Test her!" Lucy said. "Test her to see if she's telling the truth."

Lucy walked behind Luther, then picked something up. Something small and black, with a cord attached.

An electric hot plate.

"Make her prove herself, K. You know what to do."

PHIN

Phin ran outside, among the liberated prisoners, just as the rising sun peeked over the horizon.

Shots rang out.

People went down.

Phin looked around for Jack, hoping she was near, fearing she was near.

A guard came around the corner. Phin took aim, but the man was immediately swarmed, falling beneath a throng of fists and feet.

Movement, behind him. Phin swung the rifle around just in time to see something charge past.

Was that... *a pig?*

LUCY

She turned the portable electric grill up to high, and it only took a few seconds for the heating element to glow orange.

"Ten seconds," she told Jack Daniels. "The sky machines have foreseen that Luther can only trust the one who can keep their hand on the burner for ten seconds."

"Is that true?" Jack asked Luther.

K looked from Lucy, to the cop, and back again. "They tell me things. The things they tell me come true."

"If it's true," Jack said, "then I'm not the only one here who must prove their trust."

Lucy shook her head. "She's confusing you, K."

"She's the one confusing you, Luther. Like Lady Macbeth. Or Claudius plotting against Hamlet."

"She came here to kill you, K."

"I came to free you, Luther."

K made his hands into fists. "I don't know who to trust. I can't even trust myself."

"K—"

"If you can't trust yourself, Luther," Jack interrupted. "You know what you have to do."

K stared at the burner. Then he stared at Lucy.

Lucy saw her chance, and went for it. "She's right, K. How can you even trust yourself?" She held out the burner. "You have to prove it."

"My fate cries out," K said. "And makes each petty artery in this body as hardy as the Nemean lion's nerve."

And—holy shit—he stuck his hand on the burner.

There was a sizzling sound as flesh met heat, and Lucy expected him to immediately pull back, but he kept it there.

As the Hitchcock story dictated, Lucy began to count.

"One..."

Smoke began to rise. And with it, an odor not unlike bacon.

"Two..."

K's arm shook, his lips peeling back in a silent scream.

"Three..."

Now the scream was no longer silent. It started in K's throat, then rose up past his teeth, like a train whistle.

"Four..."

The scent was strong now. Meat on the grill. Fat sizzling. The acrid stench of cooking blood.

"Five..."

K dropped to his knees, but Lucy helpfully lowered the burner so he didn't lose contact. After all, what were friends for?

"Six..."

K placed his other hand atop the roasting one, pressing down in an obvious effort to keep it there.

"Seven..."

The sleeve of K's robe ignited. But it was some cheap, artificial fabric, and instead of burning it began to melt, glowing bits dropping to the floor.

"Eight..."

Lucy couldn't contain her excitement anymore. This was the biggest thrill she'd had in a long time. K had been right. The best and worst pain was what we did to ourselves.

"Nine..."

K's eyes sought hers, and Lucy drank in his pain.

"Nine..."

That's for keeping me a prisoner here.

"Nine..."

And this is for all of your not-so-subtle threats.

"Nine... almost there K!"

And this is for all the fucking Shakespeare quotes, you annoying fucking son of a bitch.

"I think I lost count," Lucy said, and K screamed "TENNNNNNNNNN!"

He pulled his hand away, and it looked a lot like perfectly cooked BBQ brisket. In fact, it looked so good that Lucy's mouth watered, even though she was a confirmed vegan.

K took his good hand off the one that was still smoking, pointed it at Jack Daniels, and said, "Your turn!"

JACK

My trick for buying time had backfired.

"Lucy should go first," I said, trying not to lose myself to panic.

"I vote for Lucy," Herb agreed.

"We're tied up," said Harry. "But Lucy has both of her hands free. I'm happy to help by counting for her."

Luther seemed on the verge of passing out. Lucy reached out and stroked his cheek. "You can trust yourself now, K. Who do you think should go next? Me, who has been your good friend for years? Or some cop who came here to kill you?"

"Hand... hurts..."

"I know it does. And I know how to help."

Lucy hobbled to the door and yelled something.

"I'm bringing you some purple, K. That will make it all better."

"You're a princess, Lucy."

"I just want you to be okay."

Luther put his head on Lucy's shoulder, and she stuck her scarred tongue out at me.

Guards came in, with a clear plastic bottle of pink syrup. Lucy took off the top and held it to Luther's mouth.

"Not too much, K. We don't want you falling asleep before Jack proves you can trust her."

Lucy ordered the guard to uncuff one of my hands.

I was out of ideas.

Was this how it all ended? Being tortured to death by two maniacs in the desert, alongside my friends? Without even knowing what happened to my husband?

"We're not the only ones here," I said, trying to lean away as the guard approached.

"Brought some more people along, huh?" Lucy asked. "Was one of them a short guy, really good at back flips?"

"Where is he?"

"That guy was fun. He died well, if that means anything."

Tequila. Oh no…

"Uncuff her," Lucy ordered.

"WAIT!" McGlade roared. "The sky machine robot things command that I go next! You must obey!"

Lucy shrugged. "Okay. Do him next."

The guard unlocked Harry's wrist, and Lucy held the hot plate in front of him.

McGlade plopped his hand down on the burner.

Unlike Luther's hand, it didn't begin to sizzle.

It began to melt.

"You have been chosen, Luther Kite," McGlade said as his prosthetic skin dripped down the sides of the hot plate, acrid fumes swirling into the air. "We are not as we seem. We are vengeful robot overlords…" He lifted his hand and his metal endoskeleton wiggled. "From the future!"

Everyone stared. Then Lucy said, "It's just a fake hand, K. Burn his other one."

"Jack should go first!" Harry yelled. "She started this!"

Then the door swung open, and Katie was there, the Colt King Cobra in her hand. She shot the guard twice, looked at Lucy and Luther, and burst into tears.

DECADES AGO

Ann Arbor, Michigan

Her baby was perfect. Beautiful. The prettiest newborn ever.

She unabashedly gaped at the child, no more than three pounds, wiggling her little hands as if she was waving at Mommy.

In the months since getting away from Ben and Winston, she'd managed to get out of Detroit, find a halfway house to take her in, and kick heroin. She was even going to try and enroll in high school next semester, even though she was only thirteen and had no school credentials. She didn't even know the last grade she completed.

Back in her maternity room, she stared at the ceiling, trying to remember the past.

So much of it was cloudy. She'd been abducted before she'd hit puberty, forced into a life of sexual abuse, violence, and drugs. Thankfully, she had very little of those years that she could recall with clarity.

But before Ben and Winston, there had been a family.

She didn't have complete recall. But bits and pieces had come back to her. The beautiful Maxine, her mother. Her sweet, sweet father, Rufus. A younger brother.

She couldn't remember his name. Or her own last name. Her counsellors said to give it time. Memory was like a puzzle, they said. Pieces may be missing for years, and then, suddenly, they pop into place.

She fell asleep, dreaming of being part of a family.

A sharp pinch woke her up.

She sat up in bed, and found herself staring into two terrible green eyes.

"Ben and I have been calling every hospital within a fifty mile radius, looking for young, single mothers. If you'd made it to Lansing, or even Toledo, we never would have found you."

Her eyelids fluttered, and a glorious rush coursed through her whole body. Winston held up the syringe.

"You missed it. Admit it."

"No..." she moaned.

"But you do. I can see how you do. Now here's what's going to happen. We're getting the paperwork ready. In a few hours, you're going to sign away your parental rights. And then you're going to come work for us again. And there'll be plenty more of this candy for you."

He tucked the needle into his pocket, then stood up.

"Just ride the wave. See you in a little bit."

He left. And she melted away.

Then she came back, not knowing how long she'd been out.

Fighting the heroin, she managed to flop out of her bed. Her clothes were in the drawers, and she dressed as fast as she could, missing a button, putting her shoes on the wrong feet.

She had to get out of there before they came back. Take little Lucy and go...

Go where?

Lucy was a preemie. She needed special care.

And no matter where she ran, Ben and Winston could find her.

She wracked her drug-addled brain, trying to figure out what to do.

Get away. She had to get away. As far away as possible. Find a job. Make some money. Become the kind of mother that Lucy needed.

The window only opened halfway, but she was still a kid herself, and she slipped through.

Katie took one last look at the hospital, and made two promises.

I'll be back for you, Lucy.

And I'm going to make those two motherfuckers pay.

It took Katie more than thirty years to make good on those promises. But when she did, she did it with a vengeance.

TWO DAYS AGO

KATIE

Kansas City

She left the fast food place dressed as a junkie, and took a cab to the pawn shop on Independence. Within two minutes of roaming the street, she found a prostitute with that vacant, strung-out look Katie knew all too well.

Katie described who she was looking for. Two men, dealers and pimps. One with a big chest and big thighs. Another with bright green eyes.

The first girl didn't know them.

Neither did the second girl, two blocks over.

But the third girl did. And the address was close.

The apartment was the kind of shithole Katie expected. It didn't even have a security door. It was nice to know that Ben and Winston hadn't become successful in their old age.

She knocked on the door, the X26 Taser in her fist, and mumbled something about needing some shit, keeping her head down so he didn't see her face through the peephole.

It wouldn't have mattered. When he opened the door, he didn't recognize her, and she almost didn't recognize him. Age had bent his back and wrinkled his face and whitened his hair.

But Katie knew those green eyes.

She shot him, the tiny electric barbs shooting into his chest and shooting a million volts through him. As he flopped around, she took out her Colt, checked the rest of the apartment.

Found a young girl locked in the bedroom, obviously high, but no one else. Katie left her there for the authorities to find later.

Using duct tape, she bound Winston to the radiator, gagged him, and then began breaking his fingers until he agreed to call his buddy, Ben.

Ben showed up twenty minutes later, dropped like a sack of shit when the Taser hit him, and Katie made sure his bonds were extra tight. Then she locked the door, put a chair under the knob to make absolutely sure no one else would come in, put on her work gloves, and began.

Katie hadn't brought much with her, other than her basic kit. But there were plenty of things around the apartment to play with.

She tried a hammer.

A clothes iron.

A cheese grater.

Pliers.

A cordless drill.

An electric sander.

Salt.

Tabasco sauce.

Even lemon juice.

She took plenty of pictures, and some of their expressions were precious.

They took a long time to die. But not long enough. Winston died first. Probably a heart attack. Ben lasted another half an hour, then blood loss took him.

After Katie was finished, she took off her bloody junkie clothes and gloves, put everything that could incriminate her in a garbage bag, and dressed in the outfit she'd worn when she left the Holiday Inn.

On her way out the door she saw a hypodermic needle on the desk. Katie didn't want the girl in the bedroom to overdose, so she dropped it in her purse, intending to throw the shit away. But just after ditching the bag in the alley, the cops rolled up and busted her for heroin possession.

Katie was barely able to keep her game face and not burst into hysterical laughter.

PRESENT

KATIE

La Juntita

It had been simple to sneak inside the mission building, but then all hell broke loose. Gunfire. Guards and servants running around. Katie had just managed to make it inside the pantry before being discovered, hiding behind several sacks of rice.

When the noise died down, she came out. The mission seemed to have been abandoned. It appeared everyone had left. Katie began checking rooms, becoming more and more frantic.

Please don't let them be gone. Please don't...

But they weren't gone. They were there, behind a steel door. Katie shot the guard, and then saw them.

My daughter...

My brother...

My family!

She immediately burst into tears.

"Lucy... Luther... I've found you both. I've been searching so long, and I finally found you."

"Who the fuck are you?" Lucy asked.

Katie could hardly speak. She'd been waiting, hoping, wishing for this moment for over three decades.

"I'm your mother, Lucy," she managed, her voice cracking. "Your real mother. When I was eight years old, I was on the beach with my family. Two men came. Do you remember, Luther? They took me."

"Katie?" Luther said.

She nodded, the tears streaming down her face. "It's me, Luther. It's Katie. They kept me for years. But I escaped when I was thirteen. I escaped… and I had you, Lucy. My precious, beautiful Lucy. I had to give you up. But I'm here now. Mommy's here now. I've been looking for so long, and here you both are, in the same place. It's a miracle. We're a family again."

"I did not see this one coming," Harry said.

"Katie?" Luther reached out his hand, and she went to him.

Hugged him.

Hugged her brother.

"I found them, Luther. The men who tore us apart. Ben and Winston. I made them pay. Look."

Katie pulled the folded front page of the Kanas City Times out of her pocket. "Two Dead In Torture/Murder," she read.

Luther held the paper in a shaking hand. Katie took out her camera and began flipping through jpegs on the view screen.

"Look what I did to them, little brother. Look. I made them suffer. They suffered a long, long time."

"Katie?" he said again. "Where have you been?"

Katie began to bawl even harder. She supposed all family reunions were tear-jerkers.

"I couldn't remember our last name, Luther. I only remembered it ten years ago, after Mom and Dad were already gone. But I've missed you my whole life, and I've been searching for you since then. I read everything I could. About both of you. I followed every trail." She sniffled, smiling through a line of snot. "I'm not close to your numbers, I know, but I've tortured and killed fourteen people, looking for you both. Sixteen, with Ben and Winston. And now we're finally together. I've never been this happy. How did you two find each other?"

"Birds of a feather," Luther said.

Katie couldn't believe this was actually happening. It was all so perfect. Nothing could ruin this moment.

"Hiya, Katie," McGlade said. "You know that sex you owe me? How about you just let us go, and we'll call it even. We had some fun times, right? Remember singing scat? Sca baa doobie do wah dee doo—"

Except that.

"Shut up, McGlade," she said, pointing the Colt at him. "Do you know how many times I came *this* close to slitting your throat while we were on that endless, terrible road trip?"

"I dunno. Eight?"

"You are pretty irritating to travel with, Harry," Herb said.

Katie switched the gun to Herb. "Shut up, fatso."

"You are pretty fat, Herb," Harry said. "And don't tell me I didn't hear your stomach rumble when psychopants here was roasting his hand."

The gun went back to Harry. "Talk again, and I shoot you."

"Shut up, McGlade," Jack said. "You're not helping."

Katie turned the Colt on Jack. "And you. I am so tired of your mouth. You condescending, self-righteous, sanctimonious, whiny, neurotic bitch."

"I don't think you're whiny, Jack," Harry said.

Katie aimed and shot him.

McGlade flopped forward onto his face. Herb turned to him. "Harry!"

"I hit him in the shoulder," Katie said. "He'll live. Or he won't. It doesn't matter. Me, my brother, and my daughter are going to hurt the three of you in ways you've never even imagined."

"You're not my mother," Lucy said.

"I am, Lucy," Katie nodded, lowering her weapon. "I had to give you up for adoption. Do you remember when I visited you at the playground? You were just a little girl. I promised I'd be back for you." She kept nodding, and crying, finding herself unable to stop either. "And I did it. I found you. We're all together again."

"So you're my mother, and he's my uncle?" Lucy asked.

"Yes, baby."

"Then who's my father?"

Lucy!" Donaldson exclaimed, swinging open the door.

But Lucy wasn't there.

It was a pantry.

He gummed his lower lip, then went to check more rooms.

"Lucy!"

Bedroom.

"Lucy!"

Another bedroom.

"Lucy!"

Another goddamn bedroom. What was this place, a hotel?

"Lucy!"

"D?"

And there she was. His Lucy. Standing right there, like something out of a dream.

Her eye went wide. "D! You're alive! I can't believe you're alive!"

"Donaldson?"

He turned. Saw some woman with a gun. "Do I know you?"

"You raped me, you son of a bitch."

"You kinda need to narrow that down a little more."

"You're her father."

Donaldson looked at Lucy. "Her father?"

"D?" Lucy said. "Dad?"

"Lucy is my kid?"

"Whoa," said some guy who was hunched over and bleeding on the floor. "This is some fucked-up Jerry Springer shit right here."

"Donaldson?" It was Jack Daniels talking now. "You were on top of the RV. How did you make it through the minefield?"

That was a minefield? Good thing he decided to avoid all those big white Xs painted on the ground.

"I can't be stopped," Donaldson said. "I'm indestructible."

The woman with the gun fired twice, blowing out both of Donaldson's knees. He fell over, and then she took a knife out of her pocket and cut him open from his catheter to his breastbone, and Donaldson watched in surprise as his insides became his outsides.

LUCY

D!" she screamed. Then she whirled on Katie. "You bitch!"

The razor in her hand, Lucy pounced, catching Katie deep on the side of her neck.

Katie turned to Lucy, an expression of shock forming on her face, as the arterial spray hit the ceiling.

LUTHER

Katie
Sister
Mother
Beautiful
Father
Sweet Sweet
Hand
Pain
Hand Pain
HANDPAIN
Syrup
Syrup
Voices
Voices?
The sky
Voices in the sky
Sky machines
Beaming voices
Voices beaming
Crazy
Crazy?
Who, me, crazy?
Andy
Andrew

Luther
Andrew
Luther
Orson
Thomas
Thomas
Lucy
Lucy
Lucy
Katie
Sister
Katie
Sister
A ministering angel shall my sister be
SISTER
LUCY
LUCY
KATIE
SISTER
LUCY
DYING
SISTER
DYING
SISTER DYING
LUCY...
NECKTIE

KATIE

She fell over, the whole world going wonky, and looked up just in time to see her brother hugging her daughter.

No... that wasn't a hug.

Luther was slitting Lucy's throat and yanking her tongue out through the newly made hole.

LUCY

How about that? Lucy thought as she gagged. *A Columbian necktie actually is a horrible way to go.*

DONALDSON

He tried. He tried to crawl to his Lucy. He tried to crawl to his Lucy while pushing his insides back inside.

But someone was on him. Kneeling on his back.

The woman who cut him. She had a neck wound that looked pretty fatal, if he was any judge of fatal neck wounds, which he was.

Katie. He remembered her name was Katie. She was one of Ben and Winston's girls.

"Gotta say, Katie. You haven't aged well."

Katie shoved her knife up inside him and stabbed his beating heart.

Well, Donaldson thought. *Guess I'm not indestructible after all.*

KATIE

She fell next to Donaldson, reaching for her brother.

Luther stared down at Katie like she was a mildly interesting insect.

Katie blinked, her own blood stinging her eyes, and she wondered if perhaps some families were better off not being together.

JACK

Luther Kite stared at me, his niece's blood still dripping from his Spyderco Harpy.

"I don't trust you," he said, raising the blade and taking a step forward.

There was a noise at the door. Like a knock, but lower down.

"You should get that," I said, raising my eyes toward the ceiling. "Could be the sky machines."

Luther opened the door—

—and in trotted Herb Bacondict.

"What's that in his mouth?" Herb Benedict asked.

"Pigs root," said Harry, his voice weak. "That's a landmine."

Luther stared down at the pig.

"Herb," Harry said. "Play fetch."

And Herb Bacondict let the landmine fall from his mouth.

PHIN

The bodies of the dead were everywhere. Gunfire was still heavy. Phin was still twenty meters away from the mission building, and couldn't get any closer without risking a bullet in the head.

"Jack!" he yelled.

Jack didn't answer.

She had to be in the mission.

Had to be.

Phin ducked down his head and ran for it.

JACK

The mine didn't go off. It hit the floor, spun like a coin, and then landed right side up.

"You gotta be shitting me," Herb said.

"Get down," Harry told us.

"You're a little late on that, McGlade," said Herb.

"No, I'm not. Both of you, get down on the floor."

Herb and I obeyed. Luther began to step around the pig.

"Have at thee, coward," Luther said. "Once more, on pain of death, all men depart. All are punish'd!"

"Herb," Harry told his pet pig. "Roll over."

He made it inside the mission just as an explosion blew a door right past his face. Leading with the rifle, Phin went into the room.

It was a slaughterhouse. Blood and guts everywhere.

And there, lying on the floor between Herb and Harry, covered in gore...

"Oh, no."

Jack.

Not Jack.

Phin dropped to his knees, and he wailed like it had been torn out of his body.

"Goddamn, you're loud," said Harry McGlade.

JACK

blinked away the blood. "Hi, babe," I said to my husband. "We're here to rescue you."

Phin crawled through the carnage and hugged me.

"We're handcuffed," Herb said. "But there are bolt cutters on the wall there."

"I saw the blood, and I thought..." Phin looked over the mess. "What the hell happened in here?"

"My loyal pig sacrificed himself to save us all, and was blown to bacon bits. The rest of the mess is the Guinness World Record winner for Most Dysfunctional Family."

Phin glanced at me.

"I'll explain later," I told him.

It only took a minute for Phin cut all of us free. I took his rifle, and Phin and Herb helped Harry.

"How many guards still out there?" I asked.

"At least a dozen," he said. "We should wait in here."

"If we don't let my friends know I'm alive, they're going to blow up this place with us in it."

"Some friends."

I took the lead, and we moved quick but careful, stepping over the dead, staying low.

A guard peeked out from behind a corner, raising his rifle. Before I could raise mine, half his head vanished.

Another opened fire from our left flank, but dropped his weapon as his hand disintegrated.

Thank you Val and Fleming.

When we reached the front of the arena, I was feeling hopeful.

By the time we neared the middle of it, I was sure we were home free. But the moment we stepped past—

"Get down!"

It happened in slow motion.

Leaning against a small divot in the arena wall, covered in blood with bullet holes in her Kevlar, was Chandler.

That was who yelled.

She was pointing up, and I looked in time to see the guard with the mounted M60. But it wasn't mounted anymore. Apparently he'd taken it off the tripod to shoot things that were directly below him. Such as Chandler.

And me.

He was aiming right at me.

There was no time for me to fire back.

No time for me to even react.

I saw the muzzle flash, and heard the *TAH-TAH-TAH-TAH!* of big caliber machinegun fire, and then I was on my back.

Someone had pushed me out of the way.

Herb.

Our eyes met just as the 7.65mm rounds tore into him.

I raised my rifle, emptying my magazine at his bulletproof shield and making him fall back. Then I crawled to my best friend.

I didn't know how to stop the bleeding. There were too many holes, and even all of us put together didn't have enough hands.

I knelt next to him. It was tough to see because of my tears.

"Hey, buddy," I said.

"Hey, buddy." He chuckled. "This kinda sucks."

"You're not going to die here, Herb."

"Yeah, this time I am." Blood bubbled out of his lips. "But it's okay. This is what I wanted, remember? The selfless hero ending. I'm glad the life I saved was yours."

I shook my head. "No. This isn't... it's not supposed to..."

Herb looked at Phin. "Take care of our girl. She seems a little upset."

"I will," Phin said.

I reached over, held Herb's hand. Held it so tight. Noticed Harry was holding his other one. Gunfire, to the east, chewing up the arena wall immediately above us.

"I'm not leaving you, Herb." The sobs were making my whole body shake. "I'm not leaving you."

"You have to, Jack." Herb smiled, then winked at me. "I gotta do this one alone, partner."

And then he closed his eyes.

And then he stopped moving.

This couldn't be happening.

This wasn't happening.

Chandler reached over, feeling under Herb's pant leg. "He's gone."

"Phin," I said, "take his arms. We're bringing him home."

"Leave him," Chandler said.

"I can't leave him!"

"Then figure out how you, Phin, and Harry can carry both me and Herb."

"We can call Val and Fleming. They can drive in and—"

Chandler grabbed my shirt and pulled me close. "And risk their lives, too? How many people do you want to die for this rescue attempt, Jack? Tequila's dead. Herb's dead. I'm down two pints of blood and counting. And you want to risk my sister and your friend, just to bring a corpse back home? We need to blow this place and get out of here before we're all dead."

The pain was overwhelming. But I put it away. Compartmentalized.

So I could deal with it.

"Okay," I said. "Okay."

I reached for Chandler to help her up.

She held up a finger. "I'm detonating."

"Won't it kill us?"

She shook her head. "We set the charges to implode the structure."

"Cover!" Phin said. "The gunner is back!"

We all threw our backs against the arena wall as the machine-gun tore up the ground a few inches away from our toes.

"I'm blowing!" Chandler yelled. "Now!"

She pressed a button.

Nothing happened.

"Heath, copy. My detonator didn't work."

More bullets whipped past our faces, so close I could feel the wind.

"His detonator won't work either. He's pinned down. I think the receiver detached from the main charge. Or there's a radio issue." Chandler punched the wall with the back of her fist. "I don't know what the goddamn problem is. And Heath said the other M60 gunner is headed our way."

"How do we blow the main charge?" Phin asked.

"Shooting it would work."

"Can Val or Fleming hit it?" I asked.

"It's facing the wrong way, on the other side of the arena."

Phin held out his hand. "I need your gun."

Chandler raised her weapon, butt-first. "I have one round left. How good a shot are you?"

"I'm okay."

"You have to be close enough not to miss," Chandler said. "And if you're that close, you'll be within the blast radius."

"I won't miss," Phin said.

I knew what my husband meant. He wasn't going to miss, because he was going to be standing right next to it.

Chandler handed him the gun.

Phin and I looked at each other.

He said, "I'm sorry, Jack."

I said, "Me, too."

Then I punched Phin in the face, knocking him over.

I squatted, prying the gun from his fingers and said, "I love you, Phineas Troutt. Forever and beyond."

And then I took off running, gunfire stitching ground around me.

A second gunner joined in. The other M60. Pinching me in a crossfire.

I dodged away from the arena wall, bullets at my heels, and then circled back, wondering what the hell I was supposed to be looking for.

There. Stuck to the wall. The main charge.

I couldn't miss. And the only way to be sure was to get close enough.

So I got close enough.

Stopped.

Looked at my wedding ring.

Thought of my daughter.

Thought of my husband.

Thought of everything I'd done in my life. All the victories, and all the mistakes. And maybe it wasn't a perfect life. And maybe I hadn't always made the right decisions.

This decision was right. The compound would blow, the arena would collapse, and my friends would get away.

But this was about more than just the moment. This was about the future.

There was only one way to I could fully protect people I loved. To make sure no more monsters ever came after them.

I'd been thinking about it for a while. And I felt I had no other choice.

Jack Daniels had to die.

I cocked the weapon, certain there was no way I could miss when I was this close.

Then I fired.

The sound of the world exploding was so achingly beautiful, it was all I needed to take to my grave.

TWO MONTHS LATER

PHIN

With his daughter on his hip, Phineas Troutt walked out the front door of his home without needing to check the video monitor.

There was no need to. With his wife dead, there wouldn't be any bad guys calling. Ever again.

He walked down the driveway, past the FOR SALE sign staked into the lawn, a bright red SOLD sticker plastered across it diagonally.

"I miss Mommy," Samantha said.

"Me too, Sam."

Phin opened the mailbox, and took out a stack of mail. Bills, crap, and two important pieces of mail, both addressed to him.

He brought Sam back inside, sidestepped several cardboard boxes filled with packed stuff, and suffered the soulful greeting of Duffy the dog, who howled like he hadn't seen Phin in years.

"I was gone for forty seconds," he told Duffy.

Duffy bumped Phin with his head and howled again, demanding to be petted. Phin gave him a scratch behind the ears, then walked into the kitchen, past more boxes. He set Sam on the counter, then opened the mail.

The first was from the Retirement Board of the Policemen's Annuity and Benefit Fund. It was a letter saying that Jack Daniels's pension had been transferred over to her surviving spouse, Phineas Troutt, and the new address was being processed.

The second was from the Coroner's Office in Mexicali.

Phin didn't like to think about Mexico. It had been, without question, the worst time of his life.

After Jack had blown the compound, a merc with an eyepatch named Heath had driven them all to a hospital in Mexicali, where Phin had stayed for two weeks under a fake name. Each day of recovery was nerve-wracking, fearfully waiting for the authorities, or Cardova's cartel, to somehow connect him to the destruction of the arena in the Vizcaíno desert. It had gotten international attention, and dozens of bodies had been recovered from the rubble.

The corpses of Herb Benedict and Tequila Abernathy weren't among those found. Phin hoped that somehow, maybe, they'd survived their lethal wounds and were sipping margaritas on a beach somewhere.

It was a nice fantasy. But there was no way it could possibly be true.

The only remains of Jacqueline Daniels discovered was a severed arm. The fingerprints matched Jack's, but Phin had identified it at first sight from the inscribed wedding band he'd bought her.

For forever and beyond.

That's what the letter referenced. That the coroner's examination was complete, and Phin could pick up Jack's remaining personal effects.

The ring.

"Are you crying, Daddy?"

Phin wiped his eyes.

"Is it because you miss Mommy, too?"

"Yes, that's why, Sam."

"Can we call her?"

Phin picked up his daughter and held her, tight.

"You're squeezing too hard, Daddy."

"That's because I love you so much. Are you excited that we're moving to a new house?"

"Yes."

"We'll be near Grandma. And we can go to the beach all the time, and swim in the ocean. Won't that be fun?"

"Yes. I want to call Mommy."

"Sam..."

"Please, Daddy. Please call Mommy. I miss her so much."

Phin set her down. Then he took out his phone and hit redial.

"Hi, honey," Phin said when his wife picked up. "Our progeny misses you."

"I've only been gone for three hours," Jack said. "I'm not even out of Illinois yet."

Phin had wanted to sell the car and buy a new one when they got to Florida, but Jack had decided she wanted to take a road trip and clear her head. He didn't argue. She hadn't taken Herb's death well.

However, Jack had been very excited about her own death. She'd even gone to her own funeral, in disguise and standing in the crowd. After coming to the realization that she'd never be free of her past, Jack took the opportunity that Vizcaíno represented and ran with it, making sure the world thought she died in that explosion. Fleming hacked the CPD database and swapped out her prints with Katie's, McGlade planted the arm with the ring, and now Jack had a fake last name and a whole new life. One without any sort of past that could come back to haunt her or the people she loved.

"Want to go to Mexico again?" Phin asked. "We can pick up your ring. Make a vacation out of it."

"I don't think I'm ready to go back. I don't know if I'll ever be ready. Can they FedEx it?"

"I'll ask."

"Hey, you know that inscription you wrote?"

"For forever and beyond?"

"Yeah. I keep forgetting to ask you, did you steal that from the movie *Toy Story 2*?"

Phin laughed. "Of course not, honey."

He was telling the truth. Phin hadn't cribbed that line from *Toy Story 2*. He'd taken it from the first *Toy Story* movie. But *to infinity and beyond* didn't sound as romantic as Phin's version.

"McGlade called me earlier," Jack said. "The dog just ate his couch."

"She's a big dog."

"Harry says she still mopes around a little. Misses Tequila. But Harry Junior loves her, and I think Harry does, too. Kinda funny. McGlade has spent years looking for a pet. He had fish and monkeys and parrots and pigs. When this whole time all he needed was a dog."

"Sometimes we don't know what we want in life until it's sitting right in front of us," Phin said, looking at his daughter.

"Indeed."

"You okay that he changed her name from Rosalina to Herb?"

"We all mourn in our own ways. I miss him, Phin."

"Me, too."

Jack sniffled, then said. "Interesting fact; Katie's last name was Glente. Glente is the Danish name for a specific bird of prey. In English, it's known as a *kite*."

"She was, as McGlade put it, crazypants."

"Crazypants McButtnutspants."

"I'm glad that part of our life is finished."

"Yeah. I feel free, Phin. Like I've never felt before. We're about to start a whole new chapter."

"Just a new chapter?" Phin said, smiling. "I have the feeling we're going to start a whole new book."

Sam had been tugging at his arm so hard she was practically hanging from it.

"Here's your daughter."

He handed the phone over and Sam blurted out, "Hi, Mommy!"

Phin watched his daughter talk to his wife, then touched the scar on his belly.

Mexico had been the worst time in his life. No contest.

But if he had to do it again for those two beautiful ladies, he would.

He'd do it again and again and again. And a thousand times again.

For forever and beyond.

THE END

The following is a preview of WHITE RUSSIAN,
the eleventh Jack Daniels thriller by J.A. Konrath

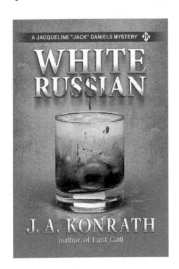

Somewhere in the USA

He opened his eyes to a world of pain. Everything hurt.

But being in pain meant being alive.

He was on his back. Immobile. Bandages covering his body.

He tried to move his arm.

Couldn't.

Not because of an injury. But because he was handcuffed to the bed.

"Nurse?" he called, his voice a painful rasp.

"No nurses. This isn't a hospital."

He turned, and saw a familiar but scarred face occupying the cot next to him, similarly handcuffed.

"Where are we?"

"I don't know yet," the man said. "But it's bad."

"How bad?"

The man frowned. "Bad enough that we're both going to wish we hadn't survived Mexico."

JACK

Fort Myers, Florida

For the first time in my life, I had a life.

I was in such a good mood that I didn't even mind getting a call from my ex-partner, Harry McGlade.

"Hiya, Jackie. How's things?"

"Wonderfully boring. I feel great, Harry. It's truly a joy not to be involved with anything dangerous."

"Good for you. I'm Glad. Now I need your help with something dangerous."

I didn't hesitate. "No."

"You didn't even hear my pitch."

"I don't care, McGlade. I'm out. No more police work. No more detective work. My guns are in storage. The only cases I'm taking are cases of beer."

"You know I've got this blog, right?" he went on, undeterred.

"Yeah. I read it all the time," I lied.

"What do you know about human trafficking?"

"I know enough that I'm not helping you."

"Slavery is still a big business, Jack. Do you know that it's estimated that there are more than thirty million people enslaved today? And we're not just talking third world. It's happening right here, in the good old US of A."

"Tragic. Heartbreaking. Terrible. I mean that. And I'm not helping you with any cases."

"Remember Mexico?"

That hit a nerve. "Of course I remember Mexico." Some good people had died south of the boarder, helping me out. "Are you calling in a favor?"

"No. I'm *doing* you a favor."

"This doesn't sound like a favor."

"What if I told you," McGlade said, "that someone we thought was dead wasn't actually dead?"

I sat up in my chair so fast I spilled my coffee.

"What are you saying, Harry?"

"I'm on my way to your place right now," Harry said. "I'll tell you in person in about ten minutes."

Then he hung up, leaving me to wonder if Harry was talking about an old friend...

Or an old enemy.

AUTHOR AFTERWORD

The story Luther Kite enjoyed from that old issue of Alfred Hitchcock's Mystery Magazine was published March 2005. It was called *The Agreement* and was written by me.

You can get it for free on my website. Be warned, though; it's a mean one.

As for who is still alive after the ending of LAST CALL, readers will find out in the next Jack Daniels thriller, WHITE RUSSIAN. But I gotta tell you; my wife threatened to divorce me if I killed any of the characters she loves.

Since I love my wife, I'll let you guess who survived.

Thanks for reading!

Joe Konrath

JOE KONRATH'S COMPLETE BIBLIOGRAPHY

JACK DANIELS THRILLERS

WHISKEY SOUR

BLOODY MARY

RUSTY NAIL

DIRTY MARTINI

FUZZY NAVEL

CHERRY BOMB

SHAKEN

STIRRED with Blake Crouch

RUM RUNNER

LAST CALL

SHOT OF TEQUILA

BANANA HAMMOCK

WHITE RUSSIAN

OLD FASHIONED

SERIAL KILLERS UNCUT with Blake Crouch

LADY 52 with Jude Hardin

65 PROOF short story collection

FLOATERS short with Henry Perez

BURNERS short with Henry Perez

SUCKERS short with Jeff Strand

JACKED UP! short with Tracy Sharp

STRAIGHT UP short with Iain Rob Wright

CHEESE WRESTLING short with Bernard Schaffer

ABDUCTIONS short with Garth Perry

BEAT DOWN short with Garth Perry

BABYSITTING MONEY short with Ken Lindsey

OCTOBER DARK short with Joshua Simcox

RACKED short with Jude Hardin

BABE ON BOARD short with Ann Voss Peterson

WATCHED TOO LONG short with Ann Voss Peterson

PHINEAS TROUTT THRILLERS

DEAD ON MY FEET

DYING BREATH

EVERYBODY DIES

STOP A MURDER PUZZLE BOOKS

STOP A MURDER – HOW: PUZZLES 1 – 12
STOP A MURDER – WHERE: PUZZLES 13 – 24
STOP A MURDER – WHY: PUZZLES 25 – 36
STOP A MURDER – WHO: PUZZLES 37 – 48
STOP A MURDER – WHEN: PUZZLES 49 – 60

CODENAME: CHANDLER SERIES

EXPOSED with Ann Voss Peterson
HIT with Ann Voss Peterson
NAUGHTY with Ann Voss Peterson
FLEE with Ann Voss Peterson
SPREE with Ann Voss Peterson
THREE with Ann Voss Peterson
FIX with F. Paul Wilson and Ann Voss Peterson
RESCUE

THE HORROR COLLECTIVE

ORIGIN
THE LIST
DISTURB
AFRAID
TRAPPED
ENDURANCE
HAUNTED HOUSE
WEBCAM
DRACULAS with Blake Crouch, Jeff Strand, and F. Paul Wilson
HOLES IN THE GROUND with Iain Rob Wright
THE GREYS
SECOND COMING
THE NINE
GRANDMA? with Talon Konrath
WILD NIGHT IS CALLING short with Ann Voss Peterson
CLOSE YOUR EYES
FOUND FOOTAGE

TIMECASTER SERIES

TIMECASTER
TIMECASTER SUPERSYMMETRY
TIMECASTER STEAMPUNK
BYTER

EROTICA
(WRITING AS MELINDA DUCHAMP)

FIFTY SHADES OF ALICE IN WONDERLAND

FIFTY SHADES OF ALICE THROUGH THE LOOKING GLASS

FIFTY SHADES OF ALICE AT THE HELLFIRE CLUB

WANT IT BAD

FIFTY SHADES OF JEZEBEL AND THE BEANSTALK

FIFTY SHADES OF PUSS IN BOOTS

FIFTY SHADES OF GOLDILOCKS

THE SEXPERTS – FIFTY GRADES OF SHAY

THE SEXPERTS – THE GIRL WITH THE PEARL NECKLACE

THE SEXPERTS – LOVING THE ALIEN

THE SEVEN YEAR WITCH

WHISKEY SOUR

Lieutenant Jacqueline "Jack" Daniels is having a bad week. Her live-in boyfriend has left her for his personal trainer, chronic insomnia has caused her to max out her credit cards with late-night home shopping purchases, and a frightening killer who calls himself 'The Gingerbread Man' is dumping mutilated bodies in her district.

While avoiding the FBI and its moronic profiling computer, joining a dating service, mixing it up with street thugs, and parrying the advances of an uncouth PI, Jack and her binge-eating partner, Herb, must catch the maniac before he kills again...and Jack is next on his murder list.

WHISKEY SOUR is the first book in the bestselling Jack Daniels series, full of laugh-out-loud humor and edge-of-your-seat suspense.

THE LIST

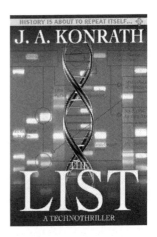

A billionaire Senator with money to burn...

A thirty year old science experiment, about to be revealed...

Seven people, marked for death, not for what they know, but for what they are...

THE LIST by J.A. Konrath

History is about to repeat itself.

WEBCAM

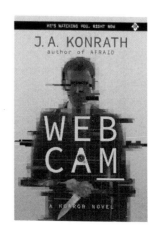

Someone is stalking webcam models.

He lurks in the untouchable recesses of the black web.

He's watching you. Right now.

When watching is no longer enough, he comes calling.

He's the last thing you'll ever see before the blood gets in your eyes.

Chicago Homicide Detective Tom Mankowski (THE LIST, HAUNTED HOUSE) is no stranger to homicidal maniacs. But this one is the worst he's ever chased, with an agenda that will make even the most diehard horror reader turn on all their lights, and switch off all Internet, WiFi, computers, and electronic devices.

J.A. Konrath reaches down into the depths of depravity and drags the terror novel kicking and cyber-screaming into the 21st century.

WEBCAM

I'm texting you from inside your closet. Wanna play? :-)

Sign up for the J.A. Konrath newsletter. A few times a year I pick random people to give free stuff to. It could be you.

http://www.jakonrath.com/mailing-list.php

I won't spam you or give your information out without your permission!

70781453R00211

Made in the USA
Lexington, KY
17 November 2017